Praise for the wo

Across :

I loved Kat Jackson's first book, *Begin Again*, and I've been not-very-patiently awaiting the release of her second. I was not in any way disappointed! If you're looking for a layered tale of wonderfully flawed people, look no further. What enchanted me so much about *Begin Again*, and what runs through *Across the Hall* is one of the things that makes humans so interesting is that we are not perfect.

Mallory and Caitlin are complex characters with great depth, who I alternately wanted to hug and shake. Their stories are carefully crafted, and I am so thrilled to hear that Lina is getting her own book!

-Orlando J., *NetGalley*

Kat Jackson's *Begin Again* was an incredible debut and she became my favorite new author of 2020. Needless to say I was really looking forward to this sophomore effort. It didn't disappoint.

It's a workplace romance featuring two mains with a lot of baggage to bring to a fledging relationship. This story is really told in third person from Caitlin's POV, so we don't really know what's going on in Mallory's head. I really enjoyed following the ups and downs of the relationship and it was hard to tell where it was going. I started reading and next thing I knew, I was finished. That's what I love about a book.

-Karen R., *NetGalley*

I completely enjoyed this book from start to finish. I thought Caitlyn was super charming and I really felt for her when she was trying to get back on the dating horse. Of course she picks a woman who's a bit of an ice queen! They are always the hot ones!! What I loved even more, though, was that Mallory was actually a great equal to Caitlyn. I really felt the ying/yang and their chemistry.

I don't want to spoil it, but there is a bit of angst between the two that I wasn't expecting, but it made it that much more entertaining. And go Caitlyn for calling Mallory out when she was, in part, being lead on. I may have cheered a little.

Overall, a very fun read with great characters, excellent chemistry, and just the right amount of story. Can't wait for the next one from Kat Jackson.

-T. Geist, *NetGalley*

Begin Again

This debut novel was well written, with a good pace, and I could sympathize with the characters.

-Michele R., *NetGalley*

Begin Again is one of the most beautiful, heartrending, and thought-provoking books I've read. Kat Jackson manages the rare feat of making a lesfic novel that toys with infidelity meaningful and elegant. While this all might sound a bit grim, it does have plenty of lighthearted moments too.

-Orlando J., *NetGalley*

Begin Again is one of the most thought provoking, honest, emotional and heart rending books I've ever read. How the author managed to get the real raw emotions (that I could believe and feel) down on paper and into words is amazing. If you read the blurb you will know, sort of what this story is about. But it's much more than that. As other reviewers have stated, it's not a comfy read but was totally riveting. I read it in a day, I just couldn't put it down. Definitely one of the best books I've read and if I could give it more stars I would for sure! Superbly written. Totally recommend.

-Anja S., *NetGalley*

THE ROADS
LEFT
BEHIND US

Other Bella Books by Kat Jackson

Begin Again
Across the Hall

About the Author

Kat Jackson is a collector of feelings, words, and typewriters. She's a teacher/behavioral coach living in Pennsylvania, where she enjoys all four seasons in the span of a single week. Kat's been consumed with words and language for as long as she can remember and continues to spend entirely too much time overthinking anything that's ever been said to her. (This is a joke, kind of, but not completely.) Running is her #1 coping mechanism, followed closely by sitting in the sun with a good book. SSDGM and snuggle your pets, y'all.

THE ROADS LEFT BEHIND US

KAT JACKSON

BELLA
BOOKS
2022

Bella Books, Inc.
P.O. Box 10543
Tallahassee, FL 32302

First Edition - 2022

Editor: Medora MacDougall
Cover Designer: Sheri Halal

ISBN: 978-1-64247-345-2

Acknowledgments

First and foremost, thank you to everyone at Bella for providing the space and opportunity for writers like me to bring their dream stories to life. I'm grateful and still a little stunned every day that I get to do this.

Medora, many thanks for your patience & keen eye during the editing process. I make no promises about giving up my use of semicolons but I'll try to at least...cut back.

Jen & Andie: Thank you for coming on this journey with me. Your input and reactions were invaluable, and your confidence in me is something I'll never understand but always appreciate. And JB, thank you for your professorial input—I hope it's hot enough for you!

Blaze: for being you, for your five-star review of "I'm interested to see where it's going," and for your uncanny ability to distract me when I need it the most—thank you.

The Roads Left Behind Us is a story that's been brewing inside me for years, and I'm thrilled that it unfolded the way that it did. This was one of those painfully beautiful stories to write, one that digs right into the quiet corners of your heart and tugs out moments and words that had been carefully packed away. I truly hope you all enjoy it.

"Every thought's a possibility…"
Indigo Girls, "Mystery"

CHAPTER ONE

The hallway in which Callie sat, her bag propped at her feet, was entirely familiar. She couldn't count the number of times she had walked (or sometimes stomped, depending on the day/class) over this aging linoleum. It had been a couple of years since she'd been in this building, but the decor was, sadly, unchanged and in dire need of a facelift. Callie slumped lower in the back-numbing wooden chair and gazed surreptitiously at her competition lining the walls in similar chairs. She was trying to appear uninterested, but she quickly realized her lazy posture showed something else—something she shouldn't be portraying at this critical moment. Sighing, she directed her stare back to the spot in front of her own two feet and sat up straighter.

She mulled over the other people she'd observed before she'd forced herself to sit up and look away. Three young women, two definitely younger than she was, and two young men—both of whom looked to be in their early twenties. Callie bit the inside of her lip. She wasn't expecting this many contenders, so to speak, and her stomach twisted in anxiety. This was only the screening interview, she reminded herself, so not all six of the candidates would move forward toward her coveted spot. Math was definitely not her strong suit, and despite what Courtney had told her, Callie was starting to feel the stress of her odds for moving past the screening.

Before Callie had time to obsess *too* much, a harried-looking young woman flew out of the conference room, a clipboard smashed against her chest. She paused to clear her throat dramatically, then cast a stoic smile at the candidates in the hallway.

"Hello, everyone. I apologize for the delay…there was a… miscommunication." The woman paused again. Callie glanced at the young woman sitting across from her, who wrinkled her nose in confusion at Callie. Callie bit back a smile. At least she wasn't the only candidate who seemed utterly perplexed by this person she'd never seen before—and here Callie thought she knew the entire English Department at Pennbrook University.

"We are now ready to begin," the woman continued, glancing at her clipboard. "We'll start with Callie Looze."

Callie scoffed under her breath, hoping the woman was too flustered to catch her. "It's Lew-es."

"Pardon?"

Callie gestured to the clipboard, then back to herself as she stood and lifted her messenger bag over her shoulder. "I'm Callie. Callie Lewes. Like Lewis with an i, just with an e instead."

The look the woman gave Callie in response to her brief lesson in pronunciation wasn't quite at the stage of withering but close to it. Callie smiled in return and motioned toward the closed door in front of them. "Shall we?"

"We shall," came the clipped response. She banged the door open, leaving Callie to follow her while dodging the door on its return swing.

* * *

As soon as Callie entered the conference room, her little twist of anxiety from the hallway edged out. She was confident:

she knew she had a certain charm that won people over whether or not she was actually trying to win them over. Beyond that, she was obsessed with reading, writing, literature, theory, analysis...she'd been studying—correction: She *had* studied—literature for six straight years during her undergraduate and graduate terms before leaving it behind to enter the corporate world because she didn't know what else to do. Because of the lapse, she might be a *little* rusty, but all things English were her passion, so she figured she couldn't really be too out of shape, linguistically speaking.

You got this, she reminded herself, catching Dr. Courtney Wincheck-Rodriguez's eye with a small nod as she sat down in the chair she was directed to.

"Our first candidate is Callie LOOZE," began the hallway woman, and Callie tensed immediately. Was she serious? What kind of game was this? "Callie has—"

"I apologize for interrupting," Callie said calmly. While she was tempted to throw her own withering glare at this obnoxious human specimen, she resisted the temptation and aimed for professionalism instead. With a kind smile, she explained again the pronunciation of her last name, throwing in an anecdote about how Lewes is actually the simpler version of her historically Welsh last name. The room was quiet for a moment, no one certain as to who should speak next. Behind her, she had no doubt, Hallway Girl was glowering.

Finally, someone on the panel spoke. "Audrey, aren't you originally from Delaware?"

Grateful the focus had been taken off her for a moment and hoping her gentle correction didn't turn around and bite her in the ass, Callie looked more closely at the four professors seated in front of her.

Courtney was on the end, her long legs stretched out under the table, carefully manicured hands folded casually in front of her, and an amused smile resting on her lips. Per usual, her brown hair was pulled back in a tight, no-nonsense bun.

Next to her was Dr. Darkler, one of Callie's least favorite professors from her graduate experience. It wasn't that she didn't like him, it was just that he wasn't exactly progressive in his studies or his teachings. She hadn't been able to fully jibe with his love for the classics during the course she'd taken with him years ago.

Dr. Renee Lawler was leaning forward, her chin resting on her fist as she took in the scene unfolding before her. Callie had always sensed Dr. Lawler liked her, especially during her undergrad years, but they didn't know each other well and now, despite being a little older and more than a little wiser, she still found the chair of the department fairly intimidating. She could rock a power suit and disarmingly high heels like nobody's business and today was no exception. Her tanned skin shone against the bold turquoise fabric of her silky shirt and Callie was certain that a matching pair of heels was hidden under the table.

Finally, her eyes drifted to the last person sitting there, the one professor she didn't know. Coincidentally, she was also the person who had asked Audrey about Delaware. Callie searched her memory for any recollection of her, but she came up empty. She studied her, hoping for something to click. Below a slightly wavy crop of dark brown hair, unblinking hazel eyes were fixed on a spot just behind Callie, which she knew must be Audrey. Her skin was a touch darker than pale, and she was dressed modestly in cropped black pants, a white top, and a nicely fitting black blazer. A pair of thin black wire-rimmed glasses sat next to her open laptop.

As Callie struggled to put her finger on something, anything, about this woman, she heard Hallway Girl—Audrey, apparently—stutter behind her. "Well, y-yes. Yes, I'm from Delaware, Dr. Jory. I don't quite know why—"

"Audrey, I'm fairly certain you have a picture on your desk that you pointed out to me and Dr. Wincheck-Rodriguez just last week, and that picture was taken on Rehoboth Beach, wasn't it?"

Callie knew from the moment the woman said Delaware exactly where this slow burn was going, and now she struggled not to laugh out loud. She avoided looking over at Courtney, knowing that she'd lose it if she did. Instead, she turned her eyes over toward Dr. Jory, happy to have a name for the stranger.

"Yes! My college friends and I love Rehoboth!"

"Right, and didn't you mention a boutique that you go to in the nearby town?"

Audrey nodded, her pale blond curls bouncing in tempo. "Shelly's. Yes, it's right in downtown Lewes."

One of the professors exhaled loudly. Callie was tempted to follow suit. A flicker of shocked irritation flitted across Dr. Jory's face before she settled back into an impassive stare. Callie wasn't sure if it was hot or intimidating. When Dr. Jory looked directly into her eyes, however, she felt her own slow burn well up from somewhere deep inside of her, finishing on her flushed cheeks. After she held Callie's stare for what seemed like five minutes but was probably more like two seconds, Callie saw a roguish smile play on Dr. Jory's mouth. Through her maddening blush, Callie returned the smile. Yes, she was in on the joke.

Dr. Jory exchanged a glance with Dr. Lawler, who looked like she could burst out laughing at any moment. She turned back to Audrey. "You know what, let's chat about geography another time. We're already running behind, and Dr. Lawler has appointments this afternoon that she can't miss."

Dr. Lawler nodded immediately, regaining her composure. "You may leave now, Audrey. We'll send Ms. *Lewes* out when she's finished."

With a huff, Audrey took her exit. When she was sure she was gone, Dr. Lawler let out a laugh and put her shaking head in her hands. Courtney rolled her eyes before raising her eyebrows at Callie, as if to say, "Can you *seriously* believe that girl?" Even Dr. Darkler had to take a moment to compose himself.

"I don't want to be the one to say it, but…"

Dr. Lawler cut Dr. Jory off with a literal chopping motion.

"Don't. We're all at fault. It was a unanimous decision to hire her."

"Some of us voted more strongly than others," Courtney said in a singsong voice, always one to add fuel to the fire.

"Courtney, I don't want to hear it. I was waiting for you to jump in and help the poor girl!" Dr. Jory leaned forward and shot a glare down the table.

"Ha! I wasn't about to. Frankly, I'm surprised Callie here didn't save her."

Three pairs of eyes suddenly swung back to Callie, as though they were surprised to see she was still there. This time, however, only Dr. Darkler and Dr. Jory worked to regain their professorial posture. Both Courtney and Dr. Lawler were looking at Callie in amusement.

"Yes, Callie, what if that was part of your screening today? Someone mark that down. 'Callie did not help Audrey with basic Delaware knowledge that correlates directly to the pronunciation of Callie's last name.'"

At Dr. Lawler's statement, Dr. Jory began typing on her laptop. The department chair physically reached over and stopped her typing. "Kate, I was kidding."

The look that Dr. Jory (*Kate*, Callie mused) gave Dr. Lawler could melt steel, but soon the two women were leaning forward, laughing. Callie took the opportunity to shoot a questioning look at Courtney, who discreetly tapped on her cell phone. *Okay*, Callie thought. Courtney would text later and explain.

"Okay, we've kept Callie waiting long enough." Dr. Lawler turned her attention to Callie, who straightened up in her chair and self-consciously tucked an escaped piece of hair behind her ear. "Callie, welcome to the screening interview, the first step toward becoming a graduate teaching assistant. Why don't you tell us about your education thus far?"

With a deep breath, Callie thanked the professors for having her and launched into her post-high school education history, which, of course, was all based at the very university in which they sat. The more she talked about her experiences there, the more relaxed she felt and her confidence returned quickly.

Maybe it was just like Courtney had told her: She had it in the bag.

* * *

Pushing through her apartment door, Callie paused to listen for the telltale signs of her roommates. Sure enough, a quiet voice filtered down the hallway. Probably Nikki, since her girlfriend, Maya, wasn't known for doing anything quietly.

She stopped to grab a glass of water before heading into her bedroom to change. She sighed contentedly as she tugged off the constricting business-casual clothing that she truly hated wearing. She had to admit, it was definitely one of the reasons she'd recently quit her professional, business-casual clothing job and decided to go back to school, yet again, for her PhD. She. Hated. Wearing. Fancy. Clothes.

More comfortably clad in worn-in jeans and an equally worn-in Brandi Carlile concert T-shirt, she went back into the living room and flopped down onto the sofa. She absently scrolled on her phone, half-waiting for Courtney to call. There were things to discuss, and she was getting antsy with too much time in her head to mull over the interview, the other candidates, and that slightly unsettling newbie, Dr. Kate Jory.

Callie knew she hadn't seen Dr. Jory before, which was confusing because even though she'd finished her master's degree almost ten years ago, Callie wasn't a stranger to Pennbrook's campus. She went to a lot of basketball games with Courtney (and therefore had become accustomed to their team losing every single game) and even popped into Courtney's office in Berringer Hall every so often. Besides those logistics, there was the small-town vibe of Pennbrook. Nearly everyone who attended and worked there lived within a five-mile radius of the school. Chestnut Hill, the city that housed Pennbrook, was not large, but its downtown area had a lot to offer, and Callie was forever running into college staff while she was out and about. Never had she crossed paths with this new professor and, weirdly, that was bothering her.

A brief knock sounded at the door. Before Callie could respond, the door opened and her best friend, Sadie, poked her head in. "Oh, you're home," she said as she came all the way in. "I wasn't sure."

Callie lived in an old, converted Victorian house. Sadie had been living in the third-floor studio apartment for as long as Callie had known her, which was since they'd met during

Callie's sophomore year. Callie, Maya, and Nikki shared the large second-floor apartment. The first floor was split into two smaller apartments. Tim, an adjunct professor in the Math Department, and his girlfriend, Jenny, who worked in the Admissions Office, lived in the front apartment. Wylie, a local musician, lived in the smaller apartment at the back.

Sadie sat down in her favorite chair, the overstuffed armchair across from the sofa, and looked at Callie expectantly. "So? How was it?"

Callie dropped her phone beside her. "Honestly? Kind of weird, but overall good. I think."

"Weird? How so?"

Callie replayed the screening interview for Sadie, trying her best to be factual and keep her emotions out of it. Sadie was an excellent barometer and could often pick up on the subtleties that Callie missed.

When she finished, Sadie was nodding to herself. "You were pretty thrown by the new prof, huh?"

"Yeah. I was. I guess I figured Wincheck would have given me a head's up or something."

"Cal, I don't think you have anything to worry about. I know, I know. You've been out of the academic game for a decade—"

"Wow, thanks for that," Callie interjected before throwing a pillow at Sadie. She was a little sensitive about her time away, mostly because she felt kind of old to be taking on a GTA position at the age of 34…especially when the other candidates were clearly a lot younger than she was.

"Well, it's true. But it gave you life experience and all that extra shit that people love to hear about in a candidate." Sadie paused, running her hands through her thick copper-colored hair. "Do you honestly think one new person could prevent you from getting this position?"

Callie considered the naked truth of Sadie's question. No, of course that's not what she thought—it was just an irrational fear, one of many she loved to mull over. "Nah. And even if she has reservations about my academic abilities, I'm sure I won her over with my dashing good looks."

"Good lord," Sadie said with a roll of her eyes. "You don't know anything about this woman."

"I don't, but a vibe is a vibe, Sade."

"You somehow neglected to mention that you got a 'vibe,'"—she air-quoted for emphasis—"when you gave me the rundown."

"I don't know…" Callie trailed off, remembering the completely impassive look on Dr. Kate Jory's face. "There's something about her that I can't put my finger on."

"Yeah, well, you literally just met her, so your fingers shouldn't be touching any part of her."

"I'm pretty sure I didn't say anything about wanting to put my fingers on her, thank you very much."

Sadie didn't dignify that with a response, which Callie was used to. The two women had known each other for long enough to recognize each other's bullshit the very moment it came tumbling out of their mouths. Callie didn't even know if she thought Dr. Jory was attractive, but Sadie already had Callie wanting to put her hands—sorry, *fingers*—on her. Maybe she *was* too hooked on Dr. Jory's presence to pass it off as simple concern over one new person tipping the scales out of her favor.

"We still on for dinner?" Callie asked, abruptly and happily changing the subject.

Sadie was looking at her phone, a mild look of annoyance stretching across her freckled face. "We were until I got a text saying my new hire is too sick to come in for her shift tonight."

Callie bit her tongue, refraining from reminding Sadie that hiring college students, especially undergrads, was a sure way to suffer many texts about being "sick" that were really code for being hungover and/or preferring to party than work a shift at an indie bookstore. They'd had that conversation too many times. If Sadie didn't want to listen to her sage wisdom, then that was on her. Then again: They *did* live in a college town, ripe with undergrads wanting a relatively easy job to pick up some extra cash…to spend on the partying that then prohibited them from working consistent shifts.

"This is a pain in my ass," Sadie muttered, caught up in juggling multiple texts as she tried to cover the shift.

"I have an idea."

"Go on," Sadie said, not looking up from her phone.

"I'll help you in the store tonight…"

Sadie looked up then, her dark green eyes glowing with relief and happiness. "You're my favorite person."

"There's an *if*."

"Of course there is, you ungenerous prick."

Callie gasped and went full Southern belle as she covered her gaping mouth in horror. "Well, I never!"

"But you have. Because you are, at times, an ungenerous prick. And don't forget," Sadie continued, pointing straight at Callie's torso, "you're still on my payroll, so your *if* better be within the terms of your employment."

Callie vaulted off the sofa, and, though Sadie saw it coming, she didn't have time to ward her off. She launched a full assault on Sadie's highly ticklish ribs, their heads knocking together as Sadie screeched and vainly tried to push a taller and stronger Callie off her.

"Stop! Okay! Whatever you want, it's yours! Just stop!" Sadie wiggled uncontrollably under Callie's unrelenting attack.

Callie abruptly pulled her hands away, then placed them on the arms of the armchair and leaned in close to Sadie's face. They stared each other down, each breathless, waiting for the next ball to drop.

Sadie straightened up, giving Callie a solid push to put some space between them. "When are you going to grow up?"

Hearing the tension in Sadie's voice, Callie pulled further away, gently kicking her bare foot into Sadie's shin to keep the mood light. "Probably never. Anyway, my condition for coming in to work is that you feed me. Preferably pad thai, but I'll allow an Italian sub from the deli if you'd prefer that."

Sadie pushed her hair off her shoulders, not meeting Callie's eyes. "I could go for Thai."

"Great. All problems solved."

Sadie nodded, a smile on her face that looked, if Callie had to guess, a little forced. She consulted her phone once more, then finally met Callie's eyes.

"I'm gonna go change and head into the store. We should be good for a couple hours, so can you come in around five?"

"You got it."

Sadie slipped out of the apartment a couple minutes later, and Callie dropped back onto the sofa, wondering what was taking Courtney so long to text her.

CHAPTER TWO

"Callie, can you take over at the register? Amanda's over in the children's section."

"No prob, boss." Callie gamely dropped the stack of historical fiction texts she was reshelving and heeded Sadie's request as she breezed by on her way to the stockroom. Cornerstone Books was strangely busy for a Tuesday night, not that Callie minded—more customers to help meant the time passed faster, which meant she had less time to obsess over the interview.

Standing at the register was a twenty-something-year-old guy who looked vaguely familiar. She tried to figure out why before she faced him but came up empty. That was the blessing and a curse of living in a relatively small college town: Everyone starts looking familiar. Just because you've seen them, though, doesn't mean you know them, even if you think you should.

"Hey there, did you find everything okay?" Callie quickly logged in to the register and reached for the three books the young man was purchasing.

"Yeah, I'm kind of shocked you had these, to be honest," he said with a touch of chagrin. He studied Callie and she stared back at him. "You look familiar."

"You do, too, but I can't figure out why," Callie said as she rang up his purchases. *Impressive choices*, she mused. Not many people came into Cornerstone looking for Derrida's *Dissemination*. In fact, only masochistic English majors would look for such a text.

She pointed at the book, about to comment on said masochistic act, and the guy snapped his fingers. "I saw you this morning! In Berringer Hall, right? Interviewing for the GTA position?"

"Yep, I was there." Callie nodded. "That's it. Glad you figured that out because I would have driven myself crazy trying to place you."

"I'm Drew," he said, extending his hand toward her, a move that surprised her given how old she assumed he was.

"Callie," she responded after shaking hands. She put his books in his proffered reusable bag. "What'd you think about the interviews today?"

He shrugged, the picture of nonchalance, and handed her his debit card. "Pretty standard, I think. The department seemed kinda…" He paused, searching for the right word. "Not strict, but—I don't know, officious?"

Callie bit back a laugh. That's the last word she would have used to describe the panel of academics she'd faced earlier that day. Then again, she had known them all prior to going into the interview. She had a feeling Drew hadn't had that advantage. No, she corrected herself: She'd known *almost* all of them.

"I'm new around here," he continued, confirming her suspicions. "So maybe that's just how things are at Pennbrook."

Callie handed the debit card back to Drew, neither confirming nor denying his statement. He was, after all, a rival. "Where are you from?"

"Syracuse. I needed a change of scenery after finishing my master's program there." Drew collected his bag and smiled at Callie. "Anyway, glad we figured out why we were staring at each other. Have a good night, Callie." With that, he was off, and Callie realized she hadn't taken the chance to ask him how his interview had gone. *Just as well*, she figured, as now she could return to obsessing over her own interview experience.

Not for long, though. A delivery person soon swooped into the store with a bag full of Thai food. Callie called over to Sadie, who paid, then passed the bag to Callie.

"I'm in the middle of helping some poor undergrad with an insane reading list. Can you hang up here until Amanda's done? I don't care if you eat while you wait for customers," Sadie called over her shoulder, already on her way back to the STEM section.

Callie sighed. She was starving and she knew she couldn't eat her pad thai as usual, i.e., by basically inhaling it. She'd promised Sadie her time this evening, though, so she sat on the edge of the counter by the registers, trying her damnedest to chew before swallowing.

She gazed around the store as she ate. Cornerstone was a privately owned bookstore that housed a small café and an extensive, if peculiar, collection of magazines. It was an incredibly smart retail venture for the small college town, one which had somehow avoided being taken over by a big-name bookstore. True, most college students were relying on the Internet to provide texts for them—whether they were buying or renting. Then, of course, there was the official Pennbrook bookstore in the student union building, though books there were grossly overpriced. Nevertheless, Cornerstone had a nice-sized market of customers, and plenty of them weren't affiliated with Pennbrook at all. Callie had started working at the store sophomore year after she'd met Sadie, whose aunt co-owned Cornerstone. Callie had since come in and out of working at the store, but Sadie had never left, eventually moving into her current managerial position.

A flash of dark hair caught Callie's eye as she shoveled more noodles into her mouth. Another flicker of recognition sounded inside of her, but this time, it came with a quick shot of understanding. The short waves, cropped to the point of being unable to be unruly, bobbed along the top of a shelf before the person attached to the hair came into view. She wasn't alone, Callie noticed—she was with a man.

Surprised, or shocked, or maybe just caught completely off guard, Callie tried to swallow her mouthful of noodles before Dr. Jory got close enough to see her or talk to her (not that she would, Callie thought immediately, *but still*). Naturally, the noodles wanted to be further masticated and rebelled against the sudden swallowing movement. Feeling the ungodly and entirely embarrassing choking feeling rising in her, she dropped her container on the counter before quietly and quickly bolting for the bathroom in the back of the store.

Locked in the bathroom, Callie managed not to choke and die on her pad thai. The mirror reassured her that her shoulder-length honey-blond hair was still secure in its ponytail, a few waves poking out as usual. Her face itself was a brilliant shade of purple-red, however, and not a hue that complimented the unique dark blue shade of her eyes. Once she got her breathing under control, she splashed water on her cheeks in a weak effort to cool down both the aftermath of nearly choking and the surprise of seeing Dr. Jory. Callie knew she shouldn't be surprised; Cornerstone was frequented by many, many professors. Dr. Jory, as a member of the freaking English Department for shit's sake, surely would make an appearance every so often.

A banging on the door jolted her out of her thoughts. "Callie?" It was Sadie, thankfully. She would have died of embarrassment had it been Dr. Jory knocking. Because of course she would go running to rescue Callie from imminent choking death, having just met her that day. Of course she would! Callie cursed as she swung the door open and then grinned, trying her best to be cool and calm. She sucked at being cool and calm actually, but Sadie was too sweet to call her out on it, though she did eye Callie suspiciously.

"You good? Amanda said you practically sprinted back here."

"Yeah! Great. Everything is good." Callie shimmied out of the bathroom and away from Sadie's questioning look.

"What's wrong with you? You're...purple."

"Jesus Christ," Callie muttered, frantically patting at her cheeks as though that would calm down her coloring. "I'm fine. Some food just went down the wrong tube, you know how that goes."

Sadie wrinkled her nose as the two women walked back into the stacks of books. "Okay, ew. Can you refrain from eating like a caveman while you're working?"

Callie hip-checked Sadie, thankful that her pulse was returning to a normal rate. "I was starving. And I got caught a little off gu—" Her voice stopped of its own volition as Dr. Jory came into sight. Immediate sight that is. As in, she walked right out of an aisle and stopped in front of Callie, a slight smile touching her lips.

"I thought that was you," she said.

It was a simple statement, Callie knew that, but she couldn't help but feel suspicion lurking beneath the simplicity. "It's me," she said awkwardly.

Callie felt Sadie's eyes boring into her with questions, but she couldn't deal with that, so she avoided her stare. "I work here sometimes," she continued, unable to stop. Dr. Jory must have seen her sprinting away in her choking furor, she realized. Mortification spread through her body...and likely back onto her face.

"It's a great little store," Dr. Jory said appraisingly. "I've only been here twice, but it already feels like home."

Callie was too busy filing away little clues from Dr. Jory's statements to notice that Sadie was about to jump into the conversation. "That's a great compliment," Sadie said as she stepped forward, leaving Callie floundering. "I'm Sadie. I'm one of the managers here."

"It's nice to meet you, Sadie. I'm Kate Jory." Dr. Jory (*Kate*, Callie thought, tossing the name around in her brain) glanced at Callie before looking back at Sadie. "I'm a professor at Pennbrook."

"Oh!" Now Sadie glanced at Callie. "What department?"

"English," Dr. Jory said, motioning toward Callie. "I guess I didn't leave much of an impression on Callie this morning or else she would have mentioned that already."

Both women turned their glances to Callie, who cleared her throat loudly and tried to regain any semblance of coolness.

"Dr. Jory was part of the interview team this morning."

Callie watched as understanding dawned on Sadie's face. She hoped that meant Sadie was ready to rescue her from her tendency to make things super awkward without meaning to.

"Oh, right!" Sadie nodded, then turned back to Dr. Jory. "Callie mentioned there was a new professor on the panel, and since she's being super weird right now, I'm guessing that's you." Callie made a mental note to punch Sadie after the store closed. Hard. A nice, friendly, hard punch in the ribs should do it.

Dr. Jory laughed lightly. "That's me. I'm the newbie, fresh from a stint at the University of Tennessee."

"That's a big move," Sadie remarked. "What brought you to New Hampshire?"

Callie revised her mental note to say "punch Sadie and then thank her profusely for being great at making small talk."

The professor's smile slipped ever so slightly. No one but Callie would have noticed, since she was concentrating very hard on everything Kate was doing as she searched for clues about her. "It was time for a change," she said, her tone still friendly but definitely terse.

Sadie nodded, and Callie joined in, finally finding her voice. "Change is good. Even when it seems like it isn't at first."

Dr. Jory's eyes focused on Callie and held her gaze for a moment, just as she had earlier that very day. *Definitely intimidating*, Callie thought. She stared right back, determined to hold her own.

"That's true." She snapped back out of impassive mode as quickly as she'd entered it and smiled at both Sadie and Callie. "Well, I better find Theo and get him out of here before he buys the entire science fiction section. It was nice meeting you, Sadie. I'm sure I'll see you both in here again soon."

With that, she was off in search of Theo, whoever he was. Sadie nudged Callie's shoulder gently once Dr. Jory was out of earshot. "Amanda's at the register, so you can chill out. But... what's your deal, Cal? You were weirder than normal with her."

Callie shook her head. "I'm telling you, she just keeps catching me off guard. I wasn't expecting a new professor on the panel today, and I sure as hell wasn't expecting to see that new professor in the store tonight."

"Ooookay. Well, go distract yourself with those books you need to reshelve."

"I hate when you pretend you can boss me around."

Sadie rolled her eyes and took off for the front of the store. "I am your boss, idiot."

* * *

There wasn't anything amazing about August, really. It was a stifling month, even in New Hampshire, which liked to give the impression that it was cool and breezy all the time. Except for winter, of course—New Hampshire, like the other New England states, loved a good blustering, blizzarding winter to show off its picturesque cobbled streets and old, clapboard homes. New Englanders really loved to shovel snow, too. It was a favorite pastime, one that was definitely preferred to sweating to death at an outdoor brewery with your friends.

Callie questioned her judgment yet again as she took a pull from her new favorite beer, Hoppin' with Demeter. She had to hand it to the guys who ran Harpy, the new-ish and fantastic microbrewery near Pennbrook's campus. They knew how to make good beer. For a Greek mythology-obsessed person such as herself, also as a person who enjoyed good beer, Harpy was the best possible place to spend a couple of lazy hours on a sweltering Wednesday afternoon. She restlessly waited for the sun to drop behind some of the neighboring buildings so that she could move from the bar to one of the outdoor tables. If at all possible, she refused to sweat, so while Nikki and a couple of her friends from school sat outside and laughed as they sipped their beers, she brooded in the air-conditioning by herself.

As she drained her glass, Callie felt her phone buzz in her pocket. She was waiting quite impatiently to hear about her GTA position, and for a moment, she wondered if this was going to be the notice. "Finally," she muttered, then shook her head. It had only been two days and not even a *full* two days. She really needed to chill out and just let it happen, whatever it was going to be.

She tugged her phone out of her pocket. Her nerves tightened as she saw a text waiting from Courtney. Confirmation of the position definitely wouldn't come in a text from her, but maybe she had news. Callie read the bland text and quickly responded, telling Courtney to meet her at Harpy. It would be easier to get info out of her in person.

As she waited for her to arrive, Callie ordered a second Demeter and took another look around her. For four o'clock on a Wednesday, there was a decent crowd in the brewery. Another thing that she loved about living in Chestnut Hill was that her "neighbors," however loosely defined by geography, were pretty laid back. The town had a relaxed, chill vibe. It was rare that there were disturbances of any real kind, other than the occasional carousing of undergrads who drank too much. Some of the people hanging around the brewery were playing the random assortment of games that were lying around, others were chatting amicably, and a few lone wolves like Callie were sitting quietly and enjoying a damn good beer.

As the bartender slid Callie her fresh Demeter, Courtney dropped into the seat next to her and leaned forward to order a Hermes Express.

"Did you fly here? How exactly did this happen?" Callie whipped her head around for emphasis, searching for an aircraft.

"I was right around the corner, if you must know." Courtney exhaled deeply, then leaned back as she rolled up her sleeves. "I also had a hunch you were here, which is why I texted when I did."

"Cool, so now I'm a raging afternoon alcoholic?"

"Nah, more like a directionless drinker."

Callie nodded, appraising that assessment. "I'll take it."

The Hermes arrived, and Courtney took a deep, satisfying drink. She held up her finger as Callie opened her mouth to speak, then took another equally long drink before placing her glass back on the bar and lowering her finger, now permitting Callie to speak.

"Why haven't I heard anything yet? And, furthermore, why didn't you text me until now? I thought you were going to call me on Monday, you asshole."

"First of all, you need to relax." Courtney leveled Callie with one steady glare. It was par for the course for their friendship, which had grown out of Callie being a highly competitive, and somewhat obnoxious, undergraduate student in several of Courtney's classes. Courtney was an adjunct at the time, just six years older than Callie and busting her ass to get a coveted tenured position, which she earned during Callie's senior year. Once Callie entered the graduate program, she and Courtney struck up a quiet friendship, realizing it was inevitable, given their identical sense of humor and similar interests. Since Courtney wasn't teaching masters-level courses then, there wasn't any professor-student oddness to navigate. Still, they kept it quiet and cool—they never hid their friendship, but neither wanted anyone to think that Callie had some kind of privilege because she was hanging out with a professor and sometimes the professor's husband too. Once Callie graduated with her master's degree, they both heaved a sigh of relief and their friendship took off running.

Callie heeded Courtney's command (admittedly, it had taken her time to adjust to calling her by her first name, having spent years as her student calling her Dr. Wincheck-Rodriguez, or simply Wincheck when they were outside of the classroom) and took a breath. "Okay. I am now relaxed."

"Bullshit, but I appreciate your effort. You haven't heard anything yet because they haven't made all of their decisions yet."

"I like how you say 'they' like you're not involved in this."

"As far as *they* know, you and I are not friends, so I'll stick with pretending like I'm not involved for the purposes of this conversation."

Callie shook her head. "Not true. Lawler knows we're friends."

"Not exactly. Renee knows we kept in touch after you graduated. But I don't make a big deal out of it, and neither does she." Courtney poked Callie, hard, in the shoulder. "And neither should you."

"You know I don't. Just stop being a freak and admit you're part of the process."

Courtney sighed heavily for effect, then downed another gulp of her beer. "Whatever makes you happy, princess. My point is, there are three positions we're filling, and there is a bit of discussion still going on regarding that third position." She threw Callie a winning smile. "And that's all I'm telling you. Oh! I lied. I can also tell you that you'll know by the end of the workday on Friday."

Callie groaned and covered her face with her hands. "No. Absolutely not. That is far too much time for me to obsess, Courtney, and you know it."

"Sadly, my friend, I cannot reveal any more than what I already have. But you really do need to relax."

In a strange attempt at getting Callie to relax, Courtney looped into a long, detailed story about a syllabus she'd been working on with Dr. Lawler and how she knew some of the undergrads would hate the works, but they were just so seminal for movement through the English program. Callie half-listened, half-obsessed about the time remaining until Friday, but she snapped back into the conversation when Courtney spoke Kate Jory's name.

"And there really isn't a way around it, you know? If one of us is teaching that essay in ENG210, then *all* of us teaching ENG210 need to get behind teaching that essay. I think Kate and Darkler are going to go at it one of these days, and I am Here. For. It."

"Hmm, yeah, that would be a wild throw down."

Courtney shot Callie a strange look as she accepted a fresh Hermes from the bartender. "What would?"

"Uh, what you just said. Kate and Darkler. Going at it. Wild."

Courtney scoffed. "That's Dr. Jory to you, young one."

Callie sat with that for a moment and watched Courtney thumb through a text message on her phone. "What? Is she, like, super professional?"

"Kate? Kind of. It's hard to say. She's not like anyone I've ever known in that department before."

This wasn't going to be easy, Callie realized. Courtney could get weird about giving information to Callie, even when she wasn't directly affiliated with the college. She did like to maintain a professional demeanor; it really only cracked after a third beer. Callie contemplated how quickly she could get her to order another beer.

"She's new, you know," Courtney continued, much to Callie's excitement.

"Well, yeah. Kinda shocked me to see her sitting on that interview panel."

"Right, right—I did mean to call you about that after the fact. Sorry about that."

Callie waited, but Courtney didn't go on. She decided to tread carefully instead of bulldozing as she often did with Courtney. "She came into Cornerstone that night. She mentioned she's from Tennessee?"

"Mmhmm, she had a really great gig there."

Dead air. This definitely was not going to be easy.

Callie tried again. "She was with some guy that night... Theo, I think his name was."

"No clue. She's pretty tight-lipped when it comes to anything other than academia." Courtney paused, visibly reconsidering what she'd just said. "That's not entirely true, I guess. She's not very forthcoming. But she's a lovely woman. Very nice. Insanely smart. Just a little closed off."

Callie cleared her throat. "If she's so new, how did she end up on the panel?"

Courtney looked closely at Callie, then laughed. "Wow, she really threw you off, huh?"

"Honestly, yeah."

Courtney shook her head. "Don't sweat it, Cal. She's a great person. Renee practically scouted her to come to Pennbrook, and she's got the kind of energy that we want to see more of. Renee figured having her on the panel would help direct more of that energy our way via the candidates." A long swig of her beer signaled that that was going to be the final stop of the information train today.

Sure enough, Courtney promptly changed the subject. "How's that editing gig going, by the way? Making any headway?"

Disappointed but understanding why Courtney hit Pause, Callie talked openly about the editing she had started doing for *Sapphisms*, a well-known magazine aimed toward the women-loving-women community that focused more on creative and memoir-style writing than on journalistic writing. Callie had submitted a piece herself a couple years ago, gotten to know (via email, naturally) the editor-in-chief, and essentially talked herself into a part-time copy editor job. She loved every aspect of the work, especially the picky proofreading element, but she didn't feel comfortable relying solely on it for a career. She wanted more, and she was determined to get it, which is why she'd quit her fast-paced corporate job and come back for her PhD in literature, of all things.

"So, you like it?" Courtney summed up.

"I do. It's not forever, but it's decent money for doing something I'm naturally good at."

"You are an ace proofreader, I'll give you that." Courtney's phone buzzed again, and she sighed longingly at her empty beer glass and then her phone. Callie was hoping that the beer glass would win, because Beer #3 meant looser talking boundaries. "Nick's shift ended early."

"Eh, he can make his own dinner."

"You think I cook for him? You're insane." Courtney dropped money on the bar and gave Callie a slap on the back, which was the extent of their physical affection. Anything else they deemed disgusting. "He made dinner reservations, and for some reason Mr. Impractical chose a restaurant that's a half hour away."

"Courtney Wincheck-Rodriguez, I cannot believe you're leaving me at your husband's beck and call."

Courtney playfully shoved Callie as she walked behind her. "Have another drink, then go home."

Sage advice, since more than three beers would put Callie on her own kind of loose-boundary fault line. She glanced outside and saw that Nikki and her friends were still there. She ordered another beer before heading outside, hoping the sun had finally calmed down and she wouldn't sweat to death while she enjoyed some conversation and Hoppin' with Demeter.

CHAPTER THREE

It was, like, such a crazy good moment, right? The way her lips smothered mine in a kiss that took all of my breath away, it was like I hadn't inhaled in years and I was floating and wow I really couldn't breathe but it was okay because she was still kissing me and I was so into it. WOW I mean just WOW I had no idea kissing a woman would be so freeing and make all my insides twist up...

With a groan, Callie banged her forehead into her palms. There was not enough coffee in the world to get through this essay, and she wasn't even a coffee drinker. She eyed the glass of water next to her desk, assessing its power to make this essay better. Futile, she knew. A cool sip helped clear her head but did nothing to improve the frenetic letters on her laptop screen.

Callie toggled tabs, bringing her email to the front. She scrolled down, nervously eyeing the four other pieces that were calling for her editing attention, and clicked on her boss's name in the chat window.

Callie: *Are you serious with this one?*
Jana: *If I sent it to you, then yes.*
Callie:*…maybe you sent it by accident?*
Jana: *Unlikely. Which title?*
Callie: *"The First Kiss"*
Jana: *Hang on.*
Jana: *Oh.*
Callie:*…OH??*
Jana: *Give me five minutes. I'll call.*

Seven frustrating minutes later, Callie trudged out of her bedroom and made her way to the kitchen. Water wasn't going to cut it. Not that tea was much more exciting, but at least the caffeine would help her get through the next hour or so.

"Good morning, sunshine," Maya greeted Callie as she entered the room. "What's got you so riled up this early?"

Callie grunted as she sifted through the variety of teas. "An utterly juvenile, haphazard essay that I'm editing."

"And Jana let it through?"

Sapphisms was well-known in their apartment. Maya and Nikki each had subscriptions to the magazine and refused to consolidate into one to share. Maya's note of confusion was appropriate, since *Sapphisms* was well-known for only publishing very polished, maturely written essays, poems, and short stories. Callie wouldn't go as far as to call it an elite literary publication, but, well, it *did* have a reputation.

Callie watched her mug spin in the microwave for a moment before responding. "She sure did. But only because her girlfriend's niece wrote it." She laughed, shaking her head at the impossible situation she'd been put in. "And Jana assured me she only did it to 'help you prepare for grading all those terrible undergrad essays.'"

"Yikes."

"Yikes is right."

"Well," Maya said, considering, "she's not wrong. I mean, you are about to be ambushed by shitty freshmen 100-level papers."

"Okay, but I expect them to be shitty. Submissions to *Sapphisms*? No. They are not supposed to be this…challenging."

Maya grinned wickedly. "Is it pure porn?"

"Hmm, no. More like the internal monologue of a thirteen-year-old who's just been kissed by a girl for the first time and doesn't know where to put her hands."

"Oh, that's precious." Maya leaned over and squeezed her arm. "I'm sure you'll be able to impart your incredible wisdom and editing skills to make that little essay shine."

Callie glared at her roommate. "It just feels a little nepotism-y."

"You're one to talk, Ms. Graduate Teaching Assistant."

It was a low blow, albeit a jesting one, and one that Callie had been ready for since the moment she'd received the phone call from Dr. Lawler yesterday confirming her GTA position. Part of Callie wished Courtney hadn't been on the screening team just so she could avoid these teasing jabs from her friends, but she knew Courtney was a consummate professional and hadn't let their friendship affect her decisions. Maya, Nikki, and Sadie, on the other hand? Just a bunch of assholes, really, but she loved them anyway.

"You've been waiting to use that, haven't you?"

Maya scrunched her nose playfully and nodded. "Nik has some stored up, too."

"What do I have stored up?" Nikki asked, her voice scratchy with sleep, as she came into the kitchen.

"Lots of love for me." Maya nuzzled her head into Nikki's shoulder.

"Only for you, baby."

Callie gagged. "Take it to your room."

"Just because it's been *forever* since you've—"

"How about we don't go down that path this early on a Saturday morning?" She gestured toward the door. "Don't you have dogs to walk?"

After kissing Nikki with obnoxious enthusiasm, Maya cuffed Callie on the shoulder and left, off to hustle some dogs for one of her odd jobs.

Silence fell over the apartment as soon as the door closed behind Maya. She was definitely the more outgoing of the couple. Nikki, who had just started work on a doctorate in psychology, was the silent observer, the thinker. Callie had been observing them for the many years of their relationship, and she envied their balance, their ebb and flow, the easy way they complemented each other in so many ways. She'd also witnessed the many imperfections of their relationship: That was one of the drawbacks of the three of them living together.

"Where'd you go?" The prod was quiet and gentle, as it always was from Nikki.

"Relationship-land," Callie admitted. "I don't know how you guys do it."

"It's pretty simple," Nikki said. "We choose each other every day. And when we hit a snag, we work through it together."

"Idyllic," Callie mumbled.

"Not always, and you know that."

The apartment may have been spacious, but it wasn't soundproof. The infrequent but passionate fights between Nikki and Maya were fairly epic, and she had the pleasure of hearing 70 percent of them thanks to the intense decibel level of Maya's voice. Nikki always bought Callie lunch the day after. She wasn't sure if it was a "thank you for putting up with that" act of penance or a tacit "I'll kill you if you tell anyone about that," but she wasn't about to turn down free food.

"Speaking of…"

Callie started shaking her head as soon as the words left Nikki's mouth. "Nope. And now I have a great built-in excuse of not having the time."

Ah, yes, Nikki and Maya's favorite topic: Callie's Nonexistent Dating Life. It came up at least once a week, usually after Maya had a couple of drinks. They were hyper-focused on her having been single for over four years. Nikki sometimes went as far as to call it a "crime against all lesbians willing to date you."

It wasn't that Callie didn't want to date or be in a relationship. She did. But she was gun-shy. It didn't help that her last relationship had a historically bad ending, complete with a push-and-pull that had lasted for over six months before she finally shut down all communication with her ex, Kelly. Yes, "Callie" and "Kelly." When they both started turning around at the sound of either of their names, it was clear they were doomed. After that shit show finally ran its extended course, she had shut down for a period of time, scorning even the *idea* of meeting someone new.

The well hadn't run completely dry. After licking her wounds, she had managed to go on a couple of dates over the past four years, even pulling off three straight months of dating the same woman before deciding they were incompatible. (She'd never let Maya and Nikki meet her, so naturally they thought the incompatibility thing was an excuse.) And then she gave up: She simply stopped looking and stopped trying. Over the past year, she had been in no-woman's-land, going on zero dates and not even seeing anyone who caught her eye. Frankly, she wondered if that part of her was dead.

More strangely, for someone who had been so invested in meeting women and dating during her younger years, she wasn't sure if she wanted that part of her to be revived.

"It's always a timing thing with you," Nikki said, bringing her back from her thoughts. "I'd say it's an excuse, but this time…"

"This time you know I'm right. Juggling the TA gig with my own PhD classes is going to suck up any remaining free time I have."

Nikki shook her head, a solemn look on her face. "The lesbian community mourns this loss, my friend."

"The lesbian community hasn't exactly been knocking at my door, has it?"

"Nice try." Much like her girlfriend had earlier, Nikki clipped Callie on the shoulder on her way out of the kitchen. "If you opened yourself up to the possibilities, we'd have to invest in deadbolts to keep that door closed."

"I'd pay to see that," Callie mumbled. If nothing else, the image of a merry band of available lesbians banging on their apartment door amused her.

Remembering the task at hand, she sighed deeply, channeling the frenetic energy of new, hungry lesbians. She'd need it to get through editing that godforsaken essay.

CHAPTER FOUR

And just like that, summer was over and Callie found herself back in the workforce. As she trekked through the still-humid town on her way to campus, she marveled at how differently she felt on this walk to work as opposed to her forty-minute commutes to a job with a nearby textbook company. She'd taken the job because, with her wealth of literary knowledge, she anticipated she could move into a position where she would have input on creating curriculum. Having never taught a day in her life, however, she wasn't a prime candidate for those types of positions. Turned out she was a proofreading whiz, though, and after a year in an entry-level sales position, she was shifted into an editing position that she didn't hate but never loved.

Corporate life wasn't Callie's dream. Truthfully, she wasn't sure *what* her dream was, but she knew that literature—reading, writing, analyzing, editing—was the place where she felt happiest. She and Sadie joked about Callie writing a book, but she didn't think she had the attention span for that venture.

Instead, she stuck to proofing and editing, doing her best to help writers improve and put forth their best work.

Jana wasn't wrong, Callie mused as she tugged open the door to Berringer Hall. After spending close to two hours muddling through the abyss of that…*challenging* essay, Callie now felt better prepared to tackle the mess of English 100 essays that would come her way in a matter of weeks. One of the joyous parts of being a TA meant that she would be on the receiving end of the less-than-scholarly assignments. *It's fine*, she assured herself. And temporary! Once she got her PhD, she could…

Could what? Yeah, that was the question everyone around her wanted to be answered, including Callie's parents. She'd been avoiding them lately, pushing her bimonthly visits into monthly hour-long stops, because she had yet to come up with an answer to please them. She put enough pressure on herself without their forceful nudges when asking about her post-degree plans. What was she actually planning on doing with her life?

"Something grand," she muttered, taking the stairs two at a time. "Something unbelievably grand."

The English Department was housed on the second floor of Berringer Hall. It had seen better days—perhaps in 1974 or so. The antique appearance added to its charm and created a very lived-in, creaky atmosphere. Linoleum floors were etched with endearing cracks and chips. The walls, while wearing a relatively fresh coat of off-white paint, held their own battle scars from backpacks, projects, and likely kicks. Thick wooden trim squared out the rectangular floor; that, too, was dented with murderous flair. Callie loved every bit of the department's vaguely Gothic character, including the classroom doors, nearly all of which stuck and had to be body-slammed to be opened. The ambiance was perfect for studying moody literature.

The one downside to the aged charm of the place was its inconsistent HVAC system. Courtney complained about it so often that Callie knew what to expect, and still she was shocked to feel the air hotter inside the building than outside. Her wavy hair stuck uncomfortably to the back of her neck. As she approached the department offices, she furiously wiped beads of sweat from her upper lip. While she was dressed in jeans and a plain black T-shirt, definitely at least a full ladder rung down from her corporate attire, she didn't want to look entirely a mess on her first day and the sweat was not helping.

Callie hip-checked the door to the bank of offices, hoping it was cooler in this area. Not much luck there. She inhaled the familiar scent of books and stress as she moved toward the secretary's desk.

"Nice of you to show up."

Callie quirked an eyebrow at the woman sitting behind the desk. Gone was good old Bertie, the legendary hard-assed keeper of all English Department secrets. In her place sat Audrey, horn-rimmed glasses perched on her small, slightly upturned nose. She was trying to look intimidating, but Callie had a hunch the girl didn't have a daunting bone in her body.

"It's a pleasure to see you, Audrey. I had no idea you were the new secretary."

Audrey tilted her chin, fixing Callie with a look that was some weird attempt at condescending. "Why else would I have been leading the interviews?"

"Leading" was not a term Callie would have used to describe her role that day. She scanned the room, leaning forward a bit to peer down the hall toward Courtney's door, which was closed.

"I'm supposed to meet Dr. Lawler at nine," she said, tapping her index finger on the edge of Audrey's desk. "And I'm ten minutes early. Is Dr. Wincheck-Rodriguez in her office?"

"She is not," came the huffed response. Audrey's eyes were fixed on Callie's tapping finger. "You can have a seat and wait for Dr. Lawler."

With a look of bemusement, Callie spun and took a seat in one of the chairs across from Audrey's desk. She had to hand it to her: She was trying really hard to be professional. It was endearing in a way, but also a bit over-the-top. Watching Audrey acclimate to the unique bustle of this department was going to be highly entertaining.

A few minutes passed before Callie heard voices in the hall. Courtney's laugh was unmistakable. She felt some of the tension slip from her shoulders. She could admit she was nervous; starting something new and unknown always made her insecurities flare. Having an instant ally in Courtney was just the balm she needed to transition into this position more smoothly.

The door jiggled, resisting the nudge of the opener. It jerked a bit but refused to open. Courtney started laughing, and Callie knew she was helpless once she dissolved into laughter like that. A mild curse was heard from the other side of the door.

Callie and Audrey exchanged a look. As the door remained stuck, their look evolved into a stare down. One of them should help. Someone banged on the doorknob. Another round of laughter joined in with Courtney's as a string of expletives flew out of someone's mouth.

Audrey cleared her throat loud enough to grate Callie's ears. With a deep, resigned sigh and a roll of her eyes, Callie stood up and wrapped her hand around the doorknob. Gently, she turned the knob forty-five degrees before jerking her arm back forcefully.

The creak of the thick wooden slab as it opened was accompanied by gasps from the other side of the door. Dr. Lawler and Dr. Jory stood in amazement, Courtney behind them still trying to stifle her laughter.

"And this, Kate, is why we hired Callie," Dr. Lawler said. "She understands the mechanics of this building better than those of us who have worked here for years."

"For decades," Courtney corrected, having regained her composure enough to toss a dig at the department chair. She entered the office area and grinned at Callie before heading straight for her office.

Dr. Lawler snapped her fingers. "After all these years dealing with her attitude, you'd think I'd be armed with comebacks. But no. I'm never ready."

Callie opened her mouth, ready to explain the impossibility of being ready for Courtney's jabs but stopped herself. Casting a quick glance at Dr. Jory, she had a feeling she should continue to keep quiet about her friendship with Courtney until Courtney told her otherwise.

To Callie's surprise, Dr. Jory was studying her as well. She resisted the urge to hold her eye contact and offered a quick smile instead. She felt a quiet heat blossom over her cheeks as she shifted her attention back to Dr. Lawler, who was still harping on her inability to nail Courtney with a solid comeback. In her peripheral vision, she could see Dr. Jory's hazel eyes lingering on her.

"All right. Callie, let's get started." Having apparently gotten over Courtney's low blow about her age, Dr. Lawler snapped back into business mode. "You don't need a tour, right? Nothing has changed around here."

"No, I'm good."

"Wonderful." Dr. Lawler glanced between Callie and Dr. Jory. "Would you two like an official introduction?"

Callie's blush deepened. "Oh... I—we..."

"We made one of our own," Dr. Jory interjected, saving Callie from continuing her embarrassed mumbling. "I ran into Callie at Cornerstone."

Dr. Lawler huffed. "So, you're depriving me of the opportunity to talk about how thrilled I am to have poached you and dragged you across several states in order to join our impressive faculty?"

"That's a dramatic explanation," Dr. Jory said. "But to please you..." She turned to Callie. "Hi, Callie. I'm Dr. Kate Jory. Former drama teacher, current professor."

"She's from Tennessee!" Dr. Lawler exclaimed as Dr. Jory offered Callie her hand. She shook it and noted the gentle but firm touch.

"It's great to meet you, Dr. Jory." Callie played along, smiling evenly. "I'm Callie Lewes, former textbook editor, current TA and doctoral student."

Interest briefly lit up Dr. Jory's face but was quickly replaced by that impassive look. "A fellow late-in-life doctoral student. We should chat sometime."

A flicker of curiosity shot through Callie. "I'd like that."

Dr. Jory pointed past Courtney's office. "I'm at the end of the hall. I know you and Renee have a lot to cover today, but I'm sure I'll see you around."

Before Callie could respond, Dr. Jory walked toward her office, and Dr. Lawler, after receiving several messages from Audrey, ushered Callie in the opposite direction toward her office.

* * *

Renee Lawler was all business. Callie appreciated that. No, really, she did. But the sheer amount of information that she threw at Callie in a matter of twenty minutes was overwhelming to say the least. Sure, she was familiar with the campus and most of the professors, and yes, she knew part of this job was a process of learn-as-you-go, plus she had to attend two full days of training later in the week, but still. *Wow*. It was a lot to process.

Noon found Callie at the desk she'd claimed as hers in the area designated for TAs. The space was bigger than an office but small enough that having three desks and chairs, plus a couple of filing cabinets, crammed into it made it feel tight. There were windows, though, something Callie appreciated. The view of trees would be lovely as summer edged into fall, and if Callie squinted, she could see the rolling lawn in front of the student union building. The room itself could use some personality. Once Callie got a handle on how to manage her new schedule, she figured she could spruce things up.

For now, however, the daunting task of creating a manageable schedule loomed before her, glimmering in its impossibility. On top of TA'ing two classes—Experiences in American Literature, and Introduction to Literary Theory, both 200-level classes, which was a most pleasant surprise—Callie had two of her own seminars to attend on Tuesday and Thursday evenings. Fortunately, Dr. Lawler had given her MWF classes, one at eight and one at eleven, so the rest of those days would be freed up for some office hours. Callie stared down at her calendar, working through times in her head. She didn't *have* to hold office hours on Tuesdays and Thursdays, but since her classes weren't until six p.m., she could swing an hour of availability in the early afternoon, closing shop by three p.m. to ensure she had enough time to prepare for her evening seminars. She wanted to be available for her students, but she didn't want to compromise her own doctoral studies in the process.

Leaning back in her creaky chair, Callie twisted her wavy hair into a knot on the top of her head. The 200-level courses were a relief (No English 101! No freshmen!) but the Experiences course was taught by Courtney. Callie turned her gaze from her calendar to the window. She was sure they would talk about it, and it would likely not be a big deal at all. But she was worried the whole situation might be weird for their friendship.

A scuffling noise at the door drew Callie's attention away from the window. A twenty-something guy was scooching past the partially open door which, shock of all shocks, was insisting upon sticking in that position.

"Okay, guess that's not opening," he muttered as he wormed his way into the room.

"It's a thing," Callie said. "The Infamous Doors of Berringer Hall."

He looked up at the sound of her voice, a grin snaking across his face. "Bookstore girl."

Callie looked at him closely. "Derrida masochist! Drew, right?"

"Yep, and you're Callie if I remember correctly." He took in the room, nodding slowly. "Impressive digs we've got here."

"Only the very best for the TAs. I'd pick that desk." Callie pointed to the desk against the non-windowed wall. "The other one is drafty, and that's putting it kindly."

Drew dumped his bag into the chair before perching on the desk and nodding toward the calendar on Callie's desk. "You don't waste any time."

"Can't. I'm a chronic planner. It's a defect I'm happy to live with."

Before Drew could respond, the door nudged open a fraction of an inch further and a pretty redhead poked her head into the room.

"TA Central?" she asked, a nervous smile painting her features.

"None other than," Drew jumped in. "I'm Drew."

"Megan." She stepped into the room and glanced around. "This is…charming."

"That's one word for it. I'm Callie."

"Nice to meet you both." Megan, a flustered look striping across her face, headed toward the open desk by the window. "I could get used to this view."

Drew hopped off the desk he was perching on. "You know what, the view from this desk is even better. Why don't you take this one? It might get cold over there during the winter."

With a grin hidden behind her laptop, Callie watched Drew and Megan begin an obvious tango of curiosity and attraction. She tuned out their slightly awkward interactions for a few minutes, letting them find their footing until Megan's casual remark about a certain new professor brought Callie back to attention.

"It's an English 101 at ten a.m. I'm a little weirded out that I'm so close to their ages." Megan shuffled some papers. "Oh, and it's with the new professor. Dr. Jory."

"Do new professors always get the low-man classes?" Drew asked.

"Kind of," Callie said, easing back into the conversation. "But since she's established with her PhD and has previous teaching experience, I'm sure she has some upper-level courses."

"Oh, yeah, she definitely does." Megan ran her finger down the sheet of paper she'd pulled out. "She's got two sections of 101, but she also has a 200-level called Women of the Renaissance." Worry crossed Megan's features. "That's definitely not my area of expertise."

"I've read a lot of British lit," Drew interjected. "I'm happy to help you."

"I did an independent study during my master's program that was focused on British women writers. I can give you tons of resources," Callie added.

Megan smiled, bits of worry still clinging to her eyes. "You guys are great. Thank you." She continued scanning her paper. "Oh, how cool. Dr. Jory's teaching a 400-level class called Queering Shakespeare."

Callie's brain perked up at that news. She hadn't even known such a course existed, and the fact that Dr. Jory was teaching it…interesting. It meant nothing, of course. *Anyone* could be told to teach anything. But Callie was pretty certain this was a new course. She had some digging to do.

CHAPTER FIVE

"So I bent down closer, trying to get a better look. I should have known better. When I tell you that sewage plants smell better than this guy did, I'm not exaggerating. I would rather spend an hour sitting in a sewage plant than ever be in the same room with this dude again. Fresh sewage," he added. "You'd never guess from how polished he was on the outside. But that odor! Fresh sewage mixed with dog shit."

"Nick." Courtney's tone danced on the edge of warning, but as usual, her husband plowed ahead.

"When Mike came in, armed with his tools, he hit the wall of stench blowing from the patient's pores. I've never seen a human face turn that color green." Nick leaned back in his chair, his brown, heavily tattooed arms crossing over his burly chest. "I could have puked right then and there. I don't know how Mike completed the exam without vomiting through his mask, directly into—"

"Okay! Great story!" Courtney clamped her hand over Nick's mouth.

Callie eyed her beer, unsure about how it would taste now. Her stomach was roiling uncomfortably just thinking about the body odor Nick had so artfully described.

"She can handle it," Nick said, his voice muffled behind his wife's firm hand. He wiggled his eyebrows at Callie. "She loves my stories. Right?"

"While I *can* handle it, I don't particularly want to."

Courtney sighed, dropping her hand. "You're incorrigible when you're around Callie."

"She's the only one of your friends who doesn't have a stick protruding from her ass," Nick generously pointed out. "She's like one of the guys."

Callie stifled a laugh and looked around the restaurant, letting Courtney and Nick battle it out yet again. They were her favorite married couple—*goals*, as the kids would say—and she never tired of Nick's bizarre tales from his career as an RN. A stranger would never guess his profession from his outside appearance. A towering six foot five, he was both tall and, as he liked to say, "built." Courtney, who was six-one herself, favored the word "sturdy." Either way, Nick was the type of guy old church ladies feared running into in a dark alley, but he was kind, hilarious, and very weird. The tattoos didn't help his intimidating image, but his kind brown eyes sparkled with humor and genuine warmth.

There was something undeniably feminine about Nick, Callie thought, and that wasn't a stereotyping of male nurses. She had picked up on it immediately when she'd first met him. Over time she realized how perfectly that soft edge of Nick fit with Courtney's sometimes rigid, borderline masculine ridges. They balanced each other beautifully.

"Sorry I'm late!" With a burst of subtle citrus perfume, Sadie bumped into Callie as she sat down next to her. "The new manager I hired is paranoid about locking up on her own, so I had to talk her off the ledge before I left."

"Sounds promising," Callie murmured, accepting the justified jab in her ribs.

"Sadie! You just missed the best story of the day!" Though

they rarely saw each other, Nick's penchant for tormenting Sadie with his most disgusting stories never got old.

Preemptively, Sadie's face lost some of its naturally pale color.

"He's done," Courtney interjected. "Don't worry. I'm glad you could make it." She nodded toward Callie. "Your friend here was just about to tell us how her training went."

"Two days of hellish boredom," she said. And it had been. The ins and outs of her TA position had been laid out with absolutely no room for confusion. Drew and Megan had taken copious notes while Callie's attention flickered in and out like a candle battling a stiff breeze. She'd been distracted, both about what it would feel like to be on the teaching side of the classroom and by what it would be like to see Kate Jory nearly every day.

It was weird and slightly uncomfortable, the way Kate had taken up residence in a small corner of Callie's brain. She kept trying to brush it off as a facet of knowing every professor but her. Something about that wasn't ringing totally true, though, and the fact that she couldn't put her finger on the bigger piece was frustrating.

Shooing Tiny Brain Kate back into her dusty corner, Callie regaled her audience with a deeply fascinating rundown of her training. As she finished and took in their glassy eyes, she nodded with satisfaction.

"Exactly. And I look forward to seeing these same expressions on my students' faces in the weeks to come."

Nick guffawed, the only term that could be applied to his laugh. "See? No stick."

As Sadie placed her drink order with the waiter, the rest of the table scanned the menu to firm up their entree plans. Sadie, as usual, suggested she and Callie get two dishes and split them with each other.

"Remind me again why the two of you don't date?"

While Sadie blushed furiously at Nick's question, Callie gritted her teeth. Why was it so hard for people (read: men and lesbian girlfriends) to understand and accept that two women who are both attracted to women could actually just be friends?

Courtney must have inflicted some under-the-table bodily harm on Nick because instead of pursuing his question, he expelled a low "not that spot" grumble.

"The better question is: Why is Callie completely shut down from dating anyone?"

The force with which Callie snapped her head to gawk at her supposed best friend was sure to give her a sore neck the following morning. In fact, she was fairly certain something there that wasn't supposed to pop had gone ahead and popped. Violently.

As she fumbled for a response, Courtney stepped in.

"I think Callie's had other things on her mind lately."

How the hell does she know about Tiny Brain Kate? Callie almost laughed at her own ridiculous thought but instead found her footing in a bit of rage over Sadie's comment.

"Dating is not a priority for me, Sadie." Her tone was firm and punched with sass. "I'm focused on completing my doctoral program. We've talked about this, so I don't know why you feel it's necessary to discuss it...now."

"Eww, don't get all offended. I just think it's a shame that you've pulled yourself from the market." Sadie shrugged as she curled a lock of her copper hair around her finger. "You're quite the catch."

"She's not wrong," Nick said. "Sassy, smart, and sexy."

Three pairs of eyes swung toward Nick. Only his wife's rolled. The others were filled with a mixture of confusion and amusement.

"Sassy and smart—I can't disagree with that."

Four pairs of eyes swung to where Renee Lawler stood beside their table, leaning toward it ever so precariously.

"Renee!" Courtney nearly jumped out of her seat. "What are you doing here?"

With a flick of her wrist and a tilt of her head, Renee smiled winningly, then loudly whispered, "I've had a few drinks."

Callie and Courtney exchanged a glance as Nick began chatting up Renee. Despite what he would certainly describe as her having a "two-by-four up her firm, business skirt-suited ass," it was well known that Nick had a special liking for messing with Dr. Renee, as he called her.

A weird look crossed Courtney's face. Callie couldn't read it, but it triggered a sinking feeling in her gut regardless. Partly to save Courtney from later mortification over whatever Nick was about to say to Renee, Callie jumped into the conversation.

"Courtney—I mean, Dr. Wincheck-Rodriguez—and I thought it would be a good idea to, um, brainstorm a bit. Before the semester starts. Officially, anyway." Callie barely managed to stammer out her weak explanation.

"That is a *great* idea, ladies!" Renee punctuated her statement with a spirited nod that brought her current state of balance into question. She staggered a bit, then tossed another large smile at everyone. "But you should be enjoying your weekend! You can't just work, work, work all the time!"

On cue, Nick started beat-boxing the intro beat to Rihanna's song. It was enough to break the weird spell Courtney seemed to be under.

"I have no doubt that Callie and I are going to work well together. She was a huge asset to the department years ago and—"

"Honey," Nick interrupted, gently patting his wife's arm. "I don't think it's appropriate to call your new TA a huge ass."

Renee found this hilarious, and Callie couldn't help but laugh as well at the vision of all-business-Lawler slightly undone by some drinks. She'd heard rumors from Courtney about wild holiday parties, but seeing it in person was super entertaining.

As Callie waited for Renee to regain her composure before firing off a retort, another figure sidled up to the table. Callie's throat went dry, any words she might have said dying on her tongue.

Kate Jory looked back and forth between Renee and the people seated at the table, a wrinkle of curiosity rippling her features. She was wearing the small wire-rim glasses she'd had next to her laptop on the day of the interviews, and Callie felt a strange little tug in her chest.

"I'm afraid to ask what's made her laugh so hard," she said in a voice both dry and amused.

"And I'm afraid to ask how many glasses of wine she's had." Courtney winked at Kate. "Spill it, Jory."

Kate raised her hands up before her chest. "I'm sworn to secrecy." She smiled broadly at Courtney, a private look passing between them. Callie took note of it, recognizing that Courtney probably knew Kate better than she'd previously let on.

"Kate, this is my husband, Nick. Nick, this is Dr. Kate Jory, the new professor I've told you about."

"Lovely to meet you, Dr. Kate." Nick stood to his full height, an absolute giant hovering over Kate's five-foot-three stature, and shook her hand. "And you know our friend Callie here. This is her friend, Sadie."

Kate nodded, seeming to put pieces together. "Sadie from Cornerstone. It's nice to see you again."

"I was going to call you tomorrow," Sadie said with a little wave. "That Elizabeth Cary text came in."

Callie felt a small surge of jealousy wash through her. Why hadn't Sadie mentioned Kate had been back to the store? Sighing internally, she gave herself a shake. The better question was, why *would* she?

"Oh, that's great news. And right on time. I'll swing by tomorrow and pick it up." She paused. "Actually, I can't. It'll have to wait until sometime next week."

"How about I give it to Callie at home tomorrow? That way you can have it first thing Monday morning."

Kate's eyes settled on Callie, a curious look in them as though she was just then remembering that she was sitting there. After a tiny hesitation she said, "If it's not out of your way…"

"Not one bit!" Sadie bounced in her chair. "I know how exciting it is to get your hands on a special edition of a prized text, so why wait?"

A giggle erupted from Renee; Callie had nearly forgotten she was standing there. Somehow, she'd gotten her hands on a glass of wine and was taking a luxurious sip from it. She set it back down in front of Courtney—aha, well that sucked for

Courtney—before whispering, again far louder than she likely intended, "A special edition? Buncha nerds."

Sadie and Callie couldn't hold back their giggles. Seeing such an intimidating, powerful professor soused by some simple glasses of wine was far too entertaining, especially when they used to be scared shitless of attending said professor's classes when they were undergrads.

"I'd ask you both to join us," Courtney began, nothing but amusement in her voice, "but I think someone has had enough to drink tonight." She looked pointedly at Renee before sending another wink over to Kate.

"You do know she's referring to you." Kate's voice was dry, but it was obvious she wasn't mad.

Renee twirled her finger in Courtney's face. "You need to loosen up, Wincheck. Have another glass." She allowed Kate to tug her back from the table.

Lifting up her now-empty wine glass, Courtney sighed heavily. "You've left me no choice. Now go home."

A chorus of goodbyes rose from the table, saluting Renee as she waved regally toward her adoring fans. Kate shook her head as she leaned in to exchange some words with Courtney. When Nick pointed out that Renee was on the staggering run, Kate closed her eyes and gave her head another firm shake.

"A little warning about her endless capacity for wine next time, Courtney."

"Consider it your initiation," Courtney said brightly. "We've all been there."

"At least she's entertaining," Callie piped up.

Kate's eyes landed swiftly on Callie, their gazes locking for an instant that felt too short and too long all at once. "That she is." Kate sent smiles to the others. "I better go catch her. Enjoy your evening."

Relieved that Nick, Courtney, and Sadie lapsed back easily into conversation, Callie allowed herself the pleasure of watching Kate walk away. It couldn't hurt, simply admiring the way her jeans snugly outlined her curvy hips and thighs. She hadn't previously noticed exactly how curvy those hips and thighs were and now that she had, she knew she would have a hard time forgetting it.

Then again, seeing the mysterious Kate Jory every day wasn't going to give her much room to forget anything.

CHAPTER SIX

Callie twisted in front of her mirror, checking every angle she could possibly see. Dark blue eyes, once described as "stormy but sexy" by an old girlfriend, stared back at her. Her summer tan was fading, taking with it the sun-kissed glow from her cheeks. She peered closer, gasping in slight horror. A sun spot boldly stared back at her. She rubbed it, succeeding in creating a red slash on her forehead. The spot remained, taunting her. Right. She'd deal with that later.

Finding the balance of TA-appropriate attire was going to be her biggest battle in the coming weeks. She knew from her own time in college that TAs could be notoriously sloppy. She would not descend to that level. Nope, not happening. On the flip side, she didn't want to look over-the-top professional. Courtney had warned her about the fine line separating students from TAs. It wasn't as bold as the line that existed between students and professors; there was a blurring of boundaries there that came from TAs being students as well. Callie figured that part of that line came down to attire, as weird as that may sound.

Huffing, Callie yanked off her shirt and pulled on a white button-down that was one step away from being form fitting. She was proud of maintaining her fit body but was well aware that a few extra pounds had snuck their way onto her five-foot-nine frame while she wasn't paying attention. Nevertheless, Callie liked her body. She felt comfortable in it and had learned to appreciate the softer lines that now covered its formerly firm, muscular structure.

She eyed herself, liking the fit of the shirt and the way it accented her still-narrow hips as it tucked loosely into her dark rinse skinny jeans. Scuffed brown leather boots completed the outfit. After tugging her shoulder-length hair into a loose knot at the nape of her neck, she grabbed her Timbuk2 messenger bag and headed for the kitchen.

"Look at you, all ready for your first day of school!"

Callie curtsied for Maya before grabbing her water bottle. "Shall we take pictures to commemorate this moment?"

Maya snorted. "Only if you have one of those chalkboard signs ready to go. Oh wait, you'd have a giant blank spot since you have no idea what you want to be when you grow up. Maybe we should skip the pictures."

"You, of all people, have literally no ground to stand on when it comes to professional goals."

A beat of silence sat between them. Callie fought her instinct to apologize. Thankfully before she could unnecessarily drop a "sorry," Maya spoke up. "Nice, Callie. Real nice."

In the wake of Maya stalking out of the kitchen, Callie blew out an annoyed sigh and finished filling her Nalgene with water. They got along most of the time, but if Maya weren't Nikki's girlfriend, a friendship would never have been forged between them. She'd been trying to put her finger on it for years, but Callie couldn't quite figure out what it was about Maya that got under her skin. Part of it was probably her haphazard attitude toward life. Maya kept herself busy with bartending, dog-walking, and, theoretically, writing. The last item remained a mystery to both Nikki and Callie. Neither had ever seen evidence of Maya's writing.

As long as their part of the rent was paid, Callie didn't care how Maya was earning her money. Nikki and Maya had a good relationship, but she worried for Nikki. There was an obvious disconnect between Nikki and Maya's life and future plans. Callie could write a dissertation on the pitfalls of a relationship between someone who didn't have defined career goals and someone who was very career-motivated.

It was, after all, the reason she was single.

* * *

In stark contrast to previous weeks, Berringer Hall was vibrating with energy. It was early, just shy of seven thirty, but already eager, anxious undergraduates were sweeping into the building. Callie smiled to herself as she observed a small group of young women hustling toward a classroom. Definitely not freshmen, she thought. While eight a.m. classes were not first choice (what college student *wanted* to have to learn at that time of day?), 200-level courses weren't typically frequented by freshmen. There were a few sprinkled into Courtney's (Callie's!) first class of the day, but the majority were sophomores.

As Callie approached the English offices, she inhaled deeply. First-day early morning scents assaulted her: coffee, never-opened textbooks, someone's overabundance of perfume (likely hiding the inability to get up early enough to shower before class), freshly cut grass stuck to the bottoms of shoes, and a tiny hint of something Callie couldn't place. It was a soothing scent, like soap and water on someone's skin, and it stuck out among the other expected hallway odors.

The mysterious scent strengthened when Callie pushed into the offices. She smiled brightly at Audrey, who sat ramrod straight behind her desk.

"Good morning, Audrey. It's lovely to see you this morning."

A sneer crept over Audrey's otherwise pretty features and her eyes squinted behind her horn-rimmed glasses. "Do you need something?"

"Not a thing." Callie wiggled her fingers in a spirited wave as she breezed past Audrey. She paused at Courtney's office door and seeing that it was ajar, she knocked lightly before poking her head in.

Courtney glanced up and waved her in. She was murmuring to herself as she stabbed keys on her laptop. Knowing the drill well, Callie perched on the arm of the chair that sat across from her desk, keeping still and quiet while she banged out what was sure to be a rather firm email to some poor, unsuspecting recipient.

"Done," Courtney breathed, then glanced up at Callie. "That's probably not going to go over well."

"Who's on the lucky other side of that email?"

"The dean." Courtney grimaced. "The good news is you'll have a job if I get canned today."

Callie laughed and shook her head. Courtney, too, was on the Let's Figure Out Callie's Life For Her bus and it was absolutely one of her least endearing qualities.

"Oh, hey. Good news. Renee knows about us."

"Oh, there's an 'us' to speak of?" Callie tilted her head at her friend.

"Please don't say that around my husband. You know it's his dream." Both Callie and Courtney made faces of disgust. "Renee, as she does, casually commented in the middle of a meeting how nice it is for me to be able to mentor, and I quote, 'one of your dear friends.'"

Callie pressed her hand to her chest. "Such kind words! But seriously, that's good. Right? A little stress off the table?"

"Definitely good." Courtney moved some papers around her desk. "So, Ms. Graduate Teaching Assistant. How are you feeling? Ready for this?"

Callie wiggled her dangling foot. Ready, yeah. She was ready. But she was also simply existing in the line, waiting for the ride of the semester to begin. She was confident in her planning and time management. *Thank you, Type A personality traits*. At the same time, she was relaxed and vibing with the idea of going with the flow. Though Callie touted her complex, difficult-to-label personality like it was the shining example of Quality Personalities, it was awkwardly mysterious and a damn challenge at times, thanks to its clash with her split Type B personality qualities.

She pocketed her conflicted monologue for another day. "Ready as I'll ever be. I think."

"That's the spirit—spoken like a true professor." Courtney stood and gathered her things, then propelled them both out the door. "Let's go terrify the children."

Hours later (How many? Callie had no idea; she'd lost track of time and life sometime after the end of that eleven a.m. Lit Theory course with Dr. Lawler), Callie found herself staring blankly out the window of her office. Drew and Megan had been there, she was sure of that, but Megan had maybe gone to another class? And Drew had possibly gone to acquire coffee? It was all a mystery, a foggy mystery in the chaotic storm of the first day of the semester.

"Two classes will not kill you." Callie nodded, appreciating that the words sounded more confident than she felt, and tapped her pen against the cool wooden surface of her desk. They wouldn't kill her; she was up for this task. The nagging insecurity arose from that hotbed of inexperience but—*come on, Callie*—her fellow TAs had the same teaching inexperience. What she had were years of life experience that would benefit her in some way.

She groaned as she hit the nail on the head. There it was: the age snag. She was thirty-four, a great age by all accounts. But working as a teaching assistant at her age had never been a life goal. All those years of school had pushed Callie into believing she'd figure out her life and career path sooner rather than later, but apparently, she'd been wrong.

The shift and shudder of the perennially jammed office door drew Callie out of her thoughts. Assuming it was Drew returning with what she believed to be the promised coffee and tea, Callie called out, "That's as good as it gets, buddy."

It wasn't Drew's head that appeared in the quarter-open doorway, however, but Kate's. Callie swallowed hard as embarrassment flushed her cheeks.

"Hey there!" She half-stood from her chair before realizing it probably made her look like she was greeting a royal instead of a mere professor. "Dr. Jory," she hastened to add, feeling they weren't anywhere near the point of casual greetings. Callie bit her lip; the shot of pain centered her. "I'm sorry, I thought you were Drew. Hence the 'buddy' comment."

Kate stepped into the office and swept the small space with her eyes. "Call me Kate," she said as she took another step closer to Callie's desk. "I know other professors have different expectations, but I don't mind a first name basis when it's just the two of us."

Callie struggled to keep her cool as her stomach executed some Olympic-status gymnastics at the phrase "just the two of us."

"Okay. Right. Kate."

Seemingly nonplussed by the wide range of awkwardness that Callie was exhibiting, Kate moved closer still. Callie took a brief moment to appreciate the extremely pleasing ensemble she'd put together for the day: black pants that were just tight enough, a plain white V-neck shirt topped by a dusky maroon blazer. Kate's curvy and petite body seemed made for the clothes that she wore—a trick of the trade called tailoring, something Courtney praised to no end.

Callie's synapses fired to attention as that clean, maybe fresh cotton, soothing scent from earlier in the day made its way over to the desk. So, she didn't just look good, she had to smell amazing, too? *Who is she and what the hell is this woman doing to me?*

"So," Kate began, leaning her hip against Callie's desk. "How did the day go?"

Right. Business talk! Of course. Confusion tugged at Callie as she glanced at her watch. Shouldn't Kate still be in class?

"I thought you had class until three?" she blurted out, entirely against her rational will.

Kate lifted a corner of her mouth in an amused smile. "Keeping track of my schedule?"

Woefully unprepared for this surprisingly coy response, Callie pressed her fists, hard, against her thighs. *Get. It. Together.* "Well, I know Megan is TA'ing your afternoon class and she's not back yet." As her moxie returned, she smiled easily. She could play the coy game, too. "You left her alone on the first day? That's a bold move."

"It would be a bold move—if I were interested in hanging the poor girl out to dry." Kate rested her palm on Callie's desk. "Did Courtney and Renee actually keep their classes full time?"

Before she could answer, and she was ready this time, Kate tilted her head toward the ceiling and gave a little laugh. "Why would I think they wouldn't?"

"And you let yours out early, I'm guessing."

"The first day of a two-hour seminar class when it's obvious no one has done the pre-reading? I gave them twenty extra minutes of freedom." Kate stood taller, an adorable feat for her petite frame. "Trust me, it's the only extra freedom they'll see this semester."

Callie appreciated the glint of fire in Kate's darkened eyes. On one hand, she wished she'd been placed in a course with Kate, but on the other hand, recognizing her growing physical response to her nearness, she realized that would have been… challenging.

"You didn't answer my question. How did your day go?"

Mildly surprised and completely impressed by Kate's directness and ability to pivot a conversation, Callie took a moment before responding. "It went well. Nothing that I wasn't expecting for a first day, and both of the classes seem mellow but engaged."

"I think you'll learn a lot from both Renee and Courtney." Kate hesitated, that impassive look falling over her face. "Courtney's probably taught you a lot already."

That's a weird way to say it, Callie thought. "Courtney and I go way back, yes. In the traditional sense, she taught me way too much when I was her student. And our friendship has taught me plenty." She grinned. "Honestly, she's a pain in the ass but a really great friend."

Kate steadied her blank stare on Callie. "Will that be difficult for you two? Being friends while being in the TA-professor relationship?"

Another five-star somersault tumbled through Callie. Was she going to read something into *everything* that came out of this woman's mouth? How exhausting. But also, how intriguing.

"I don't think so," Callie said honestly. "We've talked about it at length and set some firm boundaries. I know how she is as a professor and she knows how I function as a human being, so I'm sure we'll work it out."

"And you're close with her husband." A statement, not a question. Interesting.

"Sure. I've known Nick for years." Sensing Kate wanted more, Callie pressed on. "The three of us hang out when our schedules allow for it. Sadie, whom you've apparently gotten to know a bit, comes along too sometimes."

That drew a small smile out of Kate. "That bookstore might be the death of my bank account. Sadie does a great job with it."

"She's very happy," Callie acknowledged. "I never pegged her for a businessperson, but she enjoys it."

Silence settled between them, and Callie watched Kate work through it. She could tell, despite that unreadable look on her face, that there was something she wanted to ask or wanted to say. Or maybe she was just hoping there was something else coming. She felt like Kate was subtly digging but for what, Callie couldn't guess.

"Sadie is a lovely person," she said finally, meeting Callie's eyes steadily.

"She is," Callie said, drawing out the words. "We've been friends for, my God, almost fifteen years?" A noise of disbelief fluttered through her lips. "That seems wild but it's true. We met here, during our undergrad years. Suffered through Lawler's classes together. Dr. Lawler," Callie quickly corrected herself.

A bit of warmth spread over Kate's face as she physically brushed away Callie's correction with a flick of her wrist. "You really don't have to be professional on my accord. I know you have a long history here so it must feel strange to shift gears."

Callie was a bit unsettled at how quickly, and without warning, Kate's expression and demeanor could change. She sensed it was something bigger than she could understand at this point, but then she remembered Kate's history as a drama teacher. That begged the question: Which part of Kate was an act?

"Did I say something to upset you?" Now a gentle tone flowed from Kate. Callie struggled to keep up.

"Not at all. Why?"

Kate drew a circle in the air, aimed around the perimeter of Callie's face. "Your entire expression changed, and you went silent."

Callie bit back the urge to call this damn pot a fucking kettle. "I was just working through something Courtney suggested to me earlier." Ready to end this maddening exchange, she reached down into her bag and came back with the Elizabeth Cary book Sadie had given her the night before. "From your friend, Sadie."

"*Your* friend," Kate said, her tone now light and friendly. "Thank you, Callie. I appreciate you bringing this for me. I expected to have more time to wander through that amazing bookstore but"—she glanced back at the office door—"this job has other ideas for me."

"Well, rest assured that Sadie's an ace at getting her hands on difficult-to-find books. She was able to track down a copy of Speght's *Muzzle* for me years ago."

Kate didn't even try to hide the look of excited surprise that overtook her features. "You studied Rachel Speght?"

"She was part of an independent study I did during my master's program. Dr. O'Brien—she moved to a different university a few years ago—built an incredible study for me that was focused on women writers of the British Renaissance era. It was amazing."

"And Renee knows this?"

Callie shrugged. "I don't see why she wouldn't, but I doubt she committed it to memory."

"Hmm," came the response. "And here's poor Megan, overwhelmed with the mere idea of teaching this subject, while you sit here on a pile of amassed knowledge of the very topics I'm teaching." Kate pressed her lips together—pleasantly full lips, Callie couldn't help but notice—and nodded at Callie. "Seems like a miscalculation in scheduling to me."

After clearing her throat, Callie wagered, "But on the flip side, we all need to...learn." The thought of Kate teaching Callie *anything* sent tiny shockwaves through her body.

A genuine laugh burst from Kate. "Spoken like a true instructor." Kate tapped the edge of the Cary text on Callie's desk. "Thank you, again, for delivering this. Be sure to tell Sadie how thankful I am for her hard searching work."

"I will." Disappointed that Kate was clearly preparing to leave, Callie checked her emotions into place. "Thanks for the chat."

Kate studied Callie, her eyes drifting before settling into purposeful eye contact. "My pleasure. And my door is always open for you." Perhaps realizing the weight of her words, Kate spun and made for the door.

A bite of tension crackled in the pause before Callie found her footing. "Have a great rest of your day, Kate."

From the door, Kate looked back and nodded once. "You do the same, Callie."

CHAPTER SEVEN

Nikki leaned across the kitchen table, clearly intending to pry the pen from Callie's hand. It wasn't easy; she had a death grip on it, determined to finish skimming the pile of essays in front of her. After a minor scuffle involving a few cheap nail-digs and one mighty screech from Callie, Nikki emerged victorious, pen dangling from her hand.

"Green?"

"Red is too punitive."

"Oh, I see," Nikki said with a smug smile. "You're trying to be the cool professor, the one who goes out of her way to use special colors that don't hurt the precious feelings of the children."

Callie pushed the stack of essays away from her. It was no use fighting with Nikki to get the damn pen back, and besides, her eyes were ready to drop out of her skull. "Or I just don't like red pens?" She shrugged. "It was one of those weird things I learned along the way. There's actually some psychology behind it, Ms. Future Dr. Nikki Zullo."

A groan came from the opposite side of the table as Nikki let her head drop into her hands. "Can we not talk about my very poor decision to take four classes this semester? It's the weekend, Cal. We both need a break."

She had a strong point. While Nikki wasn't in the TA grind that Callie had willingly placed herself in, she was knee-deep in her PsyD program, which came with its own requirements and rigor. September was flying by. They both had three weeks under their belts and they'd acclimated to their demanding schedules, but they were simultaneously feeling the pressures of the semester.

"Hey," Nikki said suddenly, peeking through her fingers. "How's that situation going?"

Callie furrowed her brow, wondering when she'd so much as mentioned Kate to Nikki. She was sure she hadn't; Nikki, psychology studies or not, had an uncanny ability to see through any pretense Callie shoved into a conversation. In other words, the moment Callie even mentioned Kate's name, Nikki would be pointing out the crush Callie was rapidly developing.

Wait. What? Crush? Callie bit her bottom lip in thought. She was well aware that Tiny Brain Kate had begun to take up more space in her head, but she'd chalked that up to seeing her nearly every day. It was a natural progression, right? *Right. Sure.*

Callie admired Kate, that's all. She was a little enthralled, maybe, at how whip-smart she was and how she could hold the attention of a room (or was that just her attention?) by simply entering it. Over the past couple of weeks, their conversations had been sparse, but when they did occur, she was consistently in awe of how well-spoken Kate was, how invested she was in her studies and teaching. Yes, that was it. She simply was very into who Kate was as an academic. As a professional. She wanted to be like her.

Also, seriously. Callie was a thirty-four-year-old woman, well beyond the stage of having unattainable crushes on women who probably, in all likelihood, weren't even gay.

Right. So far beyond that.

"It's"—Callie cleared her throat—"fine?"

"Classic response." Nikki unveiled her face to roll her dark brown eyes. "So, no more rambling emails sent at odd hours of the night with preposterous questions about course material?"

Her brain quite literally snapped to attention, and TBK scurried back into her protected corner. "Oh! The Maddie thing."

"Of course, the Maddie thing. What else would I be referring to?"

"Nothing," Callie rushed. Now was not the time to discuss Kate. Never was the time to do that when it came to Nikki. "She hasn't emailed in a couple days, but she did corner me after class yesterday."

"The Maddie thing," as she so affectionately referred to it, was the student issue Callie was dealing with. She'd shrugged it off as nothing after the first long-winded email sent at 2:45 a.m., but once three more similar emails appeared in her inbox within a week, she'd brought it up with Nikki. Nikki's immediate belief was that Maddie was cultivating a massive crush on her TA. Lucky Callie. It seemed innocent enough—certainly not warranting any type of action. Callie hadn't even mentioned it to Courtney, let alone Renee—but Nikki felt a warning was needed.

Callie held up her hand, knowing Nikki's rebuttal before it came. "If it continues, I'll bring it up with Lawler. Hopefully my lack of replies to her emails sends her a message."

"Don't they teach you to be direct in your fancy TA program?"

"Funny, that hasn't come up yet. Maybe you and your precious Psych degree can help me with that." Callie stood and gathered the essays from the table. She held out her hand, and after a moment, Nikki handed over the green pen. "If you expect me to even show my face at this party tonight, I have to get through these essays."

"I'm giving you two hours of uninterrupted time!" Nikki yelled at Callie's retreating form. "Then it's outfit planning time!"

Callie shook her head as she shut her bedroom door behind her. Nikki's enthusiasm for party preparation was one of the weirdest but cutest things about her. The outfits could wait. The essays, however, could not.

True to her word, Nikki barged into Callie's room two hours later. Fortunately, the essays were finished and Callie had even had time for a fifteen-minute disco nap. Still, she wasn't ready for Nikki's obsessive outfit-planning session.

"Is there something you're not telling me?" she asked as Nikki forced her into a different pair of jeans. "This feels more intense than normal."

"Nope! Just want you to look good and also look nothing like me."

Nikki had a valid concern: Over the course of their seven-year friendship, the number of times she and Callie had shown up wearing the same exact outfit was…disconcerting. It was a lesbian thing, they joked. The truest joke there ever was.

Fifteen minutes later, Nikki was satisfied and Callie was mostly so. They both fell in the space between stereotypical butch/femme labels and appearances, and for whatever reason that meant their uniform consisted of a lot of ripped jeans and joggers, T-shirts, hoodies, and the occasional leather jacket. Nikki referred to it as "Comfort Core," but Callie just wore whatever the hell she wanted and didn't care about labeling it.

Maya joined them in the living room, and after waiting for Sadie to pop down from her studio upstairs, the group headed downstairs. Living in this house meant attendance was strongly recommended at parties hosted there throughout the year. The best part, in Callie's opinion, was that the downstairs neighbors loved hosting so she and her roommates never had to. The other best part was that even though they lived in a college town, everyone who attended the parties was well into their thirties and beyond, so while the occasional spirited game of beer pong or flip cup popped up, the overall vibes weren't reminiscent of frat parties.

After waving hello to Tim and Jenny, the sweet couple who lived in one of the downstairs apartments, Callie grabbed a beer and headed out to the wide front porch. It wasn't yet crowded inside, but it would be eventually, and she preferred to grab her spot on the porch before everyone realized it was the best place to be.

The mid-September night was cautiously warm. Some leaves were just starting to dabble in changing colors, but summer still felt very present. The sun was working its way down the sky, leaving in its wake trails of violent red and flaming pink. Callie claimed her favorite chair, the one that had the slight rock, and propped her black Converse up on the porch railing. A long, cool sip of the local IPA immediately woke her taste buds.

Her mind was starting to wander to all the things she had to do before Monday when her thoughts were interrupted by a handful of partygoers coming onto the porch. With a sense of relief, she got caught up in their conversation, not noticing as time ticked by and people came and went.

It was Nikki, of course, who got her attention a bit later. As she handed her a fresh beer, an overeager smile bent her lips.

"Why are you smiling like that?" Callie asked warily.

"Ha! No reason." Maya bounded up next to Nikki, an equally disarming smile on her face. "We have someone we want you to meet," Nikki blurted.

Sadie appeared behind them, extending a beer to Callie. "Oh," she said, seeing the unopened bottle in Callie's hand. "Guess my timing was off."

"It's not," Callie reassured her. She liked how in sync Sadie was with some of her habits, including her drinking speed. "Nikki brought me this one as a bribe."

"It's not a bribe," Nikki said at the same time that Maya proclaimed, "Totally a bribe."

Sadie and Callie exchanged a look and Sadie perched on the arm of Callie's chair. "What's going on with you two?"

Before either could concoct a story, a woman with short, tousled, dark brown hair walked up next to Nikki. "Thought I

The Roads Left Behind Us 63

lost you in there," she said, her voice a bit raspy and undeniably sexy. "Theo told me you might have gone outside."

It took Callie a moment to realize Nikki and Maya were staring at her expectantly. Sadie nudged Callie. "Say something," she said out of the corner of her mouth.

"What's up?" Callie said, looking from one woman to the other. "Did I miss something?"

"Me," the new woman said with a crooked smile. "I'm Hannah. They just introduced us, but you were clearly somewhere else."

Irritation and embarrassment collided inside of Callie, pulling a strong urge to flee. Instead, she stayed rooted in her chair. "I see." One look at Nikki's guilty expression told Callie exactly what she needed to know. "Nice to meet you, Hannah. I'm Callie, but apparently you've already been informed of that."

"Nikki! Babe, it's my favorite song!" Maya yanked her girlfriend back into the house, Nikki waving to Callie with a tiny bit of chagrin in her expression.

"I've heard a lot about you, Hannah. It's great to meet you," Sadie said, extending her hand to Hannah. "I'm Sadie, Callie's best friend."

"Sadie, right! Maya has told me so much about your bookstore. I have to check it out soon."

Callie glanced back and forth between Sadie and Hannah, admiring the ease at which they fell into conversation. Hannah was gorgeous, there was no argument about it, and she felt an immediate attraction to her. She hated the fact that Nikki and Maya had had the audacity to set her up, but she could entertain the thought of Hannah, knowing she couldn't get involved because she had zero time to date. Maybe Sadie would have better luck in that area, Callie mused as she half-listened to their ongoing chatter.

"So, you're new to the area?" Sadie asked Hannah, jabbing her elbow into Callie.

Or not, Callie thought, knowing exactly what that elbow meant.

Hannah leaned against the railing, her body facing directly toward Callie. One more inch and she'd be brushing against Callie's propped legs.

"Sort of. I lived here years ago, then left with my girlfriend when she got a promotion and transfer for work. Came back when that ended."

"The promotion or the relationship?" Callie asked, purely for clarification.

Hannah's bright blue eyes linked with Callie's darker blue eyes. "Relationship. It was amicable—still is—but I never felt at home in Rhode Island, so I came back here."

"Her loss," Sadie said, her voice coated in honey. "I'm sure Callie can help you forget about her." Before Callie could push an annoyed response from her mouth, Sadie bounced up and gave the two a parting wave.

"Subtle," Hannah said, easing just a bit closer to Callie's legs.

"That's not something any of my friends are known for, as I'm sure you've figured out."

Hannah stared at Callie, appraising her. "For the record, I've already forgotten about my ex."

"For the record, I'm not looking for a relationship."

"Honesty. I can get behind that." Hannah adjusted her position so that her arm pressed gently against Callie's leg. In a move that Callie had only read about in books, Hannah reached up and ran her fingers through her hair, landing her free hand on Callie's leg, just below her knee. She drew lazy circles as she continued speaking. "You're just interested in sex, then?"

Callie wasn't in a position to deny the obvious attraction between them, even if it was based on nothing but physical desire. "I could be."

"Honest but hard to get. Quite a combination you've got going there."

"I'm not playing hard to get," she said, dropping her legs to the ground. She watched Hannah's hand hang in the air for a moment before she let it fall to her side. "I have a lot on my plate right now. Free time isn't something I have much of."

"They told me you'd have a lot of excuses." Hannah laughed softly. "If you're not interested, just say so. I can handle rejection."

Callie's head spun. How the hell had this unfolded so quickly? "I'm not saying I'm not interested. It's just—casual sex isn't really my thing."

"Mine either. But I'm not the one who suggested that." Hannah lifted one eyebrow, waiting for her to sift through the conversation.

Sadie. Callie shook her head in exasperation. Friends with the best intentions, of course.

"Listen, I'm sorry if any of them gave you the wrong impression. I've told them repeatedly I'm not looking for anyone, but they refuse to accept that."

Hannah leaned forward and, in a move that surprised Callie, gently squeezed her shoulder. "Can we start over? This whole interaction feels like it went off the rails."

"I just told you I'm not looking for anyone," Callie said, keeping her tone firm but friendly. At the same time, she couldn't help but to admire the way Hannah's shirt draped over what appeared to be a stunning set of breasts.

"You know what they say, Callie. It always happens when you're not looking. And hey," Hannah added, pointing at her. "Eyes are up here."

When Callie dared to meet Hannah's eyes, she found a warm smile on her face. "So? Can we start over?"

Nodding slowly, Callie agreed. It couldn't hurt. A little distraction with someone this hot could only be a good thing.

"I was beginning to think you'd pulled another disappearing act." A boisterous male voice cut through the party noise, cleanly interrupting the strange conversation between Hannah and Callie.

"I wouldn't have left without telling you!" Hannah exclaimed, grabbing her friend around the neck.

"You've done it before," he replied, eyeing her. His eyes traveled over to Callie. "Oh, I see I'm interrupting." And yet he gave no indication of leaving.

Just as Callie was putting the pieces together and placing this familiar face, Hannah said, "Not exactly. Theo, this is Callie. Callie, meet my friend, Theo. Or do you two know each other already? I forget how small this town can be."

"We haven't met," Callie started as Theo said, "I know of Callie."

"Know of? Shit, what kind of reputation do you have around here?" Hannah teased.

Theo jumped in before Callie could unnecessarily defend herself. "Callie's a TA at Pennbrook. She works with Kate."

The last piece of recognition popped into place and Callie clearly saw in her memory the image of Theo and Kate together in Cornerstone.

"Kate," Hannah murmured with a roll of her eyes. "The never-ending saga of Kate The Great continues."

"You're so jealous. Once you meet her, you'll understand." Theo looked back at Callie. "I'm sure Callie can confirm how amazing she is, right?"

Callie took a drag from her beer. She weighed her words carefully, not knowing what Theo's relationship with Kate was while seeing the obvious jealousy Hannah harbored. "She's impressive."

"Ugh, maybe you two should date," Hannah said, nodding her head at Theo. "You can sit around and talk about how *amazing* and *impressive* your best friend Kate is."

Best friend. Okay. I can work with that, she thought. "We almost met," Callie said, "at Cornerstone a month or so ago."

Theo snapped his fingers. "That's right! I knew you looked familiar. I've had this image of you in my head whenever Kate talks about you, but it was so wrong compared to the truth." He laughed, a full-bellied, hearty sound. "You're much cuter in reality."

She talks about me? Callie tucked that away for later. "Thanks. Oddly enough, that's not the first time I've received that backhanded compliment."

Another laugh bellowed from Theo. "If you were my type, Callie, I'd scoop you up in a heartbeat. I don't think my partner would be too thrilled about that, though." He winked. "You kids have fun." After planting a loud smooch on Hannah's cheek, Theo disappeared back into the party.

Needing a distraction from wondering what exactly Kate was saying about her to Theo, Callie stood and realized Hannah was almost her exact height. That burst of instant attraction from earlier flared up again. There was something about Hannah that intrigued her. She might as well lean into it and see what it was.

"So, about that starting over," Callie said, her voice low and close to Hannah's ear. "My apartment is right upstairs."

"Excuse you," Hannah said, pushing a single finger into Callie's stomach. "I thought you didn't do casual sex?"

"Who said anything about sex? I thought it would be nice for us to be able to talk without constant interruptions from meddling friends."

"Smooth." Hannah looped her arm through Callie's. "Lead the way."

* * *

Rubbing her eyes only made them feel more tired. Callie rested her forehead in her palms for a second, regretting yet again her decision to invite Hannah upstairs the previous night.

It hadn't been bad—not by anyone's definition—but the night had gone on for much longer than she'd intended. It wasn't even that they'd hit it off or discovered a mess of commonalities; talking had ebbed into a heated make out session on the sofa which was promptly interrupted by Nikki and Maya coming home around eleven. Callie was grateful for the interruption. Casual sex really wasn't her thing, and sex the first time she met someone? Definitely not her thing. The attraction between her and Hannah was hot, though, and worth an hour or more of fun. It had been way too long since Callie had kissed someone, and she'd been right about those breasts.

After being caught like a couple of teenagers by Mom and Dad, Hannah had stuck around for a while, chatting with Callie, Nikki, and one very drunk Maya. It was after one by the time

Callie made it to bed, alone, having exchanged numbers with Hannah and agreeing to an actual date sometime soon.

A distraction, she repeated to herself. As long as she was clear with Hannah, and she felt she had been, there was nothing wrong with having a little bit of fun to distract her from the tedious demands of her job and academia.

Both jobs, that is. Callie pushed her eyes open and clicked on the next waiting essay. True to her word, Jana had given her a handful of much more promising submissions for *Sapphisms*. She'd breezed through two already and it wasn't even noon. One more and she could close out for the day and go enjoy the warm sunshine with a leisurely walk or something.

Jana's note on the document identified that this was an essay from a new writer, someone who would be an ongoing contributor. Callie breathed a sigh of relief, understanding this translated to "easy editing job."

And it was. The writing was damn near flawless, poetic and prosaic all at once, ebbing and flowing over the page like a soft waterfall of emotions. The diction drew Callie in, and she forgot she was reading as an editor, not as a reader. She couldn't relate to the topic. She had been aware of her sexuality by the time she turned eighteen, but this writer had taken a longer journey through life and awareness, not opening herself up to her queerness until much later. Still, Callie went along for the ride without a seatbelt, feeling every bump of uneven road and rise of a hill within the essay.

She rearranged her brain after reading through the essay once, then went back and made a few notations for adjustments. There wasn't much and she was picky. This essay was nearly perfect on its own, but more than that: It left her wanting more. She scanned her inbox, just in case, wondering if the next installment was already waiting for her. No such luck.

Satisfied with her day's work, she shut her laptop, stretched, and gave herself the rest of the day to simply breathe.

CHAPTER EIGHT

Conversation scattered across the room like essays discarded in the wind. Or maybe that was just Callie wishing for a strong gust to blow her workload far away. She'd forgotten how many assignments Courtney and Renee liked to give their students, a response that her brain adopted perhaps in an attempt to save her from traumatic memories. They were being fair about it and not saddling her with the entire load to grade, but she had a feeling they were assigning more work than normal because they had an eager TA ready to dig into 200-level essays and reader responses.

Adding to that delightful aspect of being a TA was the fact that Callie's own courses were in full swing. She was keeping up with her coursework and feeling good about the seminars in general, but she was still just a *little* worried she was in over her head.

Glancing to her left, she watched Drew and Megan, their heads adorably close, compare notes. Drew seemed to be taking everything in stride, a both enviable and annoying aspect of his personality, while Megan was a bit more high-strung and obvious about her stress levels. Callie hoped she was somewhere in the middle: appropriately stressed but appearing to be in control.

"All right, everyone, let's get started." Renee Lawler entered the room with a flourish and an extremely large cup of coffee. Kate slipped in right behind her, taking the empty seat next to several of the newer English professors. She graced them with a small smile as she opened her laptop and slid her glasses down from their perch on the top of her head onto her nose.

Callie's breath caught in her throat. She was sure she'd seen that very action performed by other people, but when Kate did it...okay, she could admit it. It was sexy. There was no discernible reason for it to be sexy, really—the woman was just trying to *see*, for God's sake—but it was.

As Renee droned on about budget restrictions, Kate looked across the room and met Callie's eyes. Kate offered a slight smile before shifting her glance to Renee. They hadn't spoken much in the past week, and Callie found that she missed their brief chats. She hoped the help she'd been giving Megan was making its way back to Kate somehow; she couldn't shake her need to impress Kate, and since they weren't working directly together, she was using Megan as her conduit.

A soft ding from Callie's open laptop grabbed her attention, and she quickly hit the mute button. Drew snickered and received a withering look from her before she maximized her email browser to see who had dared to email her at such an inopportune time.

Wonderful. Her partner from her Tuesday seminar class was cancelling their meet-up tomorrow. When she expected to get the work done without that meeting was beyond Callie, and the thought unsettled her immediately. Why professors insisted upon assigning group work was beyond her. Shouldn't that end after high school?

Callie banged out a quick response. After hitting send, she tried to focus on whatever Renee was currently blathering about but found it impossible. She worried her lip between her teeth and clenched and unclenched her fists and fingers. She'd gotten a bad feeling about her partner on the very first day of class. Like hell was she going to take on double the workload just to save her ass. But what about her own ass's grade?

Another ding sounded from her laptop, this one louder than the last. Surprised that her partner had responded so quickly and mortified that she'd increased the volume instead of muting it, Callie flicked her attention back to her laptop just in time for a third ding to sound. She frantically smashed at the mute button before scanning the two new emails.

Heat crept across her cheeks. She couldn't look up, wouldn't, as though the only way anyone could see her blush was if she removed her stare from her laptop.

> TO: Lewes, Callie
> FROM: Jory, Kate
> DATE: Wednesday, September 20, 04:10 p.m.
> SUBJECT: <blank>
> You okay over there? You're looking a little stressed.

> TO: Lewes, Callie
> FROM: Jory, Kate
> DATE: Wednesday, September 20, 04:10 p.m.
> SUBJECT: <blank>
> The mute button is on the top right corner.

A smirk made its way onto Callie's lips, easing some of the blush. She chewed on her pen for a moment, working through her possible avenues with a response.

> TO: Jory, Kate
> FROM: Lewes, Callie
> DATE: Wednesday, September 20, 4:12 p.m.
> SUBJECT: Re:
> Yes to the stress, but I'm okay. Thanks for asking.
> PS: Found and smashed mute button.

TO: Lewes, Callie
FROM: Jory, Kate
DATE: Wednesday, September 20, 4:15 p.m.
SUBJECT: Re: re:
We felt the vibrations of that Hulk-smash over here. Talking about what's stressing you will help much more than brutalizing your laptop.

TO: Jory, Kate
FROM: Lewes, Callie
DATE: Wednesday, September 20, 4:16 p.m.
SUBJECT: Re: re: re:
I don't know about that, but my laptop probably agrees with you.

Callie watched Kate read her email and felt a flare of satisfaction from the smile that appeared on Kate's lips. She could easily get swept up in watching Kate react to her lame jokes and nerdy emails. A bite of dismay hit her in the gut as she watched Kate gently shut her laptop and turn her full attention to the professor who was speaking about class attendance issues.

Before another round of email tag could begin, Renee ended the meeting and the room slowly emptied. As Callie gathered her things, Courtney came over and rapped her knuckles on the desk.

"You good? I could feel your stress across the room."

"Jesus, am I that obvious?" Callie ran her fingers through her hair. "I'm fine. A little overwhelmed and pissed off at this stupid fucking partner project I have for one of my seminars, but it'll be fine."

"Fine," Courtney mimicked. "For a wordsmith you sure have a limited vocabulary."

Callie flipped Courtney off, then remembered where she was and darted her eyes around the room. "Wow, people sure run the hell out of here."

"Lucky for you. But seriously, Cal. Am I putting too much on you?"

Callie waved her off. "Absolutely not and that's why I was hoping I was hiding my stress. It's fi—okay. Really. You're not putting too much on me, but I swear you assign more now than you did fifteen years ago."

They walked out of the room together and Courtney took a sharp turn toward her office. "You might be right. And you need to let me know if you think it's too much."

"I will. Now go away."

With a parting retaliatory middle finger aimed toward Callie, Courtney sauntered down the empty hall into her office. Callie backtracked down the hall and found her space unoccupied. She'd assumed Drew or at least Megan would be there, but she welcomed the silent room.

For the next hour, she plowed through work she'd been putting off, her focus razor-sharp. It was a strange payoff of her stress: Some people crumbled, but she rose to the occasion. She was finishing the last of the essays from Renee's class when a voice came from the doorway.

"I see you're working on that stress issue."

"The more I get graded, the less the stress tears at me." Callie looked up and smiled at Kate. "Isn't that how it works?"

"Sometimes. But other times the best thing to do is remove yourself from the stressful situation."

"Mmmhmm, I see. So you're recommending I quit?"

"That's about the last thing I'd recommend." Kate sat in the chair diagonal from Callie's desk. "You have serious potential, Callie. Renee and Courtney both talk about how easily you've acclimated to the classroom."

The tips of Callie's ears burned with the compliment— one she'd heard from both Renee and Courtney, but one that sounded vastly different coming from Kate. Callie had a feeling Kate didn't hand out compliments too easily or too often, so to be on the receiving end felt a little exhilarating.

"They're biased," Callie deflected.

"You really can't take a compliment, can you?"

"You really enjoy calling my bluff, don't you?"

"You've got me there. You make it pretty easy." Kate crossed her legs, causing her skirt to rise enough to give Callie a glimpse at the band of creamy skin just above her knee. "By the way, thank you for helping Megan with the Renaissance course. For some reason she seems to take your assistance much better than mine."

Callie couldn't bite back her smile. She leaned forward, placing her elbows on her desk. "That's because she's completely intimidated by you."

"Oh, please."

"It's true. But don't tell her I said so."

"I wouldn't." Kate thought for a moment. "She *is* kind of… jumpy around me."

"Don't take it the wrong way." Callie stopped, realizing how she was speaking to Kate, who was, in a strange way, her superior. "I mean, it's a healthy intimidation. More like awe." *Relatable*, Callie thought.

Kate waved off Callie's comment. "Nothing to be awed about. I'm a normal person."

"Sure, with a PhD and a glowing history of teaching coupled with an impressive wealth of knowledge about your subject matter. Never mind what I've heard about your ability to command attention in the classroom. Totally normal."

The look that crossed Kate's face was unreadable. She let Callie's words sit between them for several beats before saying, "Far more normal than you might want to believe. And who told you I command attention in the classroom?"

"Word gets around," was all Callie would say. She resisted the urge to wink.

"I never pegged you as someone who would cop out like that."

Callie gasped, widening her eyes dramatically. "Cop out? More like not revealing my sources."

"And have you considered a career in bad acting?"

"Coming from the former drama teacher, I'm going to take that as a compliment."

Kate laughed. "Don't." She eyed Callie. "You have an impressive memory."

"Only in regard to things I care about." The words slipped out before she could monitor them. She shut her eyes briefly, willing them out of the air and back into her brain. When she opened them, she chanced a glance at Kate and found her focused on something beyond the window.

"Since acting's off the table, I assume you're considering becoming a professor." *Ah, yes.* Kate Jory, Master of Diverting Conversations.

Callie gathered herself and her runaway mouth before responding. "I'm considering it, yes."

"Seriously considering? Or just trying it out?"

"A little of both."

Kate hummed to herself, finally bringing her eyes back to Callie, who squirmed uncomfortably under that pensive stare. She was pretty certain she'd somehow supplied the wrong answer to a very important test and there was no turning back from the shitty grade she was sure to receive.

"You're getting a good experience by TA'ing, but it's not the same as the real thing. I'd be happy to talk about it with you if you'd like. Maybe give you some input that you're not seeing or hearing from others. A Pennbrook outsider's perspective, if you will. Might be valuable for you."

Callie nodded eagerly, pleased she hadn't failed the test. "I'd really like that. A different perspective would be great."

"Are you hungry?"

The pivot caught Callie off guard. "What? I mean, yeah. Yes."

"We could grab dinner and chat." Again, a statement that could be a question, but it didn't have the lilt at the end. Callie had a massive crush on Kate's confidence.

"That sounds—shit." Callie dropped her head back for a moment. "I can't. Not tonight, that is."

"It was presumptuous of me to assume you were free," Kate said. "Maybe another time."

"I'd like that." Callie fought the urge to explain, and lost. "I have a date. It's not really my choice; my friends took it upon themselves to set me up because it's, uh, been a while."

Mortification burned her cheeks. Could she just shut the fuck up for a minute and stop using Kate as her diary?

To her credit, Kate maintained that impassive look on her face except for a light flush across her cheekbones. "Is this Sadie's doing?"

"Sadie knows better than to set me up against my will. It's my roommates. They lack boundaries."

"I'd say so. Blind dates are sure signs of poor boundaries."

"Oh, it's not a blind date." *Sure, tell her how you already kissed the life out of Hannah, oh and don't forget to mention how you felt her up like a horny teenager.* "We've already met. I, uh, agreed to the date."

If Kate was amused by her complete and total discomfort, she had the grace not to show it. With a knowing nod, she simply said, "Sounds like good stress relief."

Oh, God. Callie's brain pinballed responses she could deliver to virtually anyone except for the person sitting in front of her. And really? Was Kate seriously making an innuendo? Who was this woman?

"Hopefully," was what she settled on and immediately regretted it once she saw the sly smile on Kate's face.

"Check your schedule and let me know when you're free. Enjoy your night, Callie."

Callie watched Kate walk out of the office, feeling an acute ache at the loss of one-on-one time with her.

"Fucking Hannah," she muttered, stuffing her laptop into her bag. Well, no. That wasn't fair. "Fucking Nikki and Maya," she amended as she shut the door behind her with more force than was warranted.

CHAPTER NINE

"Cute outfit. Looks like what Nikki was wearing the first time I met her."

The sigh that fell from Callie's mouth was heavy enough to knock over a Chihuahua. She scanned her outfit, certain every garment was hers.

"Bad habit," was all she could say in return. She held open the door to Harpy and gestured for Hannah to go in.

Wednesday nights at Harpy featured half-price beers, and she wasn't about to miss out on that, even if it meant fumbling her way through a date she wasn't sure she wanted to be on. A couple of seats were open toward the end of the bar, and Callie ushered Hannah in that direction.

"What's good here?" Hannah scanned the menu on the wall, a slight wrinkle appearing on her nose. "What the hell kind of beers are these?"

A flutter of irritation bounced in Callie's gut. "These are excellent craft beers, all made on-site. Some IPAs, that one's a stout, and they have a couple witbiers." She gasped. "And a Saison! That's gotta be new."

"You're, like, really into this."

"It's great beer." At Hannah's silence, Callie pressed on. "Do you want me to help you pick one? What do you normally drink?"

"Um, Coors Light? And White Claw."

She did her best to prevent a look of disgust from appearing on her face. "Okay. Well. I'd recommend Persephone's Pils. It's a pilsner, so it'll be light."

Receiving a shrug in response, Callie picked up a coaster and tapped it on the bar while she waited for a bartender to come over. She looked over at Hannah, noting that the attraction was still there even if she had terrible taste in beverages. Her tight V-neck shirt hugged all the right places on her ample chest.

"What can I get for you ladies?"

"I'll take a Season of Artemis." Callie waited for Hannah to place her order, but she was staring outside. "And she'll have a Persephone's Pils, please."

Moments later the beers arrived and, at her request, the bartender gave Callie a quick rundown of the ingredients in the Saison. They fell into a short conversation about seasonal beers and what was selling best now that fall was coming into town.

Meanwhile, Hannah took a tentative sip of her beer, her face not hiding her distaste for it.

"Not a fan?" Callie asked after the bartender retreated.

"It's not awful, but I don't love it. Probably wouldn't drink it again." Despite her proclamation, Hannah took a deep drink of the beer before setting it back onto the bar. "I didn't know you were so into beer."

Callie bristled at her tone, not liking the implication behind it. "I enjoy good beer in moderation."

"Don't get defensive. I wasn't saying you have a drinking problem."

"You might want to consider your tone then."

Hannah widened her ocean-blue eyes at Callie, a smirk rolling over her lips. "You really don't hold back, huh."

"Not when I have nothing to lose."

A loud laugh burst from Hannah and the tension between them loosened. "I get it, Callie. Really, I do. You don't want a relationship."

"It's not that I don't want one. I don't have time for one right now."

"Then why are we on a date?"

Callie blew an exasperated breath from her lips. Hannah had a point. She knew she shouldn't have agreed to see her again after the party, but she'd gotten caught up in the idea of a distraction.

"I'm kind of fumbling here," she admitted, shooting for honesty over defensiveness. "I meant everything I said about being too busy for a relationship, but I'm also really attracted to you."

"So...you thought you'd give me a whirl?"

"Not in the casual s—"

"God, Callie, I heard you the first seventy times. No casual sex. No friends with benefits. No relationship. And apparently no casual dating, either."

Hearing it out loud, Callie winced. Maybe her honesty wasn't matching up with her actions after all.

"Like I said, I'm attracted to you. And like I said, I don't have time to devote to anything...serious. But casual dating is something I can do."

"Great. Then we'll casually date." Hannah lifted her beer to her lips. "Whatever the fuck that means," she mumbled.

"It means we hang out. Go out. Make out. All with no expectations, no pressure."

Hannah's eyes sparkled mischievously. "I knew you were just in it for the sex."

"I love that that's what you take from all of this." Callie angled her head toward Hannah. "How about we change the subject? Tell me about yourself since I know virtually nothing about you."

Fifteen minutes later, Callie subtly jabbed her house key into her thigh. Hannah hadn't stopped talking, not leaving any room for Callie to participate in the one-sided conversation, and Callie was retaining zero information from her blabbering. She was pretty sure Hannah said something about being a hairdresser? And she liked turtles, but still used plastic straws because she hated the taste of metal in her mouth? Saisons didn't normally make Callie sleepy, but if Hannah didn't shut up soon, she was going to pass out on the bar top.

"I knew it was a bad decision, but I did it anyway. That's what life's all about, right? Making the same mistake over and over again because it's definitely going to not be a mistake anymore at some point."

The fuck kind of logic was that? Callie blinked, hard, and missed her opening. Hannah was off and running again, oblivious to Callie's lack of engagement. The assault on her ears was driving some of the force of the attraction away, and, not liking that, Callie came to attention so that she wouldn't miss the next time Hannah paused to take a breath.

"Do you want another beer or do you want to get out of here?" Callie said as quickly as she could as soon as Hannah's mouth stilled.

"I definitely don't want another beer," she said, raking her eyes over Callie's body.

As Callie paid the tab, she looked longingly at the Season of Artemis tap, wishing she was on a date with that instead.

"You mean to tell me that you left the poor girl outside the bar and pretended to leave so you could circle back and get a six-pack of your new favorite beer just so you could come home alone?"

"That is correct," Callie said. She took a happy drink of her bottled Season of Artemis, pleased with her choices.

Maya and Nikki looked at each other in disbelief. "Cal?" Nikki prodded. "What are we missing here? It seemed like you two hit it off."

"Sure looked like it when you were on top of her the other week," Maya added.

"We're attracted to each other. But that's it. There's"—Callie gestured with her free hand—"nothing else there." She decided against telling them that before she left Hannah and pretended to head home, she enjoyed a very long, very satisfying kiss with her.

"It doesn't seem like you've given her much of a chance."

"Nik," Callie said, sitting up straighter. "I told you—*both* of you—that I don't have the time for a relationship. And yet you sprung this woman on me. She's hot, I'll give you that. But she has terrible taste in beer and isn't a great conversationalist."

"No offense, but you're not always the easiest person to talk to."

Callie leveled a cold stare at Maya. "I don't think—"

"Maya, back off. Why don't you get ready for work?" Nikki watched her girlfriend stalk down the hallway, then shook her head. "What's up with you two lately?"

"Did Maya decide you needed to introduce me to Hannah?"

Nikki sighed and looked across the room, away from Callie. "She thought it would be good for you."

"Good for me?" Callie scoffed. "I am completely overwhelmed with everything involving school, Nik. You know that. Maya knows that. I'm very happy that you already have a solid relationship to buffer the stress of school's demands, but I also think you of all people should understand why I can't even think about trying to find a relationship right now."

Nikki crossed the room and sat down next to Callie. "I get it. I do. But we all worry that you're shutting yourself off from even the possibility of meeting someone."

"For fuck's sake, I'm not! If I meet someone who truly captivates me then I'll acknowledge that and take it on. I'm just not looking for it, Nik. Okay?"

She nodded slowly, then ruffled Callie's hair. "I hear you. And I'm sorry."

"Well, don't be too sorry. Hannah is extremely hot."

"All that bitching at me for setting you up and you're going to continue to date her?"

"No. Well, kind of? Casually, I guess, but we really don't have anything in common, so it's not going anywhere."

"Except perhaps to your bed?" Nikki elbowed Callie. "It wouldn't hurt."

No, it wouldn't hurt, but the more Callie considered it, the less appealing it became.

CHAPTER TEN

"When we talk about deconstruction, we automatically move to Derrida. We can consider him the 'father' of this criticism, if we want to rely on gender norm descriptors, which aligns neatly with Derrida's preoccupation with unearthing the binary oppositions that dictate much of our thinking."

Callie twitched slightly as she sat in the back of the small lecture room, taking notes as Renee Lawler lectured. Something about Derrida and deconstruction made her feel like she was breaking out in hives. Must have been a literary hangover from her own graduate program.

A light tapping increased in speed, drawing Callie's attention away from her laptop. She scanned the room, her eyes narrowing as they found the culprit within seconds. She should have guessed. The difference between undergraduate and graduate students was becoming more and more clear to her each time she surveyed this class, Renee's graduate seminar in Literary Criticism, but apparently one student hadn't gotten that memo.

Maddie sat, bent so far over her desk that her torso was practically flattened to it, one leg tightly wound around the other, giving her legs the appearance of a braided pretzel stick. She seemed to be paying attention, but the foot that was toeing the floor was tapping at a speed that shouldn't have been humanly possible, ramping up the noise with each smack to the tile.

Everyone else in the room, aside from Renee, was silent and undeniably focused on the lecture. Maybe the difference didn't single her out to anyone other than Callie, who was very much aware of the special permission Maddie, a senior, had received from Renee in order to be present in this graduate-level course. Now that she'd noticed the odd behavior, she couldn't look away. That in and of itself was problematic, because if Maddie noticed she had Callie's attention... Well, Callie would rather not see what happened next. Probably six more emails by seven the next morning, if not something worse.

It hadn't escalated to the point where Callie felt she needed to address it with Renee, but she'd mentioned it to Courtney in a CYA maneuver. She'd brushed it off, explaining that students got weird around midterms. Callie didn't bother pointing out that the creepy email-stalking had started way before midterms. Anyway, she was sure it would fade out if she continued not to give Maddie the attention she was practically salivating for.

Callie snorted, then immediately ducked her head behind her laptop. Maybe she should introduce Maddie and Hannah. That could make her life a lot easier—and quieter.

She shook her head. The irony of going from a self-imposed drought to a flash flood of attention from (the wrong) women was not lost on her. Hearing the signs of Renee wrapping up class, she glanced up at the projector screen, making sure she hadn't missed anything, then slipped her laptop into her bag.

"Callie, wait. Are you going back to the offices?" Without waiting for a reply, Renee continued, "Can you drop this off in Audrey's mailbox? I forgot to do it before class, and she needs it first thing tomorrow morning."

Callie accepted the thick manilla envelope Renee extended to her. She didn't have to head back to the offices, but a few extra steps wouldn't kill her before she headed home. Plus, this was part of her job: Mail Bitch.

"No problem. And I'll email you the notes later tonight."

Renee waved Callie off, turning her attention to a pair of students waiting to hammer her with questions.

The halls were empty; Renee was prompt and ended her seminar at exactly nine p.m., but it always seemed like other professors—including Callie's—ended their classes just a few minutes before the hour. The end result was an eerie silence that followed Callie down the hall and around the corner, darkened classrooms creaking with the relief of solitude as she passed them.

Callie hip-checked the office door, cursing when she realized it wasn't completely shut and didn't require that kind of force. She rubbed her hip as she made her way to the bank of mailboxes and shoved the envelope into the one marked for Audrey. A cursory glance affirmed her assumption that her own box was empty.

Turning on her heel, she glanced down the hallway and noticed a trickle of light leaking into it. She mentally counted the doors and felt an obnoxious flutter as her curiosity got the best of her, propelling her toward the half-open door. She hesitated one step before the entryway, then knocked lightly on the door.

"I figured that was you."

Leaning in the doorframe of Kate's office, Callie raised one shoulder as she narrowed her eyes. "And why is that?"

"It wasn't a quiet entry, and it doesn't seem like you do anything quietly."

The half-smile on Kate's face didn't help Callie believe she wasn't purposely being coy, if not vaguely flirtatious. When she lowered her gaze back to her laptop, Callie took the opportunity to look around her office. Somehow, in mid-October, this was her first time in Kate's office, even though she was standing with just one foot tentatively inside of it.

It was a small space, the walls a muted off-white as they were in every other office, but a tapestry filled with curls and sweeps of earth tones covered most of one wall. The terra-cotta and golden hues brought out the warmth of the worn, dark wooden bookcases that covered the rest of the walls. A lone window anchored the center of the bookcases on the south-facing wall. Kate had positioned her desk in front of the window and the glow from a lamp on the desk illuminated her against the backdrop of fallen night. In the corner sat a well-loved brown leather chair. A far less comfortable-looking wooden chair sat at attention immediately in front of her desk. The Pleading Chair, no doubt. Pretty much every professor had one. They liked to give the appearance of encouraging students to petition for extensions and better grades; it didn't mean they granted those wishes.

"What are you doing here so late?"

Too late, Callie realized she'd let Kate's previous comment go without landing a witty comeback. "I've been unofficially surveying Dr. Lawler's Lit Crit graduate seminar."

"Dr. Lawler," Kate said, more to herself than Callie, and a small laugh followed. "You're so professional. It's cute."

"Cute? Like, overexcited puppy cute?"

Kate looked up from her laptop. Her half-smile had bloomed into a full, if teasing, smile. "Something like that, yes."

Recognition dawned on Callie, late as usual. "Wait, what are *you* doing here so late? You don't have a night class on Wednesdays."

"A perceptive overexcited puppy." Kate pulled her glasses off and touched the arm to her lips. Callie lifted her foot to move further into the office, drawn in by her evolving fascination with Kate's glasses and their proximity to her lips. "You're right—I don't have a class tonight. Sometimes I find it easier to concentrate here than at home." An unreadable look flashed over her face, taking her smile with it. "Something as simple as research just goes faster when I'm sitting here. Fewer distractions."

"And here I am distracting you."

"You're a welcome distraction. Shakespeare can take a breather, and so can I." She nodded at the leather chair as she closed her laptop. "Come, sit. Tell me what's going on with you."

Callie lowered herself into the chair, letting out an accidental moan of pleasure as she sank into its buttery, pillowy confines. "This chair should be illegal."

The glimmer in Kate's eyes was new and alluring. "I don't let just anyone sit in that chair, you know. Consider yourself lucky."

"You may not get me *out* of this chair," Callie said, stroking the arms lovingly. "Where did you get such a delightful piece of furniture?"

"Let's consider it a divorce win, shall we?"

Before Callie could react to the uncharacteristic reveal of personal information, Kate continued.

"Tell me what you're noticing about the contrast between Renee's 200- and 400-level courses." The glasses left their tantalizing dangle from Kate's delicate fingers and returned to her face. So, too, returned Kate's teacher-face as Callie regaled her with musings and thoughts, an academic perspective peppered with the unforgiving eyes of a student.

Kate opened her laptop, nodding. As Callie went on about the different work ethics she observed, she threw in some questions about how to manage them more effectively at the undergraduate level.

"I don't have the solution for that—that's something you'll work out over time, in your own way—but something you said before all that reminded me of this website I've been meaning to show you."

A little thrill of excitement spun through Callie. She liked that Kate thought of things to show her. More than that, though, she liked knowing that Kate thought about her, period.

"Come here," she said, peering at her laptop. "I want you to see this."

"You really expect me to get out of this chair?"

Kate glared at her, albeit playfully, Callie hoped. "The chair will still be there in two minutes."

With an enormous sigh of effort, Callie pushed herself out of the chair and went to stand behind Kate. Without her permission, her nerve endings lit up as though she'd had a near miss with a bolt of lightning. She'd never been quite this close to Kate, and as she stood behind her, leaning down so she could look over her shoulder, that warm, fresh scent that was distinctly Kate attacked her senses. She bit her lower lip, struggling to focus on Kate's words as the now unavoidable realization slammed into her brain.

She didn't want to be *like* Kate. She wanted to be *with* Kate. Badly.

"Do you see what I mean?"

Callie stopped gnawing on her lip long enough to say, "Yes."

Without warning, Kate turned her head toward Callie, who didn't react quickly enough to take a step back. Instead, Callie angled her head just so, putting their mouths two, maybe three inches apart. Callie froze, watching as Kate blinked once, twice, a rapid third time. Her stare never wavered in its lock with Callie's. Intimidated and reeling a bit from the realization of her attraction to this woman, Callie pressed her tongue against the back of her teeth. She couldn't look away. Kate would have to give in first.

Another moment or seven passed. And there it was: the quickest, tiniest flick of motion as Kate glanced at Callie's lips, blinking in the process. Callie admired the cover-up.

"You see what I mean." It was a statement now, delivered in a quiet, deeper voice that she hadn't previously heard from Kate.

"Yes." The same answer. Less certainty.

The moment escaped them as Kate turned back to her computer. Callie stepped back, the burn of attraction flaming through her body. She glanced at the window behind her, half expecting to see it covered with steam, before returning to her new favorite chair.

"I've been meaning to ask you how your date went."

Conversational whiplash continued to be par for the course when interacting with Kate. Still, this slam on the brakes knocked Callie completely off the road.

"My date," she stammered.

"Yes, the one you went on because you were agreeably forced to."

Callie shook her head. "Why in the world do you remember that? It was nearly a month ago."

"I—" Kate closed her mouth abruptly. She sat back in her chair before continuing, "Blind dates always grab my attention."

Callie knew that was a shit excuse for what she really wanted to say, but she also knew not to poke the bear. Not yet, anyway.

"Okay... Well, it was fine." Callie cringed. She really needed to purge that f-word from her vocabulary. "It was just a date. Nothing came of it. I don't have time to get involved with someone right now. There weren't any sparks, anyway," she hastened to add.

Kate hummed to herself, looking past Callie. "I bet you read a lot of romance."

"What's that supposed to mean?"

"Sparks," she said, now meeting Callie's eyes. "They die out after a while. You can't rely on them to show you who you'll connect with long term."

"I don't think they need to die out."

"An optimistic romantic. I didn't peg you for that."

Callie clenched her jaw. "And what are you? A cynical isolationist?"

The laugh burst from Kate's mouth, loud and unexpected. "You've got me there, Callie. But maybe it's just that I'm older and wiser."

"And jaded."

Kate shrugged. "It's possible. I prefer the term realistic."

"So, why are you such a jaded realist?"

The look on Kate's face told Callie she'd taken a step too far. The impassive look Callie remembered fondly from first meeting Kate took up residence once again. "Maybe I haven't read enough romance," she said after a moment.

"Or maybe you haven't *had* enough romance."

Kate looked pointedly at her watch, then over at Callie.

"You're dismissing me," Callie said with a smile, hoping it matched her coy tone.

"I am. This little interruption went longer than I thought it would."

Callie sighed heavily as she trailed her fingertips over the broken-in leather. "And that means you're going to force me out of this chair."

"Like I said, the chair's not going anywhere. You know where to find it."

After Callie stood, she bent down and patted the chair. "Good night, you luxurious creature."

"Is that how you ended your date? No wonder it didn't go well."

Callie spun and narrowed her eyes at Kate. "That sounded suspiciously like something Courtney would say to me."

Kate held up her hands in surrender. "We do have lunch together sometimes. She may be rubbing off on me."

"I don't know how I feel about that." Callie crossed her arms to emphasize her indignant tone.

"You feel fine about that, I'm sure of it." A soft smile lit up Kate's face, adding to the glow cast by her lamp. "Good night, Callie."

"Hey, Kate?" she said quietly, hovering in the doorway once again. "Think about it."

Kate tilted her head. The mildly confused look she wore was endearing, and Callie's heart skipped a beat. "About what?"

Callie shrugged, looking over her shoulder as she walked into the hallway. "All of it. Good night, Kate."

CHAPTER ELEVEN

Callie inhaled deeply. There was nothing like the scent of new, unopened books. She took a moment to admire the pristine, untouched, not-yet-loved paperbacks tucked so neatly in the shipping box. She hated to pull them from their cocoon, but there was a display waiting to be filled.

Her extremely part-time duties at Cornerstone had faded into the background once she'd gotten acclimated to her myriad responsibilities and towering workload at Pennbrook. Thankfully, Sadie understood and only called for Callie's help when she was backed into a corner. Tonight's corner was exceptionally fraught, so Callie gamely put her other work aside and came in for a couple of hours—but only because Sadie had promised she could do floor work and not have to interact with any customers.

It was an empty promise, impossible for Sadie to fulfill, but Callie had successfully avoided the front of the store all evening. Until now. The display she had to fill was located near the entrance of the store. She'd kept this task last on her list. It was a half hour shy of closing time, and few people, she hoped, would be trickling in.

As Callie's muscles strained under the weight of the box of books, she regretted not grabbing a dolly and pushing the books instead. By the time she reached the display, she had no choice but to unceremoniously dump the box onto the ground, providing a loud thump to startle any nearby customers.

"That's one way to get someone's attention."

Surprise wasn't the emotion that took over Callie's body. No, she'd spent ninety percent of the night wondering if maybe, just maybe, she'd hear this particular voice. And then nine had arrived and she'd mostly given up on that hope. Apparently, she'd just needed to hold out until nine thirty.

Callie shrugged, looking over her shoulder at Kate. "Someone has to make sure the old folks aren't falling asleep in those damn armchairs Sadie insists on having."

"The music choice probably doesn't help."

True. The strains of lo-fi ambient music filtering through the store didn't promote energy. Callie wondered if that's why she'd been yawning so much throughout her shift.

"Sadie thinks it's relaxing, and if people are relaxed, they're more likely to spend money. I'm not sure where she got that business strategy from, but she stands by it."

Callie turned to give Kate her full attention. She swallowed back the impulse to comment on how relaxed and cute she looked in a pair of jeans and a Pennbrook sweatshirt. Seeing her out of her polished work outfits threw her off, her brain immediately trekking down a delicious path.

"She might be onto something," Kate said. Her eyes scanned Callie. "You're looking un-teacherly tonight."

Point for Kate: an adept ability to steal and reframe the very thought Callie had been thinking about her. Callie looked down at her jeans (ripped at the knees) and her long-sleeved black Henley (not ripped, thankfully). She self-consciously touched her messy bun.

"I could say the same of you," she pointed out. "But we're both off the clock, so I think we're safe."

The smile that lit up Kate's face was one Callie hadn't seen before. She seemed different than she did at work, more relaxed for sure, but there was something else that Callie couldn't put her finger on. Whatever it was, she liked it.

"I'm glad to see you made it out of midterms in one piece," Kate said. She absently scratched the side of her neck, and Callie's eyes betrayed her, following the movement of Kate's fingers. "I haven't seen you much for the past week or so."

Callie shook her head slightly before kneeling down to start pulling the books from their box. "Someone could have warned me about how hellish midterm week was going to be."

"Just wait till finals start. Actually, the week before finals and the week after. Those are the worst two weeks of the semester." Kate trailed her finger down the side of the display Callie was meticulously setting up. "Consider that an advance warning."

"You're too kind." With a book in her hand providing a necessary barrier, Callie swatted Kate's hand away from the display. "Stop touching my books. I'm working very hard here, if it isn't obvious."

"It's very obvious. Look at you, practically breaking a sweat from the exertion of placing books on shelves."

"Did you come in here solely to harass me?" Callie raised her eyebrows. "Nine thirty on a Saturday night and you stroll into a bookstore. I'm surprised you don't have something better to be doing."

"I feel like there's an insult in there somewhere."

Callie grinned, placing the last paperback on the display. "Not at all. I just figured you would have exciting weekend plans." She stepped back to admire her work. "It's missing something."

Kate adjusted several of the books, glancing at Callie with a devious smile. "It just needs a little shifting."

They stood and looked at the display. Feeling the closeness of Kate's body to hers, Callie hesitated to move, even though she badly wanted to move one of the books so that it was perfectly on top of another. *Right, it's the books you want to be on top of each other*, she thought, battling the flush that arrived with the unbidden thought.

"I don't have exciting weekend plans," Kate said finally, her gaze still fixed on the display. "But I am surprised you don't have a hot date tonight, blind or otherwise."

"The night is young," Callie said. She glanced to her left. Sure enough, Hannah was still sitting in the café, flipping through a pile of magazines, just as she'd been for the past hour. She'd shown up unexpectedly, and Callie had gone back-and-forth between being interested and being annoyed.

Kate followed Callie's glance. Her posture changed immediately. Callie felt her straighten and the closeness disappeared. When she looked at Kate, she found that the playful expression on her face had vanished.

"That's my friend, Hannah," Callie rushed to explain. She wanted, needed, to get that blank, cool look off Kate's face.

"Hannah," Kate repeated. "Your friend?"

"Kind of." Callie busied herself by dropping back to the floor, whipping out her box cutter and breaking down the box. "Not a good friend. A new friend."

"A blind date friend?"

Callie remained kneeling on the floor, her eyes fixed on the ground. She didn't like the way this conversation had shifted, and she had a feeling it was too far off the rails to get back on track. "Actually, yes."

After waiting a seeming eternity for Kate's response, Callie pushed herself back to standing and darted her eyes over to Kate. She was looking past Callie, eyes moving as they jumped from aisle to aisle. Everything else about her was utterly still.

The silence was too much for Callie. As she opened her mouth to say something, anything, Kate beat her to it.

"I'll let you get back to work."

Callie gritted her teeth as she watched Kate stroll down an aisle, moving further and further away from their awkward, confusing moment. She grabbed the box and stormed to the storage room. She was tempted to stay back there until the store closed, but after a few minutes of energized, angry organizing, she realized she didn't want to look like she couldn't handle whatever had happened.

And, truthfully, she had no idea what had just happened.

The store was eerily quiet when Callie exited the back room. The music was off, which was Sadie's first signal to customers that closing time was nearing. Quiet murmurs came from the café where the two baristas were shutting down and cleaning up. And up front at the registers, Sadie was chatting animatedly with her one remaining customer.

Kate. Naturally.

Callie dodged down the sci-fi aisle, unable to fight the urge to get close enough to listen but stay out of Kate's sight. She found a section that needed to be alphabetized and put her visual focus there, allowing her ears to track the conversation taking place ten feet from her.

"I'm so glad the Elizabeth Cary book came in on time for you. I'm happy to order anything else you need!"

"You're a lifesaver, Sadie. I have everything set up for the rest of the semester, but I may need your book-finding expertise for something else." Kate dropped her voice; Callie strained to hear it, but she couldn't. She peered over the book she was holding in front of her face and watched Sadie react to whatever Kate was saying. Sadie looked thrilled.

As Kate continued to talk, Sadie was nodding, her eyes alight. "That sounds amazing. I'm sure I'll be able to find some books for you."

Callie unceremoniously dropped the Le Guin book she'd been using as a shield. Sadie's head popped up at the noise, and her eyes narrowed when they took in Callie clearly eavesdropping like some kind of stalker.

"I'll be in touch soon," Kate said, seemingly oblivious to Callie being a total creep behind her. With that, she disappeared into the night.

"You have five minutes to get yourself together," Sadie said as she started closing out the register. "Use that time to do a final sweep, and then meet me in the office."

Callie did as she was told, taking extra time in each aisle to scan for anything unusually out of place. She loved seeing the bizarre ways people discarded books they'd decided against.

Finding erotica in the business section always brought her joy. By the time she made it back to the office, Sadie was ready and waiting.

"When did Hannah leave?" Callie asked. They hadn't exchanged more than ten words while Hannah was in the store, but Callie was surprised she hadn't at least said goodbye.

"Around the same time you disappeared into the storage room. She got a phone call and"—Sadie thrust her arm out in front of her—"flew outta here."

Just as well, Callie thought. She wasn't in the mood to deal with that tonight.

"Are you ready to talk about the Kate thing?"

"There is no Kate thing." Callie dropped into the only other chair in the small room. "Not a thing at all."

"Yeah, well, I beg to differ. I saw that whole interaction between you two, you know."

"No, strangely, I didn't get the sense that I was being watched."

"You wouldn't have." Sadie's smile was smug. "You were so completely wrapped up in whatever you two were talking about, you wouldn't have noticed if Hannah walked by, naked."

Callie considered that. Probably not completely true, but she couldn't deny it with total confidence.

"So, are you…interested in her?"

"How many times do I have to explain that I already know Hannah and I are not a good match?"

"I heard you the first fourteen times. But I'm not talking about Hannah."

Callie sighed, picking at the frayed edges around her knee. "I don't think I'm ready to talk about this, Sadie."

"She's quite a bit older than you," Sadie said gently.

"I'm aware. Sixteen years, in fact." She'd managed to get that much out of Courtney, at least.

"That's…a lot."

"And it doesn't matter," Callie added. "Yes, she's older. She's far wiser. She's established and incredibly confident about what she's doing with her life. There's absolutely no reason for her to be even minutely interested in someone like me, but it doesn't matter. I admire her." She bit her lip. She admired a lot about Kate, more than she would admit right now. "I like the working relationship I have with her. And that's that."

They sat quietly, the somber echo of the clock ticking seconds the only sound in the room for a full rotation until Sadie cleared her throat.

"What do you think would happen if you told her how you feel?"

A shiver spiked Callie's nerve endings. *That* was not going to happen. But she could play along, even though she kind of hated Sadie's ability to clearly see the things she avoided saying.

"I think she would kindly explain that I'm too young for her, and even if I were older, she still wouldn't be interested because I have no clear life goals, and that's not something she could deal with."

"Oh, right, I see what's happening here." Sadie leaned forward and slapped Callie's leg. "I thought you were over the Kelly shit."

"It lingers," Callie said honestly. Though enough years had passed for her to fully move past it, she didn't love when her ex was brought up. This time, though, it held weight. "When a person's only reason for dumping you is because, and I quote, 'you're going nowhere in life,' that tends to stick."

"But Callie, you *are* going somewhere in life. Maybe you're not sure where the end goal is yet, but you're actively working toward it." Sadie paused. "And I guarantee Kate sees that."

"Maybe. But it doesn't matter." She smiled, doing her best to hide the disappointment she was feeling. "It's just a stupid little crush. It'll fade, like those kinds of things always do."

"Unless it doesn't," Sadie said. She got up and motioned for Callie to do the same. As she locked the office behind them, she nudged her with her shoulder. "Maybe this one isn't meant to fade."

They walked through the darkened store together. Callie fought herself until they hit the front door, and then she broke.

"Do you know something I don't?"

"Me? How could I?"

"Then why would you say that shit about it not being meant to fade?" Callie couldn't keep the exasperation from her voice.

Sadie double-checked that the doors were locked behind them before they started a slow walk back to their apartments. "That was just a statement, Cal, but you might want to look at why you're reacting so strongly to it." She wrapped an arm around Callie's waist and squeezed. "I like Kate."

Callie dropped her arm around Sadie's shoulders and held her best friend close as they walked through the darkened streets. "Me too," she said softly. "Me too."

CHAPTER TWELVE

The unmistakable click and tap of Renee Lawler's high heels began softly, far from the confines of the back office where Callie was holed up, making her way through proposed research topics. She shut her eyes, trying to shut out the foreboding noise and the indisputable fact that it was coming closer.

"Not now," Callie whispered as she cast her eyes at the door. "Really, Renee. Not now."

It had been a long week and it was only Tuesday. Callie had been predictably bombarded with emails from her student-admirer, Maddie, after Maddie had "caught" Callie "looking" at her during Renee's evening class. (Callie knew she hadn't so much as glanced in her general direction. The students had been taking their midterm and Renee and Callie had split the room for monitoring. Callie had been relieved that Maddie wasn't on her side of the room.) Ignoring the emails wasn't doing the trick, and Callie had spent too much time brainstorming for a solution that hadn't yet arrived. Aside from that, she'd started a massive assignment for one of her own classes and was kind of—totally—hating it. Not very promising for her PhD venture. And beyond *that*, she was still feeling the sting from her encounter with Kate and her conversation with Sadie, which had effectively excavated some old, dirty shit from her previous relationship.

To put it metaphorically, her wheels were spinning so hard that she was just waiting for them to fall off completely and leave her tumbled in the dust and weeds. At this point, she'd practically welcome the loss of her wheels and some subsequent impairment. At least it would give her a break.

Alas, no break was in sight: At that very moment, the click-tap sped up and stopped in the doorway of Callie's office.

There Renee stood in a deep navy power suit paired with obscenely hot pink heels. It was a combination only she could pull off.

"Let's go," she said, snapping her fingers at Callie. "That pile of work can wait."

She spun around and click-tapped down the hallway, not bothering to wait for Callie, who sprang from her chair and scampered after her. She had no idea what was going on, but when Renee beckoned, she followed, no questions asked. She was, after all, her advisor and technical boss.

"Where the hell is she?" Renee muttered, glancing around the empty hallway. She banged on Kate's closed office door, not waiting for an answer before trying the knob, only to find it locked.

Callie glanced at her watch. It was early afternoon, still Tuesday unfortunately, and she knew Kate didn't teach until six, and her office hours didn't start until four. Sometimes Kate came in earlier, but Callie hadn't seen her. Of course, she reasoned, there was always the chance that Kate was avoiding her after their weird exchange at Cornerstone.

"I know she's here. I just saw her a half hour ago!" Renee sighed heavily before spinning on her alarmingly high heel and calling, loudly, for Audrey.

With a whoosh of overachiever-scented air, Audrey appeared, adjusting her glasses, pen and notepad ready. Callie smothered a laugh.

Renee eyed the pen and notepad, cutting a sideways glance at Callie before asking Audrey if she'd seen Kate.

"Not that I recall." Audrey flipped through her notepad. "Her office hours begin at four, so I don't expect her before then."

Callie opened and shut her mouth before a snarky comment about Audrey's bizarre schedule-tracking could jump out.

"I see," Renee said slowly. "However, she was supposed to be here now so we could meet with Callie. It's not like her to be missing in action."

Callie shifted uncomfortably. "Maybe something came up," she offered.

"More likely, she got caught up in something and forgot. It's still odd," Renee added, motioning Audrey away, then gesturing for Callie to follow her. "But I'm willing to bet she's got her head buried in a book somewhere and didn't set a reminder for our meeting."

Following Renee into her office, Callie bit back the temptation to remind Renee that *she* hadn't been informed of this meeting; it was actually pure luck for Renee that Callie had even been in the office since she didn't teach on Tuesdays, and her own evening seminar had, to her utter delight, been cancelled.

"We can do this without Kate," Renee said as she sat down behind her desk. "You two have plenty of time to work out the particulars."

Callie leaned forward to take the packet Renee was holding out for her. As she flipped through it, skimming the pages and trying to figure out what was going on, Renee kept talking.

"As I like to remind everyone, I poached Kate from her previous position largely because she's a goddamned genius." Renee leaned back in her chair, clearly proud of herself. "She's also an incredible teacher, which you'll be able to witness next semester. But really, Kate's biggest strength is research and course development. She's on the cutting edge and I'm telling you, Callie, she's going to make waves. Considering you've been a part of the Pennbrook family for a long time, I'm sure you realize that we need some updating around here."

Callie nodded, also realizing that Renee wasn't going to stop talking long enough for her to get a word in.

"Kate came to me in August, right around the time of the TA interviews, with an idea for a new course. I was immediately on board. Originally, I thought she could pair up with someone from the Sociology Department, but then you came along." A mischievous smile tilted Renee's lips. "You're a far better resource than any of those wankers over in Sociology."

The words "Queer Theory," bold and underlined on the first page in the packet, smacked Callie in the face.

"I feel confident about your theory and criticism knowledge—especially since I threw you into my graduate seminar and you've handled that quite competently. Of course, Kate wants the curriculum to have a nice balance of theory *and* literature. Your brains"—Renee snapped her fingers—"are basically perfect for this. Together," she added with emphasis.

Callie took a breath and looked closer at the title page, which actually read *Queer Theory: Sex and Gender in Contemporary Literature.* Her stomach fluttered. This was Kate's idea?

"When Kate requested your assistance with developing the course, I was thrilled. I was going to suggest it, of course, but she beat me to it."

Of course, Callie thought, thumbing through the course proposal. Her mind was reeling; those wheels were absolutely going to pop right off before the end of the day.

Wait. Kate *requested* to work with her? Callie bit her lip. Then why the hell wasn't she in the room?

Oblivious to Callie's ping-ponging brain, Renee went on. "Assuming you'll agree to this, the research and development will take the place of your doctoral seminars for the spring semester." Renee glanced at her desk calendar. "Kate would like to start as soon as possible—I'm positive she already has—but we both know your schedule is packed, so don't put too much pressure on yourself until next semester begins. I'm sure you two can find some time to meet, and soon, to look over everything."

Callie swallowed, hoping the action would help her find some words. "You can do that?" was the phrase that won out. "Just eliminate two of my seminars?"

Renee leaned her elbows on her desk, the mischievous smile having edged into something slightly more cocky. "Callie. I'm the boss. Whatever I say, goes." She picked up a pen and twirled it between her fingers. "Besides, I'm confident that you working with Kate on this project is going to be far more valuable than the work you would have done in your seminars."

"This sounds like an incredible opportunity." Finally, Callie's voice had returned, and with authority. "Thank you."

Renee waved her away. "Don't thank me. I'm merely the informant. I'd tell you to thank Kate, but I suppose you'll have to find her first." There was no irritation in Renee's voice, just a hint of mirth.

"I'll be sure to do that." Callie made a move to get up and Renee nodded, effectively ending their meeting.

Back in the sanctuary of her office, Callie dropped into her desk chair and stared out the window. Her wheels continued to spin haphazardly: Queer Theory. Sex and Gender. Kate. *Kate.*

If anything, Callie thought, maybe this magical course would finally allow her to figure out if Kate even liked women or if Callie's hardcore crush was destined to dead-end.

* * *

A gust of pre-winter wind shoved against Callie as she made her way from the driveway to Nick and Courtney's front porch. They were about three weeks away from a tiny Thanksgiving break that didn't even really constitute a break but which would allow Callie to recharge a bit before the last handful of weeks of the semester. The New Hampshire weather had apparently gotten the memo and charged full steam ahead with dropping temperatures and blustery bursts of wind.

Courtney handed Callie a glass of wine as soon as she walked into the warm house. "I'm getting the sense that you need this."

"Did I sound that bad?" After her meeting with Renee, Callie had waited around to see if Kate would return to her office. By four thirty, she was getting curious enough—suspicious enough, in fact—to prod Audrey for information. Audrey informed

Callie that Kate had cancelled her office hours but not cancelled her evening class. Confirmed avoidance: check. Callie left soon after and called Courtney on her way home.

"Not bad, exactly. You sounded panicked. And that's not an emotion I hear from you too often."

Courtney ushered Callie into the living room, where a fire in the fireplace was gently roaring. Callie made herself comfortable in the oversized armchair by the corner windows, pulling her socked feet up onto the chair so she could curl into herself. After a sip of the crisp white wine, she sniffed the air.

"Nick's cooking?"

"It's his night. Prepare yourself for something spicy and random." Courtney sat diagonal from Callie and propped her feet on the coffee table. "I think you're overreacting, Cal."

Callie groaned. She knew that would be Courtney's response. She also knew she was probably right. However, the emotional turmoil she was still experiencing disagreed.

"She's clearly avoiding me. And now we have to...do this research project together. This massive, major thing that holds a lot of weight for me!"

"And for her," Courtney said calmly. "Hence your overreaction. Kate would never jeopardize her career, or yours, for that matter. She's a consummate professional."

"An avoidant professional."

"That's not the word I'd use for her. You need to get to know her better. And you will. Don't jump to conclusions about her based on your own overactive brain."

Callie rested her head against the back of the chair. "What word would you use for her, then?"

"Private." There was no hesitation in Courtney's response. "And I think you're starting to get a sense of that. But I'm also thinking that you're not telling me something."

A mouth-filling sip of wine prolonged the time between Courtney not knowing and Callie confessing. Callie bided her time with a second, long sip. She could feel Courtney's unrelenting stare, and she knew she'd never get out of this conversation without owning up to what she was experiencing.

So, she rehashed her interactions with Kate, pointing out the moments where she felt the tension crackling—that charged, too-close moment in Kate's office, their semi-flirtatious interaction and Kate's subsequent shutdown in Cornerstone.

Courtney kept her eyes on Callie after she stopped talking. Callie bit back the one piece she preferred to keep to herself: that damn crush.

Before Courtney could respond, Nick breezed into the room and set a plate down on the coffee table. "Don't ask me what exactly it is, but it's going to pair so well with that wine." He looked back and forth between his wife and Callie. "Oh, shit. What's happening here? Did Callie royally fuck up?"

"Not yet," Courtney said lightly, reaching for a crostini smothered with something unrecognizable. "Callie's having a Kate issue."

"Really, Courtney?" Callie huffed and pulled her legs tighter to her chest.

"Oooh, Dr. Kate." Nick nodded, stroking his goatee. "She's a tough nut to crack. No luck, Callie? Let me get you one of my nutcrackers. I just got a new one from Williams and Sonoma and it is *divine*."

He rushed back into the kitchen, leaving Courtney shaking her head and Callie laughing despite her desire to kick her friend in the shin.

"You realize he's not kidding about the nutcracker."

"Wouldn't doubt it." She let a moment pass, hoping Courtney would fill it. When she didn't, Callie poked. "Has Nick been around Kate?"

"She's been over a few times. So, yes. They get along absurdly well."

"And she…comes by herself?"

"Callie, just ask what you want to ask."

"Is she single?"

Courtney sighed. "Yes."

"And is she…you know."

"*I* think she is," Nick interjected as he came back into the room to top off their wine glasses. "The wife here isn't so sure."

"Don't let her off easy, Nick," Courtney scoffed. "Callie. Be fucking specific. You're a grown woman."

"Fine. Okay. Is she gay?"

Courtney shrugged. "No idea."

"Oh, fuck you."

"She hasn't said whether she is or not, and why should she? Is it that big of a deal?"

"Uh, yeah, it is if you want to date her." Callie's face flamed hotter than the damn fireplace.

"Aha, there it is. Your true motive."

"Don't be so hard on her, Courtney. Our little Callie has a crush! And finally it's on someone we'd approve of." Nick winked as he disappeared back into the kitchen. Callie missed his support immediately.

"It's not a motive. It's a feeling. A lot of feelings, if I'm being honest."

Courtney went silent, sipping her wine and staring into the fire. Having said more than enough for one evening, Callie joined in the silence.

Several minutes passed with only the sounds of wood crackling and Nick quietly singing to himself in the kitchen. A large crash interrupted the moment, followed by Nick yelling, "It's fine, baby! Nothing broke!"

"It's not a moti—" Callie repeated, but broke off when Courtney cleared her throat.

"I want you to be careful, Cal. And hear me out." Courtney tilted her head and studied Callie. "I don't want to see you get hurt, and I definitely don't want you to fuck up your career or your education. Is a relationship between you and Kate off-limits? When she's your supervisor, yes. Totally. And don't argue the details with me." Callie began working on her rebuttal, but Courtney wasn't done. "But I have to be honest with you. I don't think Kate realizes you're gay."

Callie sputtered the wine that had been on its way to her throat until Courtney dropped that ridiculous bomb. "You're not serious."

"Actually, I am. I meant what I said when I described Kate as being private. I've gotten to know her, but it's been slow. She doesn't divulge a lot of information about herself. Aside from that, she just…" Courtney swirled her wine in the glass. "I'm not sure how to explain it, but I think she's flirtatious with you because she doesn't consciously realize you would be seeing it as flirting."

"That is an utterly absurd theory."

"Think about it. Everything was fine until you pointed out that your blind date was female. Right?"

Callie shut her eyes. "Correct."

"And since then?"

"She appears to be avoiding me."

"Or, more likely, she pulled back because she felt she was getting too close and maybe that subconscious feeling kicked a little into her conscious thinking."

"That's basically just a very wordy over-explanation of avoidance."

Courtney shook her head. "Being harmlessly flirty, especially if she didn't see it as flirting, was fine until she realized you might date women. It makes sense, Callie." Courtney paused. "Kate's a complex woman. I do know some things about her and her past, but I would never break her confidence. Like I said, you don't know her that well. Give it time. Give *her* time to open up to you."

"Wait a second. What did you mean by all that subconscious feeling-conscious thinking shit?"

"I knew you'd come back to that," Courtney muttered. "Maybe Kate was flirting, and maybe she knew it, or maybe she did it without knowing and then realized days later. We don't know. But what we *do* know, and what's most important to address right now, is that you have an infatuation, and you need to handle it gracefully. We also know that is not high in your skillset."

"She has a point," Nick said from where he stood between the dining room and the living room. He smiled sympathetically at Callie. "Rein in that crush, girl."

"Consider it reined." Callie dropped her feet to the floor. "But what I'm also hearing is that you think there's a chance." She wiggled her eyebrows at Courtney. "Am I right?"

Courtney studied her, her lips pressed tightly together. With a tiny, resigned shake of her head came her warning. "Tread lightly."

"Enough with the serious talk!" Nick exclaimed. "Let's eat. I can essentially promise that it's edible, but it might be a bit overcooked."

Callie followed Courtney and Nick into the dining room as a surprising sense of calm fell over her. She could handle this. Yes. For sure.

Tread lightly. Well. Fine. The only problem there was that she was afraid she only knew how to stomp.

CHAPTER THIRTEEN

Streaks of midday sunlight painted the floor of Callie's bedroom as she sat, hunched, at her desk. She turned an eager eye to her window and exhaled slowly. She needed fresh air, and the midfifties temperatures were beckoning her. Sunday was her favorite day of the week. Or it had been, before the Sunday Scaries, that predictable burst of anxiety that popped up when the workweek reared its head. She loved to spend the day in a leisurely fashion, with a good brunch, some time outside, and typically a new book. She liked the flexibility of the days, the lack of schedule and routine—though she stuck to basically the same routine every week, she liked knowing she could flip that routine upside down if she so chose.

The fall semester had ruined Sundays for Callie. Her new Sunday routine had her chained to her desk for the majority of the day due to her habit of not doing a single productive thing on Saturdays. Sure, she knew this was all in her control and she could very easily split her workload between both weekend days, allowing her plenty of time to brunch and relax and fucking frolic if she wanted. And yet, here she was again.

Callie cracked her knuckles and studied her to-do list. Things were moving along quickly. She'd finished up an assignment for one of her seminars, and she'd finished the reading for her eight a.m. class tomorrow. She jabbed her pen at the list. Okay, the reading for her eleven a.m. class could wait until tomorrow morning. Risky, maybe, but she'd already skimmed it and realized she'd remembered more of Freud and Lacan than she'd expected. She felt confident in doing only a quick review before class.

Her pen jabbed extra hard at the last item on the list: Prep for Monday's meeting w/ KJ.

Right, that. She scribbled a dark circle next to the item, remembering Kate's rather succinct email from the end of the week. Her usual terse but playful demeanor was absent. (Callie did so love reading between the lines of emails, searching for tone and meaning. A tragic affliction, though useful in critiquing literature.) Kate had simply asked if Callie was free to meet at four thirty. After gnawing off several fingernails, Callie had responded just as curtly with: "Yes. See you then."

After casting another baleful look out her window, Callie pushed her to-do list aside and pulled her laptop closer. The meeting prep could wait till later; she only needed to look over the material Renee had given her last week.

One thing that could not wait any longer, however, was Jana's email with a submission for *Sapphisms* that needed, as she said, "Just a quick read-through, probably very little editing, just another set of eyes before publication." That, Callie could handle and then outside she would go.

A few clicks later, Callie settled back in her chair, her laptop angled and her proofreading brain ready.

Waiting: I had done enough of that. Years upon years of putting one foot ahead of the other, walking the same path without disruption. It was both comforting and maddening; there was no room for error, but also no room for movement. I was confined within the parameters that held me. I was safe and quiet, secure and silent. And still: I waited.

I had been hoping for a grand entrance, a wild unbridled moment of awareness. A lightning bolt, maybe. But what I received instead was growth within the waiting: a soft field of wildflowers threading through my brain, gently choking out the stubborn weeds. Seasons passed and the field expanded until there was nothing but a plush carpet, beckoning my fall and surrounding my landing point with smooth petals and delicate stems.

The magic of the fall was eclipsed by the strain of reality. I should have seen that coming, but I'd been so consumed by the wildflowers that I'd lost my rationality in the daydream come to life. And so came more waiting, this time harder than the last. The field swayed beneath me, silken scratches with each forward step I took, a stunning emptiness accompanying each fumble backward. I wanted to fling myself into the field for good; I wanted it to drown me. I needed it more than I dared say out loud.

When the flowers began to dull, their vivacious colors melting and subduing, I found my resolve quieting with them. Darkness fell soon after. I searched, waited, for streaks of sunlight to spread across the wilted field. Time eclipsed into connected moments of loss and fear. Those vibrant colors and their woven tangle of leaves: blurred, gone. Midnight stretched on forever in a thick drought, the field all but ravaged.

But the science of the heart is no different from that of nature: one cannot have growth without rain.

Callie stared at the screen, waiting for more words to appear. But that was it. For now? Forever? She needed more from this writer. A thought lodged in her brain, and she quickly scrolled back to the top of the document. *What the hell?* She scrolled back down to the very bottom, searching. Nothing.

"Since when does Jana do anonymous submissions?" she muttered aloud, tapping open her email tab. A few more moments of detective work and she had her answer. The author was not so anonymous, just hard to find: Katherine Pearl. Likely a pen name, Callie thought, but her first thought went to *The*

Scarlet Letter, and she laughed quietly. *Once a literature nerd, always a literature nerd.*

Since there was nothing to edit in that short but mildly gut-wrenching poetic essay, Callie tapped out an email to Jana with her seal of approval. Before she clicked Send, she added, "Please tell me there's more to this, and please send it ASAP."

* * *

Callie eyed the shut door in front of her. She resisted the temptation to check her watch, again, for something like the eleventh time in the past five minutes. Leaning against the wall, doing her best to look nonchalant and nonplussed by the fact that Kate was late for their four thirty meeting, was a challenge. The worst part was, she couldn't even tell if Kate was in her office or if she had gone MIA yet again.

"You could knock," Courtney said as she walked past, fresh cup of coffee in hand. "You know, instead of aimlessly lurking out here."

Callie gestured toward the door. "The only time her door is completely shut is when she's not there or when she has a student in there."

"Or when she's on the phone," Courtney added, tossing Callie a grin as she disappeared into her own office. "Just knock, idiot."

As Callie prepared to advance toward the door and knock—Knocking was harmless! Everyone knocks!—she saw the doorknob begin to twist. Relieved, she resumed her casual leaning position and waited for the student to emerge. Knocking crisis averted.

The student who emerged had the look and stature of someone who had just been told for the very first time that his shit, actually, *did* in fact stink. Callie gave him a sympathetic smile that stumbled into a lopsided grin at the sight of Kate, who stepped into the hallway after the student. Apparently she hadn't finished explaining just how much his shit did stink.

"I expect the rewrite by tomorrow, nine a.m. You're better than this, Chadwick."

The response came in the form of a forlorn yet somehow still cocky shrug from the retreating figure.

Kate shook her head and motioned for Callie to follow her. "Close it," she said after they'd both entered her office. "Tightly."

Having done as instructed, Callie moved to the inviting leather chair, making quick work of getting comfortable before pulling her laptop out of her bag. Then, of course, she had to find that perfect comfortable spot once more, with her laptop on her lap. She was so focused on getting settled that she felt her cheeks heat when she realized Kate was watching her.

"Oh," she deflected, eyeing Kate before flicking her glance to the dreaded wooden chair opposite her desk. "You want me to sit in the asshole-ripping chair?"

Kate stared at Callie, her mouth dropping open. After a moment, she burst out in laughter, her head leaned back, exposing the soft lines of her neck. Callie gripped the arm of the chair. The intensity of her urge to draw her tongue from Kate's exposed collarbone, slowly tracing the path of her neck until she hit the spot just behind her ear, nearly knocked the breath out of her. The sweet, contagious sound of her full-throated laughter didn't help.

Rein it in, Callie. Rein. It. In.

Once Kate regained her composure, she swiped at her eyes before picking up her glasses from the desk and situating them on her face. "I really needed that. Thank you." She smiled at Callie, all warmth and familiarity. "And no, I don't want you sitting anywhere but in that chair you so love. It's missed you."

"I've missed it." Amongst other things, but Callie was going to master the art of reining it in.

Kate hummed quietly. "Yes, I—" She cut herself off with the gentlest shake of her head. "I'm sorry I wasn't here when you met with Renee."

Callie waited for the explanation, but it was clear none was coming. Just for fun, Callie gave Kate another thirty seconds or so, pushing the limits of the silence. Kate busied herself with avoiding eye contact, and Callie bit back seventeen urges to ask her where the hell she'd been.

"Have you had a chance to look over the information Renee gave you?"

"I have. But I'm guessing you have more to share with me."

The smile that Kate awarded Callie with was beyond dazzling. "I'm just about to share my working document with you. And keep in mind, it's rough. I've been adding ideas whenever they come to me, which, unfortunately, is often when I can't sleep at three thirty in the morning."

In a forbidden flash, Callie's mind brought up the image of a wide-awake Kate at three thirty, propped up in bed, her laptop resting on top of her comforter. Or maybe just her phone in her hand, the soft glow illuminating the finest lines and curves of her face. Before Callie's brain went fully off the tracks and threw her, sleepily wrapped around Kate, into the bed, she double tapped with a bit too much force on the document Kate had just shared in Google drive.

"Haven't we talked about you being kinder to your laptop?"

"Bad habit."

"Bad or nervous?"

Callie closed her eyes briefly. "A little bit of both, I guess."

"Callie?" She looked at Kate, surprised at the kindness on her face. "What are you nervous about?"

"I'm not *nervous*-nervous; it's more of—" Thankfully, she was interrupted before her inability to rein it in tossed her into a hole she couldn't dig herself out of.

Unlatched, the door creaked open and someone cleared their throat before saying, "Dr. Jory?"

Kate's head snapped up and she shot Callie a look. "I thought you closed it."

"I did! Tightly." Callie watched as the door continued to open at a snail's persistent pace. "At least I thought I did."

"And here I thought you were the master of doors in this building," Kate mumbled. Her professional mask slid into place as the door slowly revealed its opener. "Jordan. I was expecting you earlier, at the time we agreed to meet."

The young woman flinched, clearly intimidated by Kate's tone. Callie couldn't blame her; even she felt nervous and the words weren't directed at her. Then again, she'd felt nervous before Jordan even entered the scene.

"I—I'm so sorry, Dr. Jory, I was in the library and totally lost track of time, and I just need—"

Kate held up one hand and Jordan fell silent. Callie bit the inside of her cheek. If she was going to spend the next hour or so alone with Kate, she really had to *not* be aroused from observing her professorial power.

"Let's chat in the hall. I have some suggestions for you."

"Wait," Callie said. "I can step out so you two can talk in here." She moved to stand just as Kate slipped past her, the tips of her fingers landing and pressing firmly on Callie's shoulder. The touch was more than enough to weaken Callie's will to stand and she found herself dropping back in the chair as Kate tugged the door shut behind her.

"Get a fucking grip," she whispered to the empty office. She rubbed her eyes. She almost wished Kate would flip back to being dismissive and distant. Getting through this project might be easier if she were constantly irritated with Kate instead of dizzyingly infatuated with her.

When Kate returned a few minutes later, Callie was ready. She had dived right into the document, hurriedly highlighting areas while Kate was in the hall, and now launched into a discussion of them. The distraction worked. Much to her relief, Kate didn't try to resume the conversation where they'd left off. Instead, they discussed Kate's overall plans for the course research and development. Callie complimented her on how well organized her document was and on the amount of information that she'd already included.

"It's that three a.m. brain. Highly organized." Kate leaned back in her chair, crossing her legs. "I'd recommend it, but sleep is more valuable."

Callie properly reined it in, refraining from informing Kate that if they were both awake at three a.m. and just so happened to be in the same bed, no document organization of any sort would be happening.

"Who can sleep when there are so many good books to read?" She cringed internally. Maybe the definitively suggestive awake-at-three-a.m. comment would have been better.

"That's one of the reasons I told Renee I wanted to work with you on this project," Kate said. "Your love of literature is impressive. And endearing."

Endearing. Callie filed that one away to obsess over later. "It's true, I am quite the book nerd. And proud of it." She looked directly at Kate. "What were the other reasons?"

Kate's mouth gaped before quickly closing. Callie mentally patted herself on the back; she liked knowing she could catch her off guard.

"Well, you're very smart, Callie. An excellent writer. You pay attention to detail, and that's something I tend to overlook. You also have this wonderful ability to make connections between the classics and contemporary literature." A slight hesitation, and Kate moved her gaze to her bookshelf. "I couldn't imagine a better person to work with." She cleared her throat. "Plus, you read romance."

"Romance," Callie repeated, raising an eyebrow. "That's important?"

"It's not in my wheelhouse," she said, almost apologetically. "But you already know that, so let's not make a big deal out of it."

"You mean you don't want me to call you out ag—"

"Shut it," Kate said with a laugh. "Look, I want this course to cover all the corners, and romance is one of the corners that is filled with dust on my shelf. There, I said it. Are you happy now?"

Callie grinned. "Nearly. I still think you should whip out the Pledge and get rid of the cobwebs."

An amused look passed over Kate's face and was quickly replaced with one of chagrin before flashing back to mirthful. "That's not something I can do by myself, you know."

"Well, you *could*, but I suppose it's more fun with someone else."

Right. *About that reining in, Callie, and so much for treading lightly.* She managed not to burrow so far into the chair that she disappeared. *Recover,* she commanded herself.

"You can romance yourself, that is," she added, powerless to stop digging her hole. "Self-care and self-love and all that. You can date yourself, and—"

"Callie. You can stop." While it wasn't impassive, the look on Kate's face didn't give anything away. "I can take a joke, even those of the thinly veiled sexual variety."

"You did start it," Callie couldn't help but point out.

There, a smile. Small but present. "That I did," Kate said.

Very aware of the tiny detail they'd both managed to avoid over the course of the entire meeting, Callie decided to stomp right into it.

"While we're on the topic of romance..." At Kate's nod, she continued, "I do have a wealth of knowledge about queer romance. Seeing as you're intending for this to be a queer theory course, we should probably work that in."

"That's a—that's not the angle I'm looking for," Kate said quickly, a light pink flush rising up her neck. "I mean, of course we'll be examining sex and gender through the queer lens. It's only logical that romance be included in that, since sex and gender roles in romance are complex. I'm not sure it's necessary to include specifically queer romance."

Callie felt flattened into the chair. A charge of ice shot through her veins. This was a battle she expected to fight with other professors, but with Kate? And about a literal course on *queer theory*? The fuck was happening here?

"So what you're saying," she began, slowly but confidently, "is that you want the queer theory course to examine heteronormative literature and exclude queer literature."

"No." Kate shook her head emphatically. "That's not what I'm saying."

"I'm pretty sure that is literally what you just said."

"I didn't mean it like that."

"Kate, I'm sorry but—"

"No. Callie. I said queer romance. I didn't mean we should exclude queer literature as a whole."

Callie's head spun. She knew she was missing something critical, but she couldn't put her finger on it. "But queer romance *is* queer literature."

"And your 'wealth of knowledge about queer romance'? How does that work into a course about literature and theory?" The edge in Kate's voice gave away how flustered she was, even if her facial expression didn't.

Callie took a moment to process what Kate was, poorly, saying. "I was referring to the fact that I've read a lot of queer romance. Hence my wealth of knowledge of the *genre*."

"Of course," Kate said hurriedly. "Of course that's what you meant."

"You mixed up the terms, right?" Callie asked gently.

They stared at each other, neither one breaking. Callie still felt the cold in her body and Kate's rigid posture wasn't helping her warm up. After several interminable beats, Kate spoke.

"I'll go back into the document later and work in a specific section to highlight contemporary queer romance. I'd like you to add some recommendations of texts by the end of the week. Aim for five to start with, and we'll decide together which to focus on."

A complicated mixture of anxiety and anger clawed at Callie's throat. Every fiber of her hated, absolutely despised, the tone of Kate's voice and the way she so easily shut down the camaraderie between them. Plus, she was still utterly perplexed about the bizarre turn their conversation had just taken.

"That's no problem," she said, shoving her thoughts down.

"Great." With one last long look at Callie, Kate nodded, then turned her attention to her laptop. "When you have time, take a more in-depth look at the outline. Feel free to leave comments and suggestions. I'll let you know when we'll meet next."

"Sounds good," Callie said quietly, sliding her laptop into her bag. She left in a rush, not wanting another moment in the unpleasant tension that had risen between them. Without asking, she was sure to close the door tightly behind her.

She needed to get the hell out of there. Whatever had just happened was unsettling and confusing, and while part of her wanted to march right back into Kate's office and demand a better explanation, she chose to listen to Courtney's voice in her head, repeatedly saying "tread lightly." This certainly seemed to be a moment where stomping could backfire.

Callie stopped at the bank of mailboxes, ignoring Audrey, who sat at her desk watching her like a hawk.

"You have four pieces of mail," Audrey announced.

"Thank you. I'd forgotten how to count." Callie turned and summoned up her most sarcastic smile.

"Oh, I almost forgot. There was a student looking for you while you were with Dr. Jory."

"Was it important?" Callie asked absently as she flipped through the pieces of mail.

"She didn't say. It didn't seem important. She looked like she wanted to flirt with you." A note of disdain crept into Audrey's voice, but Callie knew it was about the flirting in general, not the potential of girl-on-girl flirting. Audrey hated flirting. She openly told Megan and Drew, who had begun dating shortly after the semester began, to "keep your business in a place where I am not privy to it." Naturally, Drew made a point to exaggerate any kind of flirting whenever he was near Audrey, whether it was with Megan or Callie, who thoroughly enjoyed playing along for the sake of tormenting Audrey.

Callie groaned, knowing exactly who had come looking for her. Okay, so ignoring Maddie as much as possible wasn't doing the trick. She'd have to try a new angle.

"You told her I wasn't available?"

"I told her why you weren't available. She wasn't very happy about that," Audrey said, bemused. "But she said she would email you to set up a time to meet."

"Lovely," Callie mumbled. She stopped flipping through the mail and threw Audrey a gloating smile. "Audrey! However did this happen?"

The young woman was out of her seat in a second. "What? What is it?"

"This piece of mail! It's not addressed to me and yet it found its way into my mailbox." Callie sighed heavily. "What a tragic incident."

"Give me that." Audrey came at Callie like a pissed-off emu. "Now!"

Just as she was about to grasp the envelope, Callie pulled back and spun around. "I'm entirely capable of putting a piece of mail into the correct mailbox, Audrey. You go relax. I can handle it just fine."

"No, now I know you're lying. Give it to me. I need to see the evidence."

Callie stalled, looking closer at the envelope in question. It was absolutely intended for Dr. Jory, but the full address on the label said it was meant for one Dr. Katherine P. Jory.

Audrey's beak-like hand snapped over Callie's shoulder and grabbed the envelope, whisking it away to its proper slot. As Audrey muttered to herself, Callie stood rooted to the linoleum. Katherine P. Jory. It couldn't be. It absolutely could not be.

But if it was, Callie thought, that would explain a whole fucking lot.

CHAPTER FOURTEEN

"I tried to talk her out of the baby-blue hair dye, but she was so sure it was what she wanted. The end result was, let's just say, *interesting*." Hannah screwed up her features in horror and chewed on the edge of a cucumber slice. "It seriously amazes me when people don't listen to my advice. I went to fucking beauty school, you know?"

"Did you make that face or did you somehow manage to hide your disgust?"

"Honestly? Probably something in the middle."

Callie grinned and took a sip of her vanilla mint iced tea. Grabbing a midweek lunch with Hannah was turning out to be an excellent move on her part: She could lose herself and her thoughts in the whirling web of conversation Hannah spun practically all by herself. Plus, she was funny. Sitting in the café just off-campus, listening to Hannah's stories, was the most relaxed Callie had felt in days.

"Okay, I've talked so much that I've barely touched my

salad." Hannah speared a forkful of kale. "Tell me about your week."

Callie pointed at the plate full of vegetables that Hannah was eagerly ingesting. "You never told me you're a vegetarian."

"You're assuming my eating habits based on the one meal we've shared?"

"You specifically asked for no meat."

Hannah laughed. "So observant."

Not really, Callie thought, considering the café was quiet and Callie had waited patiently to put in her order while Hannah rattled off a list of modifications to the salad she ordered. The whole spectacle had been hard to miss.

Before Callie could bring up a single thing she'd experienced during the week so far, including the fact that her two morning classes had both been strange—one couldn't stay on-topic for the discussion about Modernism and the other was utterly uninterested in discussing anything, period—Hannah was off on another ramble, this one about her vegetable preferences and the last time she'd eaten meat. (Eight years ago, nearly to the day! A vegiversary!)

Half listening and aimlessly picking at what was left of her sandwich, Callie allowed herself to actually observe Hannah. Yep, still cute. She was wearing an outfit Callie wouldn't be caught dead in: a short denim skirt, black tights and Doc Martens, a thin red T-shirt topped with a denim jacket that was at least three shades darker than the skirt. It worked on Hannah, certainly highlighting her body's best attributes, but Callie didn't feel the little rush of magnetism that she previously had. She felt like she was admiring a cool painting in a gallery, knowing she'd remember it but having no desire to hang it on her wall at home.

"Where'd you go?" Hannah's voice, louder than it had been a few minutes prior, broke through Callie's thoughts.

"Thinking about art," she answered honestly. Mostly.

"You're so random." Hannah rolled her eyes. "It's not a bad thing, but you're really hard to read sometimes."

She snorted, then immediately apologized for the startling noise. Her? Hard to read? Hannah should meet—

A hand dove toward Callie's plate and snagged a chip before she could register what was happening. She looked up in confusion and annoyance.

Courtney shrugged, the picture of innocence even as she crunched the stolen chip. "It looked like you were done."

"Did your husband not give you money to buy your own lunch?"

"Cute." Courtney smiled at Hannah. "Hello there."

"Hannah, this is Dr. Courtney Wincheck-Rodriguez, my friend and an esteemed professor at Pennbrook. Courtney, this is my friend, Hannah."

"I'm not esteemed," Courtney said. "She's sucking up. She's very good at it."

"I've noticed that about her. It's nice to meet you. I've heard a lot about you."

Callie choked back a laugh. It was possible she'd mentioned Courtney once, during one of those rare times she'd managed to get a full sentence out during their conversations.

"Well, you two enjoy. I'm going—"

"Why don't you join us?" Callie gestured toward the empty chairs at their table, pointedly ignoring the slightly crestfallen look on Hannah's face. "Plenty of room."

Courtney hesitated, taking a step to the side and smoothing a nonexistent stray hair into her tight bun. Callie saw the stall and knew she was hiding something. Before she could press her, the hidden piece of the puzzle approached the table.

"Hi there."

Callie had seen Kate every day that week, and still she was unprepared for the tiny tornado of emotions that whipped through her at the sound of her voice. Part of the storm was major unresolved feelings from their meeting on Monday. She hadn't processed it with anyone other than herself, and she was trying like hell not to believe that Kate had some kind of internalized homophobia going on. She was doing quite poorly with talking herself out of that belief. Even now, she was having a hard time meeting Kate's eyes. Something was off, and her discomfort with it was shaking her at her foundation.

"Kate, this is Callie's friend, Hannah." Callie made her way back to the conversation when she heard Courtney's voice. "Hannah, this is—"

"Kate Jory." Hannah nodded, boldly looking Kate up and down. "We have a mutual friend."

"Other than Callie?" Courtney asked, her voice far too bright. Callie continued to slowly pass away in her chair.

"Yes," Kate said, smiling widely. "Theo has nothing but great things to say about you, Hannah. It's wonderful to finally meet you."

Hannah's mouth open and shut rapidly, her eyes darting from Kate to Callie. "Oh. That's, wow, that's really nice of him."

"He told me you work at his salon. Has he ever told you how he got started on that path?" Hannah shook her head. "Theo was the best hair and make-up artist in Tennessee. He worked on several theater productions with me before moving here. Even with the distance, he's been a very good friend to me for many years." Kate went on, pointing out various ways Theo had, indeed, been a good friend to her. As she spoke, Callie watched Hannah's defenses melt. Courtney went off to secure a table, leaving Callie to handle her women alone.

"He really is a great guy," Hannah said, agreeing with Kate's latest praise of Theo. "Actually, Theo was there the night Callie and I met."

The saccharine tone of Hannah's voice made Callie's lunch flip-flop in her stomach. "There were a lot of people at that party," she said hurriedly. "But yeah, I remember meeting him."

"That was such a fun night. I'm so happy Nikki and Maya invited me, otherwise who knows if we would have ever met!" Hannah batted her eyelashes at Callie.

She shot a glare at Hannah, wondering what the hell she thought she was doing. They'd been over this. They were just friends, not even casually dating. Friends did not bat their eyelashes at each other.

Callie cautiously turned her head, bringing Kate into her line of vision. If there was a polar opposite for Hannah, there she was, in the flesh. Actually, more accurately, she was in a pair of maroon dress pants, a soft white button-up, and a camel-colored blazer. Her cropped dark hair was tousled from the wind. She looked amazing, miles beyond Hannah's cute get-up. Her shirt had at least three buttons undone at the top, and a simple gold necklace hung in a place Callie dreamed of pressing her lips.

As Callie's eyes drifted to Kate's face, she found the look she'd been dreading: utter blankness. *No. Wait.* There, in her eyes. That was something new. Not registering that Hannah was still talking—*fucking shit of course she was and oh God what was she saying?*—Callie locked her eyes on Kate's. A flicker of emotion sat there, unguarded, and the thrill Callie felt was addictive.

Kate held eye contact for a few seconds before turning to Hannah and exchanging a few words with her. She smiled coolly at Callie before leaving to join Courtney.

"So that's Kate the Great."

Callie straightened her back against the chair, trying to focus on Hannah and ignore the fact that Kate was directly in her line of vision. "That's Kate," she echoed.

"She's not exactly what I expected. I thought—"

"What the hell were you going on about?" Callie asked, her voice low and on edge.

Hannah's eyes popped. "What do you mean? I was just telling her how we met and stuff."

"'And stuff'? There is no 'and stuff,' Hannah, and you know it."

"Why are you—" Hannah's eyes narrowed. "Oh. I get it."

"I don't think you do." Callie balled up her napkin, fighting every instinct to look across the room and see what Kate was doing.

"You don't want Kate the Great to know about us."

"Jesus, Hannah, there is no *us*. And stop calling her that."

Hannah shook her head. "I mean, you don't even want her to know that we've hung out." She wrinkled her nose. "I don't get why it's a big deal, though."

Callie stood and gathered their trash. When she returned to the table, Hannah was waving goodbye to Kate and Courtney. Callie nodded in their direction and walked outside, Hannah at her heels.

"Callie? Stop being silent. What's your problem?"

She stopped abruptly and shoved her hands in her jacket pockets, then turned around to face Hannah. "It's too much to explain. Okay? Please just let it go."

Hannah rested her hands on Callie's shoulders. "Chill out. You're all freaked out over nothing." She squeezed gently, then dropped her hands. "I'm the one who should be freaking out. Turns out Kate the Great *is* actually kind of great and now I can't hate her."

* * *

The sound of someone clearing their throat brought Callie out of her deep dive into an assigned reading about Whitman. A pit of nervousness settled in her belly. One glance toward the open doorway of her office confirmed her worry.

Kate stood there, one foot tentatively placed past the threshold. She'd rested her hand on the door frame and was illuminated by the light from the hallway, giving her a bit of a glow. "Are you able to meet on Friday?"

Immediately, Callie missed their normal, easy conversation. She bristled at Kate cutting right to the chase but followed suit. "Sure. Twelve thirty work for you?"

"That should be fine."

At a loss, Callie simply nodded her agreement. Her eyes dismissed the avoidance memo, however, and remained glued to Kate, searching for a sign of, well, anything.

"How was your lunch date? I told Courtney we shouldn't interrupt, but she didn't listen to me."

Callie stiffened. This was not the conversation she wanted to have. She also wasn't terribly fond of Kate's lighthearted tone.

"It wasn't a date. Hannah is just a friend." She tried to keep her voice level, tried to keep those swirling emotions reined in and not splayed across her face. She had a feeling she was failing and steadied herself with a deep breath.

"Hmm," came the reply, followed by, "You might want to take a closer look at that."

"No need," Callie said, as tersely as possible.

"I don't mean from your end." Kate let out a short laugh wrapped in frost. "Your *friend* seems to be quite interested in you."

Steeling herself, Callie leaned back in her chair and crossed her arms over her chest. "And what if she is? Would that be so terrible?"

After a moment, Kate said, "That's entirely up to you."

They remained on opposite sides of the room, their unspoken battle simmering beneath the surface. Callie kept her mouth clamped shut, fully aware of her agitation and how the things she desperately wanted to say would only come out laced in irritation, anger, and confusion: not exactly front runners for an air-clearing conversation.

In that moment, she wanted nothing more than the ability to read minds. A glimpse at Kate's inner workings would give her a tiny leg up in their troubling, distracting, arousing silent fight.

"I'm sure you have work to do," Kate said. Her hand drifted from its position on the frame and landed softly against her thigh. Callie ached, watching such a simple movement. "I'll let you go."

She was gone before Callie could catch her breath, having been knocked back, hard, by the power of those four simple words.

Don't, she thought, furiously. *Don't let me go.*

CHAPTER FIFTEEN

Wednesday ended up being an all-around bad day. The uncomfortable lunch situation had happened, followed by that unsettling conversation with Kate. And then, because the day simply had to get as awful as possible, she'd had the most frustrating encounter to date with Maddie, who apparently had never learned the meaning of boundaries.

On Friday, Callie was still carrying large parts of Wednesday on her shoulders, and when Courtney pulled her into her office after their eight a.m. class, she didn't take "nothing" for an answer when pressing Callie about what her problem was.

"You're being dodgy, and that's not like you," Courtney said as she shut the door behind Callie. "Spill it, kid."

With a huff, Callie dropped into the chair by the window. "It's this ridiculous student issue. It's driving me crazy. The girl just does not take hints."

"I thought that had gone away, since you haven't brought it up for a while. Did something else happen?"

Callie briefly covered her face with both hands, then launched into the unfortunate tale of Wednesday evening. Renee had handed over her class to Callie, citing some tele-meeting she had to attend. Fortunately, the class was working on something that demanded little of Callie other than her presence and answers to questions about various literary theories. She purposely kept her distance from Maddie and the young woman she was working with, hoping that if any questions arose from that duo, they would come from Maddie's partner.

Alas, no luck there: Maddie had called Callie over, loudly, with, "Callie, I need you over here," and while Callie fumed internally, she put on a placid expression when she approached them. The interaction was over within seconds, and Maddie stayed quiet for the rest of the class.

Callie let them out precisely at nine p.m. and hightailed it back to the relative safety of her office. She found she was alone—surprisingly, Kate's office was closed up and dark—and she relished the peace even as she idly wondered where Kate was, since she often worked late on Wednesday nights.

"When I heard the main door open, I assumed it was Kate."

"What, do you two have some secret special Wednesday night meetings?" Courtney joked. When she saw Callie's pained expression, she raised a hand. "Sore subject, apparently. We'll come back to that."

"We will not."

"Oh, but we will. Go on."

It truly did not occur to Callie that it would be anyone other than Kate coming into the office at that time. Not until Maddie was standing in her office, arms tight across her chest, eyes wide and watery.

"What are you doing here?" Callie had asked, standing immediately.

"I just—I really need to talk to you." She stepped closer, no hesitation in her movement. "I don't understand why you ignore me all the time."

"Maddie. I don't ignore you." Callie pressed her knuckles into her hips. "You asked for help in class and I responded right away."

"No, not that." She shook her head, hair bouncing over her shoulders. "My emails. Why don't you ever reply?"

Because you've sent me hundreds and not a single one has needed a response. Callie clenched her jaw. "Okay. Look. I think we're—" She dug her knuckle into her hip bone, needing the pain to ground her. "I need you to cut back on the emails."

A tear rolled gracefully down Maddie's cheek and Callie hated herself for feeling responsible. "But I just really want to talk to you. I don't get why you don't want to talk to me."

"It's not that I don't want to talk to you. That's not it at all."

The tears disappeared and Maddie's posture snapped from forlorn to bold. She moved until she was pressed against Callie's desk, her eyes now shining with happiness. "I could give you my number," she said quietly. "In case you're worried about people finding out by looking at our email or whatever."

Callie took a step back and felt the edge of her chair poke into her knee. "That's—no. Maddie, it's late. Why don't we meet during my office hours tomorrow and resolve this?"

Maddie's eyes scraped up and down Callie's body, the movement causing bile to rise in Callie's stomach. She needed Maddie to leave and right away. With a jolt of energy, she grabbed her things and jammed them into her messenger bag. Before Maddie had a chance to restart the conversation, she was ushering them both out of the office.

"I see," Courtney said as she leaned back in her chair. "So it's escalated."

"No shit." Callie ran her fingers through her hair before pulling it into a messy bun atop her head. "What do I do?"

"You're meeting with her today?"

"That's the plan. Wait. Shit." Callie let loose a few more expletives. "Kate and I are supposed to meet at twelve thirty."

"Meet with Maddie at twelve. Email her. You know she's waiting to hear from you. Does Kate know about this?"

Callie looked at Courtney, aghast. "No! Absolutely not."

"You might want to run it by her. She's weirdly good with things like this. Topnotch people skills."

Callie snorted. "Does her resume say that? Because I beg to differ."

With a wave of her hand, Courtney blew off Callie's callous observation. "I assume your collaboration with her is going swimmingly."

Their bizarre conversation from earlier in the week and its curious snags filtered back into Callie's mind. She debated sharing it with Courtney, but something stopped her. Callie flashed back to her evening with Courtney and Nick and how little bombs had been dropped with zero resolved explosions. Whatever piece of the puzzle she was missing, she knew for certain that it wouldn't be coming from Courtney. She'd have to go to the source herself.

Courtney's office phone buzzed. "What's up, Audrey? Wow, great detective skills. Yes, Callie is in here. Mmhmm." Courtney raised her eyebrows. "Wonderful, I'll let her know." After hanging up, Courtney said, "She's not able to meet with you today."

"What? Why would Kate tell Audrey instead of just telling me directly?" A mild feeling of doom swept over Callie. "What the fuck, seriously."

"Whoa, easy. I'm not talking about Kate. That was a message from your student. Maddie."

"Oh. Right. Okay."

"And since you're meeting with Kate later," Courtney began, smiling like the know-it-all she was, "you can talk with her about that situation before approaching your student. Sounds like a win to me."

Callie slid down in her chair, pressing her fists into her thighs. Sure. Wins all around.

* * *

Maddie was suspiciously absent from Renee's eleven a.m. class, not that Callie was too upset. Then again, nearly half the class was missing. Renee muttered something about typical low attendance prior to break starting and recommended Callie go on with her plans regardless of the poor attendance, then disappeared back to her office. Renee seemed to enjoy passing off her teaching duties to her, not that she minded terribly. Courtney, on the other hand, hated giving up control and held her to more typical TA responsibilities. Callie was learning a lot from both of them.

Callie tried to end class early, but there was a handful of overachiever undergraduates in the class who wanted to stay and continue the discussion. She tried not to be obnoxious about looking at her watch too often, but when the class crept past its ending time of noon, she started feeling antsy. It was the last day of class before Thanksgiving break. Didn't these kids want to get the hell out of there? The rumor was that most professors had cancelled their afternoon classes, and here Callie was, stuck with a group of students who *wanted* to be in class.

The conversation reached a natural conclusion around ten after twelve, and Callie ushered them out of the room, wishing them a restful break. She hurried back to the office only to be intercepted by Audrey.

"Dr. Lawler would like you to take care of this before you leave." She handed Callie a thick envelope. "I didn't look at it."

"Why would you? It's not for you."

She received a stony glare in response. She moved across the entryway and flipped open the envelope, then groaned. She debated waiting until after her meeting with Kate, figuring she didn't have enough time to get to the library—

"You could go now," Audrey said in an eerie moment of mind reading. "Dr. Jory had to run an errand. She told me to let you know that she'll be back by twelve thirty."

Of course. Their meeting time *was* twelve thirty, so Callie had no reason to be panicking about running her own errand; it was only twelve fifteen.

"If I'm late, tell her I'll—wait a minute. You said you didn't look at this."

Audrey smirked and pointed at the front of the folder. Callie looked down to see "LIBRARY" written across it in bold letters.

"Right. Well, tell Dr. Jory I'll be back." Callie darted out of the office and hustled to the library.

Despite her best attempts to be simultaneously meticulous and speedy, Callie didn't make it back to the office until nearly twelve forty-five, slightly out of breath and definitely anxious. That left brain was *not* okay with being late. Seeing the main area of the office dark didn't help her increasing agitation. Audrey was gone? Long before nightfall? Something was very wrong.

Her heart skipped several beats as she stood, motionless, in the darkened office. It was unnervingly quiet except for soft shuffles of foot traffic in the hallway behind her and the muted sound of pages turning somewhere down the hallway in front of her. After depositing the folder back on Audrey's desk, Callie made her way down the hall.

The relief that washed over her when she saw Kate's open door was palpable. Callie peered in, taking a moment to observe the woman who was crushing her with confusion and wild attraction. She was sitting at her desk, both elbows propped, her right hand cupping her pale cheek. Her left hand hovered next to her face, her index finger gently brushing against her temple as her hazel eyes scanned the book opened on her desk. Callie lost another heartbeat or two as she took in the simple sight of a tired, beautiful woman waiting for her.

"I'm sorry I'm late," she said softly as she entered, not wanting to startle Kate. "I—"

"It's okay, Callie. Audrey told me where you were." Kate's voice was gentle, soft, inviting. "I was a little late myself."

Callie settled herself in the leather chair. "Did Audrey get violently ill? I can't believe she's not still here."

"No." Kate smiled, but it didn't quite reach her eyes. "I told her to leave early. Everyone else is gone so it seemed silly to make her stick around."

A little lurch in Callie's stomach bounced about. It rose again when Callie looked back up at Kate, finally noticing *how* tired she looked.

"Do you want to reschedule?" Callie asked. "You look exhausted. I'm sure you've had a long week, and—"

"No, no. I'm okay. Tired, yes, but ready to get to work with you." Kate dropped her hands from her face and fixed Callie with a stare. "But before we do that, I want to say something."

Callie gulped, wildly unprepared for any Kate confession that was about to come her way.

"Our last conversation—I mean, our last meeting—didn't end the way I wanted it to." Kate paused, her gaze flicking to the open door of her office. "Would you mind closing that? I think everyone is gone, but I'd rather be certain we have privacy."

Callie managed to shut the door without tripping. She plopped back into the chair and leaned forward, propping her chin in her hands.

"You're sure it's closed tightly this time?"

She smiled at Kate, grateful for her ability to joke through whatever serious topic she was about to broach. "It's latched. I promise."

Kate exhaled slowly, taking a moment to shut her laptop and refocus on Callie. "I feel like everything I said in the last five minutes of our previous meeting came out completely wrong. Horribly wrong, if I'm being honest. And I'm sorry about that. I think…" She nodded, her eyes cast down briefly. "I misunderstood what you were saying and got stuck on that."

It was clear to Callie that Kate was done with her apologetic explanation. It was also clear to Callie that while it was fine, good even, her brain wasn't totally satisfied with it. But the clearest thing of all was: Kate was definitely done talking about it, and she was going to sit and accept that instead of stomping.

"I appreciate you clearing that up," she said, keeping her tone even. "I was definitely confused after that conversation." *Okay, that's enough.*

Kate cracked a half-smile. "I can imagine that you were. I'm impressed that you didn't come and beat down my door, asking for an explanation."

"Again, I think you've been spending too much time with Courtney." At Kate's laugh, Callie continued, "I'll have you know that I've been working on my banging and stomping."

This time a full, warm smile graced Kate's face. "The gentle thing is working for you, Callie, but the stomping is cute, too."

It was the second time Kate had used that word to describe something about Callie, and the repetition seared itself into her brain. Before she could stop herself, she blurted, "You think my stomping is cute?"

Kate looked down and shook her head, but Callie didn't miss the smile that stayed on her lips. "We should probably get to work. I don't want to keep you here too long, especially since everyone cut out early today."

The truth was, Callie wouldn't have minded spending hours in that office with Kate, and they did as much that afternoon. Time passed without either of them noticing; they were so far into discussions about books and topics to cover for the sex and gender course that time seemed to disappear. However, Callie didn't miss the part where Kate confidently asked her to summarize the handful of queer romance titles she'd added to the outline. Her reactions and comments were a far cry from her previous response, but a shield remained in place.

"I can't believe it's getting dark already," Kate said quietly, having spun around in her chair to look outside. Suddenly, she sat up straight. "Callie. What time is it?"

"It's almost four thirty."

"So much for not keeping you too long."

"I'm not exactly being held hostage."

Kate turned back around and tilted her head as she looked at Callie. "You're sure about that?"

"Are you asking me if I want to be here with you?" At Kate's silence, Callie went on. "Because the answer is yes."

Kate remained silent as she started moving items around on her desk, signaling the end of their meeting. Finally, she said, in a voice low and inviting, "You're something else, Callie Lewes."

Callie grinned, wanting both to lighten the moment and leap across Kate's desk to take her breath away with a built-up kiss that was threatening to explode. "You may be surprised to learn that's not the first time I've been told that."

"I am not," Kate said pointedly. "I've been meaning to ask you how everything's going with the end of the semester."

Callie took the subject change in stride. She was about to tell Kate some of the things she'd learned about managing a college classroom when Courtney's voice snuck into her thoughts. Right. The Maddie thing.

"Actually," Callie began, easing into the awkward topic. "There's something I was hoping you could help me with. I, uh, Courtney suggested I talk to you about it. I believe her exact words were that you have 'topnotch people skills.'"

Kate laughed. "She's obsessed with that. But go ahead, try me."

Callie launched into the story of Maddie, taking care to spare no detail. If Courtney was right about Kate's people talents, she wanted her to have the full scope in order to best lead Callie to a successful ending. She jabbered along, occasionally jumping around chronologically to make sure she hit every moment.

"Cut to the chase, Callie," Kate said, effectively cutting her off as she retold the latest encounter. "What kind of advice do you want from me?"

Surprised, Callie reeled back a bit. "I guess I was wondering… how you deal with students who have crushes on you?"

"I don't know. How am I dealing with you?"

Whatever breath was left in Callie's chest knocked itself out in a solid whoosh. She fumbled for words but found none that could suffice. Meanwhile, Kate leveled a look on her that revealed absolutely nothing, her posture unmoving. The lack of emotion sitting opposite her ignited a fury inside of Callie. Still waters raised a tsunami.

"What makes you think that *I* have a crush on *you*?" she spat, more embarrassed than angry, but alas, the anger won.

"Well, I don't get the impression that my feelings are one-sided." Kate's voice, surprisingly gentle, barely cut through Callie's internal storm, but she clearly saw how Kate remained blank and void of any emotional signifier.

"I—what? What did you just say?"

"You asked me how I'd deal with this," Kate began, "and my

answer is that I would deal with it by addressing it directly." She paused, waiting for Callie to catch up. "Like I just did."

In the realm of fight, flight, or freeze, Callie had always prided herself on being a fighter. She didn't back down. No, she addressed. She stomped. She fought where fighting had to be fought. But right now all she wanted to do was flee.

"You're right," she said, standing. "I did ask you how you'd deal with a student having a crush on you. But I'm not your student, Kate. I may not be your peer, exactly, but I'm much closer to that than a student." She jerked her bag over her shoulder and stood at the door, turning to meet Kate's eyes. "And if I'm learning from you in this situation, I'll be closeted and constantly running hot and cold without a care for someone else's emotions. Thanks for the lesson, Dr. Jory." She yanked open the door and left Kate behind her, not wanting to witness the aftermath of her stomping.

CHAPTER SIXTEEN

Callie's favorite tree outside her office window wasn't handling the shift into late fall. Its leaves were gone and the low-hanging branches looked weighted with sadness. Even the bark looked like it had seen better days; strips of it hung miserably from the weathered trunk. The poor thing had an entire New England winter to get through and the prognosis was not good.

Relatable, Callie thought as she turned back to her laptop. She was feeling less than positive about, well, everything. She'd upped her monthly one-hour family visit to two full days over Thanksgiving break. Her parents had had the grace to go easy on her for an entire day before peppering Callie with questions and strongly worded suggestions about her unplanned future. Coming home to her apartment had been a fantastic relief, but she'd replayed that interaction with Kate so many times that she was no longer sure what had actually happened. Right, except for the part where Kate admitted she had feelings (*Feelings* feelings? Of course, yes, what other kind of feelings were there, for shit's sake?) for Callie, and she had freaked out and blown up instead of hearing what Kate was saying.

If she were being honest with herself, Callie wasn't even sure that had happened. Did Kate really say that? Or was she just role-playing, and as she said, showing Callie how she'd "address it directly." She rubbed her temples, willing insight and reality into her brain. Okay, fine, but if *that* was the case, then did that mean Kate—

"Stop," Callie said aloud, punching her thigh lightly. The mindfuck was wearing her down. The only way to get through it was to talk to Kate, she knew, but the idea of being face-to-face with her after having acted like such a weird idiot…not exactly thrilling.

"Let's go, Lewes!" Renee's voice pounded into Callie's office as she click-tapped down the hall with authority. Callie jumped, cursing as she realized she had exactly one minute to get to class.

"Thank god it's fucking Friday," she mumbled as she ran out of the office.

* * *

"Oh my God, I thought Friday would never come." Megan sighed dramatically as she practically melted into one of the chairs across from Audrey's desk. "How was this the longest week ever when we just had an entire week off?"

"Well, your body and brain got accustomed to having downtime, and being back in the working environment was a shock to your system. Which likely made time seem longer. In fact, time didn't change. It's one constant we can always rely on."

Megan wrinkled her face in confusion as Callie and Drew exchanged amused looks.

"Oh," Audrey said, adjusting her glasses. "I see. You weren't looking for a literal explanation."

"No, but that was…interesting?" Megan smiled widely at Audrey. "I always like to hear your perspective on my rhetorical questions."

"You don't like when I answer your rhetorical questions," Drew said, pouting. He sat down next to Megan and wrapped his arm around her shoulders. "Just last night, I tried—"

"Absolutely not!" The exclamation from Audrey caused all three TAs to turn and stare at her, all in various stages of amusement. They knew exactly what was coming.

"We are *at work*," she said, her voice low but authoritative. "This is not the place to discuss anything other than *work*."

"I was referring to a conversation we had about work—"

Audrey shook her head emphatically, so hard Callie worried she might strain a muscle. "I don't believe you and I don't want to hear your explanation."

Callie whistled. "Audrey, I'm beginning to think you're maybe a little jealous." At Audrey's aghast expression, she held up her hands innocently. "It's just that you're very sensitive about Megan and Drew's relationship, which is actually super cute, and they do keep it professional when they're here. I'm wondering if maybe you feel like you're missing out on something."

"They're touching," came the stern response.

Drew, at the pace of a drunken snail, lifted his arm from Megan's shoulders and clasped his hands on his lap, the very picture of a scolded little boy, complete with a shit-eating grin.

Audrey released a long-held breath and fixed a firm stare on Megan. "Don't you worry about working with your boyfriend? What happens if you have a fight? Or you break up? You still have to see him every day."

"Oh," Megan said softly. She leaned forward, careful to avoid touching any part of Drew's body. "Audrey, did someone hurt you at your last job?"

The swords shooting from Audrey's eyes were powerful enough to maim. Callie peered at Megan, half-wondering when she would start bleeding from the visual attack.

"Absolutely not," she said once more. "However. I would like to go on record with my belief that inner-office relationships never work. It's a bad idea. Very bad." A pointed look was thrown in Callie's direction and Callie leaned against the wall, trying to avoid being targeted. She was sure Audrey knew nothing about her maddening crush on Kate, but that look was freakishly all-knowing. Fortunately, Audrey moved her gaze off Callie and focused it on Megan. "Someone once said to me, 'Don't shit where you eat.' It's advice you might want to take."

Drew fell out in laughter. He apologized immediately after seeing Audrey's continued serious expression. "That's brilliant advice. Really. Thank you."

"Here's the thing, though," Callie started, unable to stop herself. "We spend so much of our time at work—more time than at home, during our waking hours, anyway. Work is an enormous part of our lives, and we meet so many people here." She shrugged. "Isn't it kind of inevitable that workplace romances happen?"

Audrey nodded slowly, appearing to actually consider Callie's words, which was a minor miracle. "You're right. But mixing work and romance is messy. End of story."

As if on cue, the door shuddered, sticking a bit and earning a kick from Kate as she managed to thrust it open and enter. Four pairs of eyes swept to her, then two quickly departed. Callie bit her lip, willing herself not to turn her head, but she couldn't help herself. And the look on Audrey's face said it all: She had learned to read Callie's damn mind, and she knew.

"Am I missing a meeting?" Kate asked, looking around the room.

Callie remained leaning against the wall, cursing herself for being any kind of obvious. She'd show Audrey she was wrong. Yes! She'd show her by being completely silent and still and having zero reactions to Kate's presence.

"A meeting of the minds," Drew responded. "You're welcome to join us. Audrey was sharing her opinions about finding love at work."

Do not look at her. Don't do it. Avoid. Callie fixed her eyes on the ground.

"Ah," Kate said. "That's a touchy subject."

"I didn't say anything about *love*," Audrey said. "That's different. And if you two"—she pointed at Drew and Megan—"already love each other, I don't want to hear a word about it."

"Lips sealed," Megan said. She turned her attention to Kate. "I have those notes ready to go over if you have time."

Kate beckoned Megan to follow her and disappeared down the hall without so much of a glance in Callie's direction. The sting landed firmly in Callie's chest, taking up sharp, needled residence.

Audrey scowled at her remaining distractions. "Don't you two have work to do?"

"Waiting for Courtney," Callie said. She grinned, knowing how much Audrey hated when she didn't use the official professorial titles.

"Waiting for Megan," Drew said with an exaggerated wink.

Before Audrey could launch another polemic about either of the issues raised, the door swung open with more gusto than Callie had ever witnessed.

"*Fuck!*" The yell arrived with as much fervor as the swinging door. Renee stormed into the office, eyes blazing. Seeing she wasn't alone, she slapped a smile on her irritated face and smoothed her already perfect hair. "Well. Hello everyone."

Courtney slipped in behind Renee and darted toward her office. Callie made a move to follow her but was stopped by Renee.

"No. Whatever you need her for can wait. Everything can wait!" she yelled. "Kate, I know you're back there! Enough. This is enough for today."

Drew looked at Callie, a mixture of question and mild horror on his face. Seeing Renee Lawler unhinged was a rare thing indeed and something inspiring of fear.

Kate and Courtney crept back toward the main area of the office, the latter hiding behind the former, which was ridiculous considering their height difference. Megan lurked somewhere further down the hall.

"We're going out," Renee announced, checking her watch. "We are all done for the day, including you, Audrey. And we are going out."

"It's three o'clock," Courtney said.

"The phone calls," Audrey protested. "And emails! I haven't even sorted the mail yet!"

"I. Don't. Care." Renee sealed it with a maniacal smile that looked more like a sneer. "Get your things. All of you! Get your damn things and let's go."

A half hour later, they were all settled, drinks in hands, at a local bar. Callie had suggested Harpy but was shot down by Renee, who wanted "a goddamn glass of wine." And wine she had, a full bottle ordered and deposited to her with a single glass. Renee waved off Courtney's comments and proceeded to pour until she was satisfied.

"You're not in charge of me," she said. "You know how badly I need this after today."

Callie had decided to keep her distance from Kate, who still wouldn't meet her eyes despite the fact that she was sitting directly across the table from her. So much for physical distance; verbal distance would have to do. Kate made that easy for Callie as she fell into conversation with Drew, Megan, and an adjunct professor who had joined them at Renee's behest.

In her corner with Courtney and Renee, Callie gently pressed for details of the terrible afternoon that had led them to the bar.

"Budget bullshit," was all Courtney would say. She signaled the waitress for another drink, having quickly drained her gin and tonic.

"We should tell her," Renee said to Courtney. "She's potentially choosing this career, and she should know the bullshit behind it."

"Fine. You can tell her." Courtney crossed her arms like a petulant child while she waited for her fresh drink.

Renee, both emboldened and soothed by her wine, launched into the sordid story of the meeting she and the others had attended earlier. As the story went on and the wine went down, she became more and more animated. She also got louder, at which point Kate turned and said, "The entire bar doesn't need to know, Renee."

"Maybe the entire bar *should* know, *Kate*," Renee said, then puckered her lips in a disarming kissy-face. "You know I adore you."

Kate, who was nursing an Old Fashioned, nodded at Courtney. "It's your turn."

"Oh, come on, Jory. We all know how much you love being Renee's wine-babysitter."

"Not tonight," she said. "I'm still mad at you for not warning me about how…affectionate she gets when under the influence."

Renee laughed loudly and leaned over to Kate, planting a smacking kiss on her cheek. "I'm so glad I found you. You're the perfect fit here."

A surge of jealousy flooded Callie's nervous system, which she knew was absurd: Renee was the straightest woman she'd ever met. But despite the miscommunications and lack of resolutions, she could only focus on that spot on Kate's cheek, wishing it had been her lips instead to brush against what appeared to be the softest skin. She wanted to be able to be close enough to Kate to inhale her warm, clean scent—the scent Callie practically chased after in their offices.

Her eyes had rested for too long on that highly kissable cheek and she'd been caught. As she came out of her reverie, she locked eyes with Kate. There weren't any words that could describe the invisible waves that passed between them. Callie sank further into her seat, unable to look away and utterly hooked on the glimpse of actual emotion, real feeling, showing on Kate's face.

A not-very-gentle shove from her left knocked her into Megan, who sat at her right, and kicked her right out of her moment.

"You have to hear this story," Courtney said as Callie apologized to Megan. Once Renee started talking, Courtney widened her eyes at Callie and said out of the corner of her mouth, "Snap the fuck out of it, Cal."

Callie took a steadying sip of her drink and focused on Renee's words. She felt Kate's eyes trail over her several times, but she refused to make eye contact again, knowing she couldn't hide a damn thing. Plus, Audrey was sitting next to Kate, and there was no need to add fuel to that bizarre fire.

When Renee made the request for a second bottle of wine, both Courtney and Kate jumped in to interfere. Callie sat back and watched the arguments ensue, only then realizing that it was just the four of them left at the table. The others had trickled off over the course of the afternoon, which had sneakily become evening. Audrey was the last to go, and despite Renee's attempts to get her to stay and "loosen up!" Audrey had excused herself, citing plant-watering duties. She'd smiled knowingly, a bit like a creep, actually, at Callie as she squeezed past Kate.

"Listen. Neither one of you is the boss of me. If I want more wine, I am going to have more wine." Renee eyed Callie. "Her glass is empty. She'll help me." And with that, she was off to the bar.

Callie shrugged. "I mean, if she insists."

"Are you driving her home?" Courtney tapped the table. "Are any of us sober enough to drive?"

"I've only had one drink," Kate said.

"Two for me. Though apparently I'm having a glass of wine now." Callie grinned. "Besides that, my car is at home since I walked to work and walked here."

Kate stifled a laugh. "Me too."

Courtney exhaled loudly. "I guess I better give Nick a head's up."

"He'll be thrilled," Callie said. "Nick loves drunk Dr. Renee!"

Drunk Dr. Renee returned to the table, prized wine bottle in hand. "God, I love this place. Bottle service in a college town. Who knew! Give me that glass, Lewes."

Callie slid her glass back in front of her after Renee filled it, daring to make eye contact with Kate as she did. Kate's cheeks were flushed, likely from her drink, and her eyes were bright. The dusky light in the bar smoothed her features and gave her skin an intoxicating glow. Callie's fingers gripped her glass.

"Well, I'm relaxed now," Renee said.

"I'd fucking hope so," Courtney said. "Hey, Kate. Think it's time we told Renee about that thing we agreed not to tell her?"

Kate smiled, her lips parting to reveal her teeth. "This seems like the perfect time."

"Christ, let me fill my glass for this," Renee muttered.

Callie tuned in and out of Courtney and Kate's story, one she'd already heard from Courtney weeks before. She sipped her wine slowly. She had a nice buzz, nothing too major, but she really didn't want to be drunk. If she left it up to Renee, however, she'd be hammered. Callie glanced over and realized that Renee had in fact refilled her glass, leaving maybe a quarter of the bottle left. If she drank slowly enough, she'd be in the clear. Relieved, she fell back into the conversation.

"Hey. You two." Renee wagged her finger between Callie and Kate. "How's that course coming? Did your genius brains finish it yet?"

A laugh burst from Kate. "Finish? You're not serious."

"Why wouldn't I be?" Renee batted her eyelashes. "You do realize the waves you're going to make with this, right?"

Kate looked over at Callie and smiled reassuringly. "We've got it handled, Renee."

"Okay, but how far along are you?"

"We're exactly on target with our pace." Kate patted Renee's arm. "Don't worry. It's going very well. We'll be finished on time, maybe even ahead of schedule. Right, Callie?"

Callie nodded, a bit too eagerly. "Definitely. We're on the same page and it couldn't be going any better."

Something like a snort came from Callie's left and she decided not to jab Courtney in the ribs.

"Good." Renee put on a bright smile, one that was bent from the wine but dazzling nonetheless. "I knew you two would be good together."

Callie caught the flash of surprise on Kate's face before the mask slipped into place. She took a sip, draining her glass, and told herself it would be very rude if she got up and ran away from the table and the truth.

"That's us, Renee," Courtney said, pointing at her buzzing phone. "Our chariot has arrived."

"Oh God," Renee drawled. "I need a cheeseburger."

After smooshing another loud kiss on Kate's cheek and blowing one to Callie, Renee was swept away by Courtney. Suddenly silent, the table seemed far too big and small at the same time.

"Hey," Kate said, her voice quiet and warm. Callie looked up at her and was rewarded with a tentative but tender smile. "Take a walk with me?"

CHAPTER SEVENTEEN

"The fresh air feels so good," Kate said, tugging her jacket closer to her body. "Sometimes I forget how much I like the colder weather."

Callie blew out a slow breath, watching the air steam in front of her face. "I don't mind the cold, but I think I could do without the harshness of New England winters."

"It's supposed to snow this weekend." A look of elation danced across Kate's face.

"Forgive me for sounding like a grumpy old man, but it's too soon for snow. It's barely December."

"I don't know. I think there's something magical about frosty air and snow-covered streets. Waking up and seeing the snow falling is so peaceful."

Callie looked over at Kate in disbelief. "And you say you're not a romantic."

Kate laughed and bumped her shoulder into Callie's arm. "If I recall correctly, you're the one who called me cynical and jaded. I never said I'm not romantic."

Caught off guard by the casual touch as well as Kate's words, Callie stumbled over a response. She didn't want to go down that dangerous minefield of *romance* with Kate. She knew exactly how that would end. Weren't they talking about weather? Right. Callie could talk about snow for days. Before she had time to pull more meteorological thoughts together, Kate went on.

"I feel like you and I have had some miscommunications lately. And honestly, Callie, some of that is my fault." She moved out of the path of accidentally bumping Callie and stared down the empty street ahead of them as they walked. "*Most* of that is my fault, and also my issue to work through. But something you said to me recently hit me in a way that surprised me."

Kate fell silent. Callie let the quiet surround them as they walked. She knew Kate would begin again when she was ready. She gave herself a mental pat on the back for knowing now was not a time to stomp.

They rounded the corner of the main street of town and found themselves on a street filled with bungalows and Cape Cods. Callie was following Kate's lead, assuming she had some kind of plan for where they'd end up.

"I'm not closeted, Callie." Kate's voice was strong but warm, quiet, and firm all at once. "I'm not hiding anything. And when you threw out that line about ending up like me, closeted and running hot and cold—it hit me. Harder than you might imagine."

"Which part hit so hard?"

"All of it." Kate sighed. "I may not be as out as some people, but I'm not in denial of who I am. Maybe I don't announce it, and maybe I'm not obvious about my sexuality. *I* know and a big part of me feels like that's enough. I don't want to make a big deal out of it." She laughed, but it was a clipped laugh, not one filled with any real mirth. "You know, in my Shakespeare class, a student was talking about a woman she met who's a lesbian, and the student's comment was, 'She doesn't look like a lesbian.' I couldn't help but ask what a lesbian looks like. She got so flustered and gave a PC, stereotypical answer." Kate glanced over at Callie. "And I realize this will shock you, but I looked right at her and said, 'Do I look like a lesbian? Because I am.'"

Despite the flickers of anger she felt zipping around inside her, Callie laughed. "That does shock me."

"Exactly. But why does it shock you?"

"Because in all our conversations over the past four months, you haven't once mentioned the fact that you're gay." A little of her anger leaked through Callie's emotional dam. "And you must know by now that I'm gay, so why would you tell an entire class about your sexuality while actively choosing not to tell me?"

Kate's hand rested on Callie's arm for a split second, long enough to ignite goose bumps beneath Callie's two layers. "I can't tell you how many times I've asked myself the same question."

The white noise of the suburbs enclosed them as they continued walking. At the end of the street, Kate guided Callie around the corner.

"I can't believe people have their Christmas lights up already," Kate mused.

"Don't change the subject now," Callie said. "Please."

She laughed softly. "You've noticed that's one of my perfected defense mechanisms?"

"You could say that." Callie blew out another long breath. "There is something ironic about this conversation, you know."

"I think I do, but I'd rather you say it."

"Of course you would," Callie scoffed with a smile. "I'm hung up on you not disclosing your sexuality to me when I technically haven't told you that I'm gay. Not that I need to announce it, but still. I could have mentioned it instead of assuming you'd read between my lines."

"Truthfully, I didn't realize you were gay for a while." Kate rolled her eyes at Callie's mock-shock. "It's true. But understand it's because I wasn't…how do I explain this? I wasn't looking for it. I was aware of the fact that I felt pulled to you, but I didn't think much of that for some time. I assumed it was a working-relationship connection. So, your sexuality wasn't a factor. I liked you instantly and wanted to get to know you better. But whether or not you were gay—it didn't matter. I didn't care."

"And now you care?"

Kate's eyes were bright again, mirroring her expression from earlier in the evening.

"Yes. Now I care."

They stopped in front of a light blue bungalow set back a bit from the sidewalk. Kate nodded toward the house. "This is me. Will you come in? I'd like to continue this conversation."

Callie followed Kate into the house and stood in the entryway as she turned on some lights. The house blinked to life, and Callie turned her head, taking in the decor. A very warm feeling rose within her chest. She had a lot more to learn about Kate, but she knew enough to see her in every visible corner. Kate led her into the living room, which was anchored by two luxurious-looking sofas. Soft earth tones dominated the multicolored rug; the neutral walls highlighted the brick fireplace with a stunning wooden mantel. Callie watched as Kate lit the scattered line of candles on the mantel.

"Would you like me to start the fire? It's already warm in here, but I'm happy to light it."

Callie cleared her throat, resisting the urge to blurt out the fact that Kate had been lighting her fire for months. "I'm okay."

"Have a seat," Kate said as she moved toward what seemed to be the kitchen. "I'll be right back."

Callie settled into the corner of one of the sofas, noting with appreciation that it felt similar to that chair in Kate's office. She looked around the room, taking in the stuffed bookshelf, the array of vibrant hanging plants, and the collection of framed photos on the wall. It was all so simple, but all so Kate.

"I used to be married to a man." The announcement came as Kate reentered the room with a bottle of wine and two glasses. "I know I mentioned that I was divorced, but there's the real truth of it." She poured the wine and handed Callie a glass. "If you're imagining that I realized I was a lesbian while I was married to a lovely but distant man who was stunned when I told him I was no longer sexually attracted to him and possibly never was to begin with, you're correct."

"That must have gone over well."

"I did get your favorite chair out of it, so not all was lost." Kate sipped her wine, not taking her eyes from Callie. "The process of my realization wasn't smooth. The acceptance part wasn't much better. It got a bit ugly. My family didn't take it well at first—the divorce or my coming out. But that's my past. A road left behind me, one I don't travel on any longer."

Callie watched Kate as she spoke. There was a calmness to her that was new, a lightness now that the air had been cleared. She was more alluring, more open and beautiful than ever, and Callie bit her bottom lip in anticipation.

"How's Hannah doing?"

The thought of kissing Kate came to a screeching halt. She gave herself a quick shake, not caring that Kate could see it. "You're deflecting."

"Yes and no," came the response, but before she could elaborate, Callie jumped in.

"Why are you so consumed with my dating life?" She caught herself, shook her head. "Not my dating life—the lack thereof, because I am not dating Hannah. Or anyone else, for that matter."

"And Hannah knows that?"

Callie placed her glass on the coffee table and angled her body so that she was facing Kate, who had chosen to sit one seat cushion away from Callie. "Yes. Hannah knows that, because I've told her repeatedly that we're just friends. I don't have feelings for Hannah, Kate. Not a single feeling."

Kate blinked and held her glass in front of her lips like a shield. "I need you to stop stomping for a minute."

They stared at each other for several beats before Callie acquiesced. She leaned back against the plump cushions and waited for Kate.

"This isn't easy for me, Callie. I need you to know that." Kate waited for Callie to look at her before she continued, "I meant what I said about believing my feelings for you aren't one-sided."

"Can you please just say it simply?" Callie asked, unable to stop herself from interrupting. "These miscommunications keep happening because you talk around what you really want to say."

Kate cracked a smile that was not mirrored in her eyes. "It's both comforting and mildly terrifying how well you know me already. Okay. Simply? I like you. I'm attracted to you. I have actual, real feelings for you." Her eyes, a darker green than her usual hazel, glistened. "But I can't have you. This can't happen. So I ask you about your dating life, and Hannah in particular, because I want whoever gets to have you be deserving of you."

The weight that had been suspended in Callie's chest dropped heavily into her stomach. A residual splash of wine inched up her throat and she swallowed hard. "Kate," she began. She was promptly cut off.

"We can't, Callie. We just can't. I'm so much older than you. We're in different places in our lives and I would never want to hold you back. You're confident in who you are, beautiful and assured and proud, whereas it took me four months to admit to you that I'm a lesbian. I just—I can't have you."

Callie stared at Kate. This wasn't happening. She'd fully expected Kate to freak out and pull away after something physical happened between them, but cutting it off *before* anything even unfolded?

"I hear you," Callie said slowly. "But I also know how I feel. And I haven't felt like *this*, well, ever." She tried to get Kate to meet her eyes, but she stared off toward the dining room. "Sixteen years isn't insurmountable. It doesn't even matter to me. You're shutting us down before we even—"

"Callie, let it be. Please. Just let it be."

And for once, Callie did as she was asked. They sat and drank their wine in silence. Callie settled herself and recalibrated to the best of her ability, figuring she could make a run for it after she finished her glass of wine. But the longer they sat quietly, the slower Callie drank. Kate, too, seemed to be sipping at an unnaturally slow pace.

"I'm not trying to get you drunk," Kate finally said. "But we might as well finish the bottle. I thought maybe we could look at some resources I've pulled for the course?"

It was the tentative hope in her voice that buckled Callie's waning desire to escape. She didn't want to leave. She didn't ever want to be far away from this woman, even after she'd doused their growing flames. And so she gamely agreed to stay, have some more wine, and turn to the purely academic side of their relationship. *No, scratch that. Friendship.*

Kate returned with her laptop and several books. Callie was no longer amazed at her ability to switch gears at the flip of a coin. Instead, she shook off their heavy conversation and rolled with it. They really did work well together. Naturally, Callie thought that could transfer nicely into other areas of their *friendship*, but she focused on the video Kate was excitedly playing for her instead of spinning into fantasyland.

A bit later, the wine bottle was empty, a couple of videos had been watched, and, after an animated argument, Callie had talked Kate into reading an entire romance novel.

"Fine. I'll do it. You make a strong case for Sylvia Brownrigg. I'll give *Pages for Her* a fair shot." Kate's face was flushed from their friendly argument and probably also the wine. "When you talk about things you're passionate about, your entire face lights up and your excitement is contagious. It's incredibly cute."

Callie side-eyed her. "If you expect me to accept the fact that you don't want me, you're going to need to stop saying everything I do is cute."

"You're right," Kate said with a firm nod. "I'll do that."

Callie typed a few final words into the outline, then set Kate's laptop on the coffee table before sitting back on the sofa. She inhaled sharply, not having realized how close they'd moved together. She expected Kate to slide back and increase the distance, but she didn't.

"I wonder if Nick was able to wrangle Renee home without incident," Callie said, itching to move out of the space of rejection.

"Oh God, I hope so. She's very demanding when she's drunk."

"And affectionate?"

Kate laughed and closed her eyes briefly. "Yes. She loves kissing people on the cheek. Loudly. And a bit wetly."

Callie raised her eyebrows. "'Wetly'? Is that a word?"

"Unfortunately, yes. Even if it wasn't, it would be now. English professor laws and all."

Callie was laughing when Kate reached through the small space separating them and picked a piece of lint off the collar of Callie's quarter-zip sweatshirt. Callie stilled, her laugh clipped short by Kate's movement, as she warred between grabbing Kate's hand and pulling her closer or holding this quiet moment in space, letting the closeness come naturally or not at all.

When Kate's knuckles grazed Callie's neck as she moved her hand to the zipper, Callie flushed deeply.

"There's quite a bit of heat coming from you," Kate said.

"Yes," was all Callie could manage.

"Callie?"

"Yes," she repeated.

"It's not a matter of want," Kate said, her voice a trace above a whisper. "Because I do want."

The moment before Kate's lips touched hers, Callie met her eyes long enough to see the lightning bolt of emotion flash through the deep green of her eyes. The kiss itself was soft, searching. Callie cupped Kate's face with both of her hands, thumbs stroking the softness of her cheeks. Kate's lips moved over hers, the hesitation quickly disappearing as intensity mounted. This was not a kiss of uncertainty. It was the kiss of withheld passion and desire.

Kate pulled back as she placed both hands on top of Callie's hands and gently guided them back to Callie's lap. "You were taking too long to do that," she said.

"I was going to do it."

"You were not."

"Considering you pretty much told me not to..." Callie shrugged. "You make me nervous. It's not a bad thing. It's kind of a good thing. But you're also very confusing. The hot and cold thing is *really* confusing. That's a very true thing." She clenched her jaw. "I really like you, Kate. I'm beyond attracted

to you, and your brain is so fucking sexy. Is that weird? It's true.
I don't care if it's weird. I've wanted to kiss you for months.
There. That's the truth."

"Callie?"

"Yes?"

With one hand, Kate squeezed Callie's hand, and with the
other, she tapped a finger on her lips. "Stop telling and show me
instead."

Forgoing the warning bells and caving to the siren song,
Callie leaned in and pulled Kate to her. Their lips met, heat
rising instantly. Callie lost herself in the soft movements of
Kate's lips, the closeness of her skin, the lure of her warm, clean
scent. The moment Kate's tongue slid against Callie's bottom
lip Callie hushed the warning bells completely, giving in fully to
the intoxicating power of a very hot, very wanted kiss.

CHAPTER EIGHTEEN

Callie rubbed her eyes, pushing the lingering sleep from her fuzzy head. Time had done a disappearing act the previous night. She knew it was morning, but the darkness of the bedroom gave no indication what time it was. She pulled the sheets up to her chin and snuggled down. It wasn't time to face the day and its ramifications. Not yet. She needed more time.

The memory of how Kate's lips felt on hers flooded her brain, and she tugged the sheets over her head. That kiss… those kisses. Her mouth, her lips, her tongue: The memories were dizzying with arousal. At one point Kate had pulled back, surprise decorating her features, and said, "Did you know it would be like this?" Callie could only nod, mute and already leaning in for more. She could have gone on kissing Kate all night. As it was, by the time they did manage to separate their lips, both women's mouths were bruised and swollen.

Callie tightened her arms around her pillow. The image of Kate's face, her silky pale skin dusted with an impassioned glow, bobbed in her mind. Her attraction to Kate had grown quickly over the past months. Last night, it had reached an epic height.

Any uncertainty about that attraction had been blown out the window.

She had done everything in her power to take it slow. Knowing that Kate wanted her, feeling the unmistakable pull of those kisses—that would have to be enough for now. She desperately wanted to forget the part of the evening where Kate had pointblank said nothing could happen between them. But it hung in the background of her mind, spotlit by a harsh glow of discomfort. Believing that this was destined to blow up in her face was decidedly *not* the tack she wanted to take. However, optimism wasn't her forte. Neither was trust, unfortunately.

With a deep sigh, she emerged from the cocoon of her blankets. Whatever was unfolding between them was going to take the path of most resistance—there was no doubt about that. The matter of how to deal with that reality, and Kate herself, was the pressing issue for Callie. She'd figure it out. Somehow. But for now, staying in bed and replaying the night was only going to kick her arousal back into explosive gear, so she forced herself out of bed and into the shower.

* * *

"I can't believe how slow it is." Sadie handed Callie a pile of books and peered toward the registers. "Did I read the calendar wrong? Shouldn't we be in the holiday rush by now?"

Callie arranged the books on the shelf, taking care to ensure they were alphabetized. "It's a Saturday night, Sadie. I'm sure everyone is out enjoying their lives and not thinking about Christmas shopping."

"I think there's a dig in there. Oh! Right, got it." Sadie planted her hands on her hips and glared at Callie. "Are you inferring *I* should be out enjoying my life instead of working my ass off to keep my beloved store up and running?"

"Definitely not. I was referring to myself and how I keep handing over the best nights of my life to come work for you."

"Funny," Sadie said, "but I believe you had a rather late night last night. Are you gonna try to tell me you didn't go out and live it up?"

Callie stilled. She cleared her throat, stalling while she tried to come up with a plausible lie. "Wait," she said, looking directly at Sadie. "Since when do you keep tabs on my comings and goings?"

"We do live in the same house." Sadie bent down to pull out more books. "And I couldn't sleep last night. I just so happened to be gazing out my window, watching for snow, when I saw your dumb ass stumble up the sidewalk at one a.m."

"I was not *stumbling*," Callie huffed. "I was very tired."

"Uh, yeah, I'd say so. Now tell me what delightful experience you were having that kept you out so late so I can live vicariously through you."

"Nothing!" Okay, yeah, that response came way too fast. Sadie would see right through—

"I love how obvious you are when you lie." She grabbed Callie's arm and spun her around so they were facing each other. "Spill it."

Callie yanked her arm away and grinned. "Nothing to spill, Sades, so sorry! My life is super boring."

"You are honestly the worst liar I've ever met." They worked in silence for a couple minutes, Sadie occasionally looking at the registers to make sure her new hire wasn't overwhelmed with the nonexistent holiday book-buying crowds.

Once their task was complete, Sadie instructed Callie to get the new display up for an upcoming release. Thankful for the break from Sadie's penetrating glares, Callie scampered back to the safety of the storeroom, where she took her time finding everything she needed to put the display up. As she slowly made her way back to the sales floor, she saw the front door open and a handful of customers enter.

"Maybe Sadie will get her little rush after all," Callie muttered as she walked toward the empty section where her display would go. She looked up again and the poster that was hanging from her fingertips slipped and fell to the floor, followed by the box of promotional materials that had been precariously tucked between her arm and side.

Not ten feet away, Sadie turned at the noise and looked at Callie questioningly. "What the fuck?" she mouthed.

Callie hustled to grab her dropped items and made it without further incident to the empty endcap. She took a deep breath and shook out her shoulders. Sadie was at her side in less than a minute, a coy grin on her face as she leaned against the shelves.

"Well, well, well. She's really gotten under your skin, huh?"

"I have no idea what you're talking about." Callie refused to meet Sadie's eyes as she started organizing the items on the floor.

"You so do," Sadie said, dropping her voice. "Kate takes one step into this store and you lose your damn mind. And everything you were carrying."

"I didn't drop *everything*," Callie argued. She stood and pointed at Sadie. "This conversation cannot happen right now. Not with"—she looked over her shoulder—"her close by." She stepped closer to Sadie and whispered, "She could be anywhere."

Sadie laughed loudly. "She's in the café, you freak." Her eyes widened and she put her hand over her mouth. "Oh, holy shit. You were with her last night, weren't you?"

"Sadie! Stop!" Callie grimaced at the volume of her voice. "Please shut the fuck up, I am begging you," she hissed. Without thinking, she looked down and assessed her outfit, making sure she looked presentable.

"Again, worst liar. So," Sadie said quietly, "did you two finally sleep together?"

"I could murder you," Callie said through clenched teeth. "But to answer your question, no. We did not."

"Oh, bummer." She sounded truly disappointed. She perked up quickly. "But you *were* with her? So did you at least kiss her?"

A smile popped onto Callie's face without her permission. It was probably accompanied by a starry look in her eyes, one she would deny was there if challenged. She nodded in Sadie's direction.

"Finally!" Sadie pumped her fist. "And? Sparks?"

"A fucking forest fire," Callie admitted. "It was…she was…" She shook her head reverently. "I knew there was something there, Sades, but I was not prepared for how much is there."

"That's adorable." She grinned at Callie's scowl. "Seriously. You deserve a forest fire. But if it was so hot, why did you stop?"

Callie bit her lip and focused on assembling the bizarre statue that the author was demanding be a part of the display. "Because she told me to go home."

A smothered laugh snuck out as a snort. "She told you to go home."

Callie couldn't help but to laugh. "Yes. We kissed for hours, and I'm not exaggerating, and then she looked at me and said, 'You have to go home now.'"

"Oh," Sadie said. "She freaked out?"

"I don't think so." *Maybe*, she thought. "I think she wants to take it slow." *Or not at all.*

"I'm dying for more details, but she's headed this way, so perk up and talk about these books," Sadie rushed in a hushed tone. "Oh, I know, Callie, this book is going to sell so well! Oh! Kate! Hey!"

Callie, with her back to Kate, shot a menacing look at Sadie, who was about as good at being unobvious as she was at lying.

"Big seller," she said, rolling her eyes. She took a moment to compose herself, hoping her racing thoughts weren't displayed on her face.

"Hi, Sadie. The store looks great. I like the holiday theme you've got going on."

Sadie started gushing about how much planning and work she'd put into "jazzing up the place" for the holidays, then spun easily into her worries about the lack of customers for "the rush!" Callie continued working, pausing only to look over at Kate and smile.

"Well! I better go see if my new hire is doing okay." With a wave, Sadie scurried away.

"She really puts you to work, doesn't she?" Kate moved so that she was standing where Sadie had been, giving Callie no choice but to gaze at her.

"I'm convinced she leaves all the displays for me," Callie said. "But it keeps me busy while I'm here, so I'm okay with it."

The smile on Kate's face was mixed with several emotions. Callie inhaled deeply and took her in, loving the way her jeans hugged every single curve of her hips and thighs. She hadn't moved her hands too much last night, too worried she'd scare Kate off and also confident she wouldn't be able to stop if she started exploring. She was dying to touch every curve and swell of this woman's body.

"I thought I might find you here," Kate said, her voice low and slow.

"You were looking for me?"

She gave Callie a look that said about sixteen things at once, but predominantly, "Yes."

"Well…here I am." Callie stopped moving and locked her eyes with Kate's. "What would you like to do with me now that you've found me?"

The animated look on Kate's face disappeared, sealed up behind that unreadable mask. Callie sighed inwardly. Note: Obvious flirting in public was a NO.

"I meant to bring you a book that will be a good resource for our—the course we're designing." Kate took a sip of her drink. "But I forgot to grab it when I left the house."

Callie regained her footing, shoving aside any impulse to flirt. "Why don't you bring it to work on Monday? I'm sure I'll have time to meet with you if you want to talk about…the book."

"I was hoping you could read through some of it tomorrow," Kate said, apology in her voice. "I know it's presumptuous to ask you to do that, but I'd really like to get moving on this particular text."

"Yeah, that's—it's fine. I have plenty of time tomorrow." Callie raised her eyebrows. "But the book is missing in action," she stage-whispered.

Kate smiled, her confidence back. "What time are you off?"

"Whenever the boss decides to let me go."

"Hmm." Kate looked over at Sadie, who was chatting with her new cashier. "I bet I could convince her to let you go once you're done with this project."

Callie narrowed her eyes. "Do you have some sort of power over Sadie that I haven't developed even though I've known her for far longer than you have?"

"No, but I know how to be convincing when I need to be."

Callie grinned, not taking her eyes off of Kate. "I have to agree with that."

Flirt accepted: Kate's eyes dropped to Callie's lips, hovering for a span of seconds that made it increasingly harder for Callie not to kiss her right there by the new historical fiction display. "I'll go talk to Sadie. Come by my house when you're finished here?"

Without waiting for Callie's answer, Kate strode up to the registers and pulled Sadie aside. Callie could only watch, her mouth hanging open in several shades of shock, as Sadie laughed and nodded, and then Kate left without even glancing back at Callie.

Before she could be caught staring, Callie jumped back into the display, working at a new, invigorated speed. This would only take her ten minutes, max, and then she could—

"I've never seen you work so quickly," Sadie said. "Amazing what the promise of sex will do for you."

"I hate you."

"Do you? Because I've been convinced that you're a very dedicated worker who deserves to be let go early tonight." Sadie picked up the empty box. "She's got it bad, Cal."

"She doesn't, actually," Callie said as she quickly shifted some of the materials. "She told me we can't do this before she kissed me, so there will be no sex when I leave here. She wants me to pick up a book and read it tomorrow."

"Is that academia-style flirting? I think it is."

Callie glared at her friend. "It's not going to happen, so let it go."

"But the forest fire!"

"Just because I felt it doesn't mean that she did."

Sadie put her hand on Callie's arm, slowing her frantic movements. "Get out of your head, Cal. I saw the way she looks at you. She wants you to leave work early so you can come to her house tonight, for fuck's sake. You may not want to believe it, but I can see it. She's into you."

The fight left Callie's body and her shoulders slumped. "Even if she is, she's not going to let it happen. Her words, not mine."

"And we know how much you rely on words." Sadie squeezed Callie's arm. "Give her a chance to show you how she feels. I think she might surprise you." She gathered up the trash from Callie's project and looked pointedly at the front door. "Now please leave before I change my mind."

CHAPTER NINETEEN

Shifting her weight from one foot to the other, Callie stood in front of Kate's front door. She could see lights on inside and the aroma of a fire tickled her nose. Thanks to Sadie's encouragement, only a half hour had passed between Kate leaving the store and Callie finding herself standing here.

She took a couple deep breaths. There were several scenarios that could unfold once Kate opened the door, and she wasn't sure which she favored. Yes, there was no doubt in her mind that she wanted this woman more than anything, but the nagging reminder of Kate's resolute statements from the previous night kept ringing through her mind. Couple that with the fact that Callie didn't know where Kate was. Yes, she was divorced, and yes, she stated she was a lesbian. But...had there been a woman, or even *women*, before Callie? The thought didn't appeal to her one bit, but on the flip side, she had a growing concern that she was Kate's experiment.

It didn't matter, she decided, and stood up straight. She was here to pick up a book. That's all.

Before she could complete a second rapping of her knuckles on the door, it swung open and Kate stood before her, a teasing smile on her face.

"I was wondering how long you were going to stand out here."

"I was thinking," Callie said, figuring honesty was her best move.

"You're always thinking. Doesn't your brain deserve a break?" Kate held open the door, and she walked in, instantly feeling the warmth from the fire and breathing in the combined scent of crackling wood and Kate. She felt the closeness of Kate's body, the enticing warmth of her body tag-teaming with her unmistakable scent. The rational thoughts from her porch-pause twirled off and away, out of reach.

Callie was doomed.

Too soon, Kate moved past her into the living room. She was talking, but Callie wasn't hearing a word she said. She followed, dumbly and nearly stumbling over her own feet, and while she stared at the floor she missed the point at which Kate stopped walking, causing her to stride directly into Kate's back.

Consumed by the softness that padded her collision, Callie regretted the moment she'd have to take a step back. Neither woman moved, allowing her to savor the feeling of Kate pressed against her. Definitely doomed.

Kate was the first to take a baby step away from the spot that marked their collision. And a baby step it was: not far enough to completely break the contact, but enough to let a rush of crackling air whip between their bodies.

They looked at each other, both seemingly unable to find words that could define or explain the moment they were caught in. Kate was the first to break the silence.

"The book," she said, pointing at the coffee table, "is right there."

Callie cleared her throat and put her hands on her hips, nodding sagely. "I see it. It looks great. Nice cover."

The teasing smile reappeared, and Kate cocked her head slightly as she peered at Callie. "I have to admit, I'm surprised that your cool demeanor can slip away so easily." She sat down on the sofa and patted the spot next to her.

Callie sat, fixing her words as she got comfortable. "Like I said last night, you confuse me. And while I disagree about this 'cool demeanor' you claim I have, I am very aware that being around you tends to…knock me off balance."

Silently, Kate studied Callie, her eyes traveling over her face before dropping down to Callie's hands, which were resting loosely on top of her thighs. "I don't mean to."

"Of course you don't. But it's out of your control." Callie smiled to reassure Kate, while she struggled to ignore the attraction that was stimulating every nerve ending in her body. "It's not a bad thing."

"I meant what I said last night, Callie." Her voice was mellow, her hazel eyes betraying her tone with a darkened, desire-filled glow.

"I believe you." Callie leaned back against the pillows. "Tell me about the book."

"Right," Kate said quickly. "The book."

Distracted by a safe topic, she picked up the book and launched into a passionate description of its value and why she liked it so much and why she was equally certain Callie would too. Their conversation eased away from the distraction of intense attraction and ebbed effortlessly into nerdy shit that they both loved.

"Anyway," Kate said after some time, "I don't expect you to read the whole thing tomorrow, but I'd like to start talking about how we can fit it into the course on Monday, so…"

Callie leaned forward and pushed the book further back on the coffee table, then rested her elbows on her thighs and turned to look at Kate. "I'm sure I'll be able to get through a good chunk. And I'm also sure you'll be happy to tell me all the things I've missed by not reading the entire thing in one day."

Kate laughed and brushed her hand against Callie's outer thigh. "The way you see me, Callie…it's really something."

"'Really something'? You know, all this time I've heard you speak so eloquently and now you throw that lame line at me?"

A pillow landed squarely against Callie's forearms, brushing the edge of her chin. Callie gasped and reached up to touch her stung skin.

"What the hell do you have in that pillow? Razor blades?"

"Of course not, it's just a standard—oh my God, you're bleeding!"

As Kate jumped up and hurried into the kitchen, Callie inspected her fingers. Sure enough, there was blood.

"Hence my question about the razor blades," she said when Kate returned with a paper towel.

"I think it was the zipper." Kate pressed the folded paper towel against Callie's chin. There was a glimmer of mirth in her expression. "I'm so sorry." The words were barely out before a laugh snuck out after them.

"There are many ways you could get me to leave you alone, Kate. You don't have to physically harm me."

Another laugh escaped as Kate pressed harder on the tiny wound. "You're lucky I understand your humor."

When Callie didn't respond, Kate nudged her with her free hand. "Hey. That was a joke, wasn't it?"

"Which part?"

"Oh, Callie," Kate said, her voice barely above a whisper. Her eyes searched Callie's, and her thumb stroked the unwounded flesh of Callie's cheek. "The last thing I want is for you to leave me alone."

A small dam of resolve broke within Callie. *Doomed.*

She met Kate's searching gaze and without waiting for a sign, a signal, a word, a breath, she closed the small distance between them and kissed her. Kate dropped the paper towel, her arms reaching around Callie and pulling her closer, tugging until Callie was practically on top of her. Their bodies moved with instincts and minds of their own, limbs shifting to accommodate the press of their torsos. Lips and tongues moved with urgent speed, harder and faster as the minutes ticked by.

A thick sigh floated from Kate's mouth as she finally broke the kiss, pulling away so that the tips of their noses were touching. Those hazel eyes bored into Callie's, the need and want in them unmistakable. Callie knew the words before Kate spoke them, but still, her entire body pulsed at the throaty, whispered sound. "I want you to fuck me."

Callie held her gaze for a few seconds before nodding and leaning back. Kate sat up, her short hair adorably mussed. Untangled, they stood and Kate led the way to her bedroom upstairs. She filled the short trip with words that didn't land on Callie's ears, words that didn't seem to hold grave importance.

Once inside the bedroom, Callie wasted no time in grabbing Kate and melding their bodies together as they stood by the bed. With one arm wrapped tightly around her waist, Callie stroked the back of her hand from Kate's temple to her chin to her lips, holding her gaze the entire time.

"You're sure about this?"

Kate nodded, her eyes feverish with desire. "Very."

The kiss that reignited there, in the silent space of Kate's sanctuary, was charged with the awareness of what was to come. Callie's hands moved to Kate's hips, her fingers gripping the curves she'd been admiring for months. The first touch of Kate's skin jump-started her already fiery arousal and she made short work of moving them both onto the bed.

Kate ran her hands over Callie's shoulders, pulling her as close as possible as Callie lowered her body onto hers. A soft moan slipped from Kate's lips and Callie toyed with the bottom of Kate's shirt.

"I need to touch you," she whispered, planting kisses down Kate's jawline between the words.

"Please," came her response. "Please, Callie."

A few tugs and Kate's shirt was flying toward the floor. Callie's breath hitched in her throat when she looked down at Kate's exposed torso. A pale blue bra, sheer lace lining the tops of her breasts, shone against her skin. Callie ran her fingertips over that strip of lace, her mouth moving faster as she trailed her lips from Kate's jaw to her throat to her cleavage. She dipped the tip of her tongue under the lace, encouraged by the speed of Kate's heartbeat and the shortness of her breath.

"Take it off," Kate said, her voice thick with emotion.

Callie slid her hand under Kate and unhooked her bra. Before she could slowly, tantalizingly, remove it for her, Kate had wiggled out of it and tossed it to the floor. If not for the intoxicating and wholly distracting sight of Kate's round, bare breasts, Callie would have commented on her impatience.

Tight, pale pink nipples waited for Callie's touch. She took one in her mouth, swirling her tongue and gently biting. Kate squirmed beneath her, hands tightening around Callie's shoulders. The softness of Kate's skin was turning Callie inside out. She felt pristine, untouched.

"Your skin," she said around the responsive nipple in her mouth, "is unbearably soft." A sighing groan was the only reply. Callie kissed her way from one breast to the other, taking her time to soak up as much of the silken skin as possible. She reached down and unbuttoned Kate's jeans, knowing that Kate would do the rest of the work for her. Sure enough, as Callie focused on licking and sucking her way across Kate's full breast, the jeans disappeared.

A deeper wave of arousal hit Callie as she stroked the top of Kate's stomach. She pulled away from her breasts and looked down, taking in every valley and curve of the body beneath her. Her hands traveled the path of her eyes, sliding and stroking the hills and swells of Kate's skin. The softness was never ending. Callie felt like she was drunk on the best possible emotions and sensations.

Kate shifted beneath her, pulling her glance back to her face. And there it was: the mask. Callie's stomach dropped and her hands stopped their journey at the lacey top of Kate's underwear.

"What's wrong?" Kate said immediately, scanning Callie's face.

Callie swallowed. There was no way she was going to get to this point and back away because of that frustrating, unreadable expression. "Sometimes I can't read you. Right now, Kate. You're just…blank."

Kate shut her eyes and nodded, then reached up and pulled Callie back on top of her. "I know," she said softly. Her lips pressed against Callie's, drawing them into a deeply passionate kiss. She broke it only to say, "Can you read that?"

"Yes, but—"

"No buts. That's what counts." Kate kissed her again, her lips swollen and achingly soft against Callie's mouth. "This is what counts."

As they kissed, Callie hooked her finger around Kate's underwear and thrust downward, not caring if she ripped the delicate fabric. If they survived, she would ask Kate to put them back on later so she could properly admire the gorgeous scene she'd witnessed a few minutes earlier. For now, she had one goal and nothing was getting in her way.

Kate had just finished kicking away the final barrier when Callie shifted and skimmed her fingers over the top of Kate's thigh. The thrust of her hips was all Callie needed to feel. She eased the crushing pressure of the kiss until their lips were barely moving.

"Say it again," Callie breathed, her fingers scratching gently against the delicate skin of Kate's inner thighs. She felt her own body tremble, matching the vibrations of Kate's, when she felt the hot, wet arousal on her fingertips.

A strangled moan leapt from Kate's lips, and her eyes, dark with pent-up desire, fixed on Callie's. "I want you to fuck me." She gripped Callie's wrist and pulled it closer to where she wanted her touch. "Now."

Callie rocked back and swung one leg over Kate's before she moved her fingers against Kate's clit. She was soaking wet. She groaned as Kate unleashed another unbridled moan, her hips rolling in invitation.

The sight of Kate, naked and waiting, *wanting*, to be fucked, was overwhelming. Callie felt the surge of need quake through her as she slid into Kate. Her body pressed down, pulling Callie in deeper. With each flick of her wrist and push of Callie's fingers, Kate's breathing came faster and her hands gripped, twisted, the sheets. She fucked her, hard and deep, trying like hell to ignore her own orgasm, which was creeping closer with each thrust inside of Kate. She ghosted her thumb over Kate's hard clit, gritting her teeth as she called out, *"Fuck!"* Callie pressed deeper inside, matching the rhythm to the circling motion of her thumb. She watched as Kate arched her back, her head pressing into the pillow, and with a guttural sound came undone.

Kate's hips rolled with each wave of her orgasm, her voluptuous body otherworldly with sweat, glow, and arousal. She threw her arm over her eyes as she continued to come. Callie stayed put, Kate holding her fingers in a vise grip until she relaxed and rode out the last few aftershocks.

Silence trickled into the room. Callie, her hand finally freed, stroked Kate's body as she moved up next to her. She rested on her side, her head propped with one hand while the other drew lazy circles around Kate's nipple. There was no rush, but waiting for Kate to remove her arm and look at her was driving Callie crazy, so she leaned over and bit her wrist.

"Biting," Kate said, "is just going to start that all over again."

"And that's a bad thing?"

She dropped her arm and rolled onto her side, coming face-to-face with Callie. "God, no. But I do need a minute."

Callie kissed her, lingering in the salty-sweetness of her lips. "Take all the time you need. I've got all night."

A laugh-sigh escaped from Kate's lips. She put her hand on Callie's hip, then pulled back. "Your clothes," Kate said, seemingly shocked. "Why are they still on?"

"I think we were both focused on one goal." Callie grinned. "But—"

"No more talking." With the speed of someone bolstered by determination, Kate removed every item of clothing Callie wore in less than a minute. "Much better."

Before Callie could say anything, Kate had her rolled onto her back and had moved on top of her, straddling her thighs. The image was enough to rev up Callie's already bursting arousal. She reached up and touched Kate, palming her breasts. She didn't move her hands when Kate leaned down and took her nipple into her mouth.

The sensations of Kate's mouth and hands on Callie's body brought her right back to the edge. By the time Kate's fingers skimmed against her clit, she was ready to burst.

"It's not going to take much," she managed to say as Kate started a dizzying tempo on her clit.

"Then I better make the most of my time." To Callie's delight and surprise, Kate moved further down the bed, making herself comfortable between her legs. The first touch of her tongue against her clit caused Callie to twitch and groan. The wet heat of Kate's mouth was exhilarating, the feeling so incredible she wanted to hold out, but *so incredible* that she knew she was merely moments away from explosion.

Sure enough, after what seemed like only delirious seconds, fire-laced pleasure seared through Callie's body, the power of her orgasm bringing tears to her eyes. She shook as Kate sucked her clit, the dueling softness and tension bringing Callie a second crashing wave of pleasure.

As she caught her breath, Callie felt Kate lie down next to her. Arms wrapped around her, and she found her face buried in the crook of Kate's neck. She held on tightly, knowing for absolute certain now: She was utterly and completely doomed to love this woman.

CHAPTER TWENTY

The whir of a bicycle and its rider calling out, "Head's up!" pulled Callie from her overlapping thoughts. She stepped off the sidewalk and continued her aimless midweek, midday walk on the semifrozen grass, figuring she was safer from errant bike riders there. It wasn't like her to be distracted to the point of oblivion, but considering the events of the previous weekend, she had no say in the matter.

Clutching her bag tighter against her chest, Callie summoned up the indelible memories of her time with Kate. The feel of Kate's body against hers, the silkiness of her skin, the touches of lips and tongues and fingertips… Callie smiled to herself. It had all surpassed any fantasies she'd had prior to the weekend. And she couldn't wait to refill the bank of memories. Until then, she was happy to replay their time together.

Saturday night, Kate had declared that it was too late and too dark for Callie to walk home. While Callie hadn't wanted to leave, she also knew that the more time she spent with Kate, specifically in bed, the harder it was going to be to leave with her "in control" feelings intact. Against her rational mind, she spent the night and slept maybe two hours. It was all too much to take in: the intensity of touching and being touched by Kate, the back-and-forth of Kate's display of emotions, the lingering drag of the "we can't do this" speech from Friday night. Kate had seemed to sleep soundly, tucked into her side of the bed— while Callie had wrestled with her mind and her desire to wrap herself around Kate while she slept.

When Sunday morning had dawned, Callie blinked awake from her small amount of slumber to find herself alone in bed. While she knew nothing about Kate's sleeping and waking habits, she couldn't help but feel slighted by her absence. Slighted and unnerved. She'd found Kate downstairs, glasses on and coffee in hand, eyes glued to her laptop. The smile she'd given Callie when she walked into the room was reassuring, though, and settled some of her nerves. Conversation came easily, nothing seemed weird, and she let herself relax. Catching herself feeling at home when Kate made them breakfast, she had shoved that feeling down as far as possible.

After they'd eaten, Kate had come back from getting the newspaper from the front porch and dropped the assigned book in front of Callie. "You have work to do." The slip back into professor mode was sexy; Callie couldn't help but fan the flames.

"I could go home and read this, or I could stay here and you could read it to me."

To her surprise, Kate had snatched the book back and ushered them into the living room where they got comfortable on the sofa. Kate read to Callie, stopping often to expand on the text and share her input or to ask Callie questions. They started off not touching while sitting, but after some time, Kate propped her feet on Callie's lap. Callie absently rubbed her legs as she listened to Kate's animated inflection as she read.

Looking back, it was that moment when Callie felt the unmistakable trip-skip of her heart. Despite it building for months, she would have sworn she wasn't falling for Kate. Right then and there, however, she realized she'd been lying to herself.

If Kate felt the shift, she didn't let on. When she'd tired of reading, Kate put on a documentary she'd been praising for weeks. Time moved quickly and pleasantly, but Callie didn't want to push it; around two p.m., she told Kate she should head home.

"Do you have to work?" Kate had asked.

"No, but I do have more reading to do." Callie had nodded at the book, still in Kate's hands though she'd stopped reading quite some time ago.

At the door, Kate had pressed the book into Callie's hands before reaching up to pull Callie's head to touch hers. They'd stood for a moment, eyes closed, before Kate placed a delicate kiss on Callie's lips.

"Thank you for coming over for the book," she'd said.

Callie had cupped Kate's face in her free hand. "Anytime you want me to come over for a book, just let me know."

That had earned her a sweet smile. "Callie…"

"Kate."

She'd wrapped her hand around Callie's and leveled her with a serious look. "We need to keep this quiet. Just between us."

A rock of doubt had lodged in Callie's throat. The words she'd been waiting—expecting—to hear sounded much worse out loud than they had in her head. So this was just a secret hook-up situation for Kate. Right. Okay. (*Not okay*, Callie thought, but she'd figure it out.)

"I know," she'd said simply, and leaned in for a quick kiss before leaving. It wasn't Kate's voice that followed her home, though, but Courtney's, reminding her that Kate was right—no one could know.

Callie looked up at Berringer Hall, having—not for the first time that week—a strong feeling of regret. She should have stayed on Sunday and asked Kate to explain. She shouldn't have agreed so easily; she should have never gone over for that damn book (which really was incredible, but that was beside the point). In the days that had passed—just two, but they'd felt like eternities unto themselves—she and Kate had only had work interactions, and Callie had discovered on Monday exactly how firmly Kate could draw a boundary.

Very firmly and very well, it turned out.

She hated it.

But until she got Kate alone, outside of work, she wouldn't dare bring it up.

* * *

Audrey had a pleasant smile waiting for Callie as she entered the office. Callie knew not to trust that smile.

"What's going on?" she asked as she cautiously approached Audrey's desk.

"I think you're the only one who can answer that question."

"Audrey," Callie said firmly, "I'm not in the mood for your little mind games today. Out with it."

Audrey beckoned for Callie to come closer. After scanning the room for any witnesses, Callie leaned in.

"The rumor mill is spinning," Audrey whispered loudly. "Do you want to know what I've heard so far today?"

Callie's stomach turned. There was no way Audrey could know that she and Kate had...hooked up. (It was more than that, Callie knew, but how else could she say it?). "Sure," she said against her will.

"Changes are coming!" Callie jumped back. So much for whispering. That was a downright gleefully loud exclamation.

"What kind of changes?" Her patience, already thin, was waning.

Audrey's eyes glimmered with know-it-all excitement. "I can't tell you, but I've heard some big rumblings about schedules and TA switcheroos."

Callie opened her mouth, ready to rebuke Audrey's claims—she already had her schedule for the spring semester—but shut it promptly when the door swung open.

Kate and Renee came in, immersed in a conversation that had them so engaged that neither one so much as acknowledged Audrey or Callie. The latter watched them disappear down the hallway and into Kate's office. The door shut, sealing their privacy.

"See?" Audrey said excitedly. "That's been happening all day, each time with a different professor. Dr. Lawler is"—she twirled her finger in the air—"making a classic switcheroo."

Again, Callie opened her mouth to respond but decided it was futile. She made her way back to her own office, slowing as she passed Kate's to see if she could hear any of the conversation. No luck.

Just as she'd settled in her chair and opened her laptop, readying herself for the potential line of incoming students during her office hours, Callie heard Renee's voice booming in the hallway. She perched on the edge of her chair, straining to make out what she was saying. Renee was talking too quickly and her words were muted just enough to blur into noise instead of sentences.

Once the hallway was quiet once more, Callie stood and walked to Kate's office. Her door was open; she, too, was in office hours. With less than two weeks remaining in the semester, Callie was surprised that the office was quiet and devoid of students. Then again, she noticed Courtney's door was shut and heard some tense words leaking out.

Kate looked up when Callie paused in her doorway. The smile she delivered was kind but guarded; it was the same smile she'd been offering all week, except for when they were behind her closed office door and Kate relaxed a bit.

"Everything okay with Renee?" Callie asked.

The smile slipped. Kate took her glasses off and rubbed the bridge of her nose. "Yes. Just some changes she wants to make."

Callie waited, but no more information came her way. She stepped into the office and shut the door behind her. Kate looked up, a curious expression paired with a genuine smile on her face.

"Hey," Callie said, her voice low.

"Hi. Your chair misses you."

Knowing that was code for "sit down and spend some time with me," Callie quickly made her way to the chair.

"This week feels interminable," Kate said, putting her glasses back on before turning to her laptop. "How's yours been?"

"Equally long. I'm shocked there aren't more students banging down the doors."

The "ha" that came from Kate's mouth was cynical. "Wait till next week. It will be a madhouse here." She looked over at Callie. "Whatever you think you're going to get done next week, plan to get it done between now and Friday."

"Speaking of Friday…" Callie knew she was pushing her luck, but if she didn't get her mouth back on Kate's soon, she was going to combust.

"Why don't you call me later and we'll talk about that." Kate pushed around a pile of papers on her desk before asking Callie if she'd had a chance to read the article she'd sent her, ending the conversation before it began. If she hadn't behaved the exact same way on Monday, Callie may have felt off-kilter, but instead, she felt herself getting used to the firm boundary Kate drew while they were at work.

Several minutes into their purely academic conversation, a knock sounded at the door and Courtney's head popped in. Despite the fact that their conversation was entirely appropriate and work related, Callie saw Kate slip her mask on immediately.

"You've got some kids out here, Kate," Courtney said. "And since the door wasn't closed all the way, I figured you were available." She tossed an amused smile at Callie. "Your company isn't very important, I see."

Callie rolled her eyes and got up. "We do have a course to plan."

"I'm beginning to think that's just an excuse for the two of you to hang out." Courtney grinned. Her comment, Callie knew, was innocent, since she had no idea what had transpired the previous weekend.

Kate, however, must not have seen it that way. Callie watched as a panicked look flashed across her face before the steel of the unreadable mask fell into place once more.

"How many students are we talking?" She deftly avoided the topic, as expected.

"Four," Courtney said, holding the door open for Callie to squeeze past. "You've got one lingering, too, Cal. Chop chop."

CHAPTER TWENTY-ONE

Courtney handed Callie a glass and nodded, a deeply pleased look on her face. "This may be the best winter beer Harpy has in their collection. Full-bodied but not filling, refreshing and full of flavor." She took a languid sip from her own glass, nodding again. "Phenomenal."

"What's the alcohol content on this one?"

Courtney narrowed her eyes. "Since when are you worried about that? You're at a party, Callie. Tomorrow's the final day of the semester. Loosen up and enjoy the damn beer."

All of her points were valid, Callie knew, but Courtney was missing a couple of puzzle pieces. Nevertheless, as her eyes continued to scan the room for that familiar crop of dark hair, Callie took a sip of Hip Hop Horae. Her taste buds leapt with joy.

"Holy shit," she said before taking another sip. "You weren't kidding."

"Why would I ever lie to you about the quality of a beer?"

"Because you want me to get drunk." Which definitely

wasn't going to happen, but Courtney didn't need to know that.

"Correction," Courtney said, wrapping her arm around Callie's shoulders. "I want you to loosen up and have fun. You look like you're waiting for a bomb to explode."

Callie didn't bother defending herself; Courtney would see through any of her lies anyway. Thankfully, Courtney pulled another professor over, and she half-listened to their conversation as she continued to peer around the room, waiting.

Kate would be there. That much Callie knew for certain. The matter of when was the unknown. Though no conversation about it had taken place, Callie was hoping they would leave together. It was a long shot, she knew, but she remained cautiously optimistic. The memories of nearly two weeks prior were still vivid, but she hadn't seen Kate outside of work since then. It was frustrating and confusing, and Callie knew, she *knew*, she had to be patient with Kate, but that was proving difficult.

She continued looking around the room, which was Renee's palatial expanse of kitchen-dining room-living room. The space wasn't crowded, but a good number of English Department professors wandered around with drinks in hand. Renee tolerated a few of the other departments at Pennbrook. Since they were also housed in Berringer, professors from Psychology and a few non-wankers from Sociology were in attendance. There was a catered spread of hors d'oeuvres and an actual bartender. For what was supposed to be a modest end of the semester/pre-holiday get-together, Renee had pulled out a few big stops.

Callie didn't find it too odd that she was the only TA present. Her relationships with the professors and her age set her apart from her fellow TAs. Being in the inner circle felt good, even if she had to hide it from Drew and Megan.

The breath ran right out of Callie when she saw Kate walk into the kitchen. Her cheeks were red from the cold, and she looked authoritative-sexy in tight black pants, a forest green low-cut silky shirt, and an unbuttoned black blazer that was rolled up to her elbows. Her collection of blazers was one of the hottest things about her, Callie had decided. Kate was made for blazers.

When Callie managed to peel her eyes from Kate, who was making no move to visit her area of the room, she made the mistake of looking at Courtney. The look on her face said everything Callie didn't want to hear. And when she opened her mouth, Callie immediately raised her hand.

"Not now, Courtney."

"You don't even know what I was going to say."

"Maybe not exactly, but I have a hunch. And my hunches with you are rarely wrong."

Courtney flicked her gaze over to Kate, then back to Callie. "It seems my warnings fell on deaf ears…though I can't say I'm surprised."

An exasperated sigh shot from Callie's mouth. "There's nothing to be surprised about."

"Callie, come on. You know I know you better than, well, most people." Courtney's expression faded into compassion. "You looked like you were knocked sideways when she walked in."

Shaking her head, Callie refused to meet her eyes. "She gets under my skin. That's all."

"Right," she said under her breath. "Well then, brace yourself because she's headed this way."

Glass of wine in hand, Kate approached Callie and Courtney. Her smile was full, her eyes bright. Callie's heart leapt with innocent hope. Maybe Kate was only reserved at work. Maybe that firm boundary was flexible after all.

"Ladies," Kate said by way of greeting. "I see you're drinking matching beers."

"Really? That's your opening line, Jory? And I thought you were creative."

Callie listened to the back-and-forth between Courtney and Kate, figuring it was best to observe for a bit before talking with Kate. She didn't miss the quick glances her way or how Kate was leaning closer to Callie than to Courtney.

"How'd you swing an invite, Callie? I thought this was professors-only." The amusement in Kate's eyes tempered Callie's emotions.

"Turns out the spectrum dictates I'm closer to the professor side than the student." Callie shrugged. "Must be because of the reviews the students are giving me."

"Oh God, here we go again," Courtney said. "The ego on this one is unreal."

Kate, however, looked thrilled. "You're getting good reviews? I'm so happy to hear that. I know how hard you worked this semester."

"And she'll be working even harder next semester," Courtney said. She held up her empty glass. "If you'll excuse me."

In Courtney's absence, the air between Callie and Kate was charged, tension spiking and swirling. Kate kept her eyes locked on Callie as she took a slow sip of her wine.

"You look incredible," Callie said, speaking softly.

"Thank you." Kate lifted a corner of her mouth. "Are you having another drink?"

She looked down at her glass, which was nearly empty. "I could. But I don't have to."

"Don't." One word, simple and clear, was all it took for Callie's body to flood with need.

Kate turned and looked around before settling her eyes on her once more. "I need to make some rounds. But I already told Renee I can't stay for long." She stepped forward and pressed something into Callie's hand. "Why don't you head out when you finish your drink?"

Callie ran her fingers over the key in her hand. "Don't take too long," she said quietly.

"Knowing you're waiting for me will make me move faster." With a final lingering look, Kate stepped away from Callie. "By the way," she said, "you look absolutely beautiful."

Watching Kate walk away was a highly enjoyable moment. Callie admired the perfect, rounded curves of her hips and ass, her fingers clenching into her palms with excitement about getting to touch that sensational body again and soon.

* * *

Callie perched on the edge of the sofa, taking in the silence of Kate's house. She'd been sitting there for merely fifteen minutes, but she was already getting antsy. The wall of framed photographs called to her. She strode to that side of the room in hopes of learning more about Kate.

As she examined a very well-composed shot of a lake that didn't look familiar, she heard the front door open. She spun around and was in the foyer in a flash.

Kate barely had time to drop her purse on the ground before Callie had grabbed her and pulled her into a deep kiss. A satisfied moan came immediately from Kate, spurring Callie on. Every movement of her lips and hands let her know that Kate wanted, needed, this as bad as she did.

"You took too long," Callie said between kisses, pulling Kate into the living room.

"I did my best." A searing kiss left Callie breathless, and Kate pulled back, a confident smile on her lips. "I liked knowing you were waiting for me."

"I bet you did." Callie wasted no time in stripping Kate's blazer off her and tossing it onto an armchair. She skimmed her hands beneath the flowing fabric of Kate's shirt, groaning audibly as her hands met incredibly soft skin.

Kate pulled Callie back into a long kiss as her body smashed against Callie's. Wrapping her arms around Kate, Callie spun her around and nudged her into a sitting position on the sofa. She knelt between her legs, sparking fire with every press of her lips against Kate's. She pushed her shirt up and over her head, inhaling sharply at the sight of a sheer black bra. She dropped her mouth immediately to her hardened nipples, biting at them through the fabric of her bra. Kate's hands wound through Callie's hair, holding her head tightly to her chest. Not missing a beat, Callie flicked open the button of Kate's pants, yanked down the zipper, and leaned back to pull them off. She took a moment to sit on her heels and admire the sight of Kate, flushed and aroused, wearing delicate, sheer underwear and a bra that left nothing to the imagination.

Callie stroked her fingers from Kate's collarbone, between her breasts, around her belly button, over her belly, to the top of her underwear. Her winter-pale skin shone against the sheer black fabric, each curve of her full body demanding to be caressed. Callie could stare at this beauty all night. A glance up at her face revealed eyes full of yearning, lips parted slightly.

"You are so beautiful," Callie whispered reverently. "So incredibly beautiful."

Kate shivered, then reached out to bring Callie's mouth back to hers. The kiss started slow, tender, before speeding into one torched with arousal. Not breaking the kiss, Callie took off what little clothing remained on Kate. Her hands cupped her full breasts, thumbs rubbing not-so-gently over her nipples. Kate began to squirm, her back arching to meet Callie. Tiny sighs escaped between kisses. Kate gripped Callie's hips, yanking her closer to meet her need.

Callie slowly pulled back from their kiss, giving Kate a sultry smile before she lavished her breasts with kisses and licks, leaving no patch of skin untouched. Her mouth traveled south, each swipe of her tongue earning a gasp. When Callie's mouth arrived between Kate's thighs, Kate pressed her hips forward, making it clear what she wanted.

The first press of Callie's tongue against Kate's clit drew a loud groan. Callie, nearly overcome by the heady scent and taste of Kate's arousal, wrapped her arms under Kate's thighs, gripping her hips, spreading her wider. She let herself fall into the moment and everything else disappeared, leaving her only with the questions of her tongue and the answers coming from Kate's body. She opened her eyes to peer up at Kate and found her fully engaged with the pleasure she was receiving: Her neck was thrown back, eyes shut, mouth agape, chest heaving, and her fingers were twisting her own nipples.

Callie thought, again, she might come just from that sight.

As she increased the speed and pressure of her tongue, Kate's hips began bucking and her legs started twitching. A series of moans floated down to Callie. Kate pushed her hips up slightly and Callie met her there, not losing the motion of her tongue. Seconds later, Kate's body tensed before exploding into shakes. Callie pressed her tongue flat against Kate's clit as she came, relishing every sound and vibration.

When Kate stilled, Callie rocked back and looked at her, running her fingers up and down her thighs.

"You couldn't wait to take me upstairs?" Her voice was hoarse, drowsy, tinged with amusement.

Callie grinned. "No. I needed you right here, right now."

A serene hum came in response. With effort, Kate straightened up. Her eyes were glassy, her lips wet and full. Callie took in the sight of her.

"I want you in my bed."

Callie stood, obedient, and offered her hand to Kate. "Then take me there."

Moments later, Kate positioned Callie next to her bed and undressed her with painstaking patience. Callie watched her, memorizing every emotion that fluttered over her face. Even in her most vulnerable and exposed moments, Kate didn't display any one emotion for too long. It was as if her feelings were betraying her by trying to be seen, and she silenced each one as it arrived, only for another to pop up, unbidden.

Naked, Callie stood before Kate, allowing herself to be seen. Unrushed kisses began raining over her body. Light touches followed the path of Kate's mouth. When she reached Callie's hips, Callie, already at the tipping point of arousal, gripped Kate's hands.

"Please," she said.

As they lay down, Kate resting her body fully on top of Callie's, the sensation of their naked bodies coming together trickled into the darker corners of Callie's most buried feelings. She bit her lip, focusing her attention on the feeling rather than the *feelings*. When Kate shifted and slipped her fingers inside of Callie with little preamble, Callie gasped and thrust her hips up to intensify her touch. A pleased murmur echoed from Kate's mouth and her touch sent ripples of pleasure through Callie's body. Steady and strong, Kate's fingers brought her straight off the cliff, and she nosedived into a burst of an orgasm. She rode it out to its shuddering end, hips pressed hard into the bed, breasts shaking with each labored breath.

It took a bit for Callie to come back to earth, and when she did, she felt Kate lying next to her, her hand resting on Callie's stomach.

"You really are something else," Kate whispered.

Callie grabbed her hand and laughed. "And you really have a way with words."

"I do when I'm not overcome with—when I don't—" Kate paused. "I don't think my brain is working very well."

Callie studied her, filling in the blanks of her fragments. "Try," she said.

Instead of speaking, Kate smoothed Callie's hair off her forehead, then continued to run her fingers through her hair. Her touch was so peaceful, Callie felt her eyes start to close. Overcome by the intensity of their connection, she was soon nodding off.

Somewhere in the hazy space of near-sleep, she heard Kate whisper, "Don't doubt how much I want you." The strength and energy it took to open her mouth and form words was missing in action, and Callie fell asleep with Kate's words ringing in her head.

Callie woke with a start, blinking furiously against the sun filtering through the blinds. She was disoriented. She'd intended on napping for a bit, then rousing Kate for another round. Instead, she'd apparently slept, hard, through the night.

Kate wasn't in bed, but when Callie managed to open her eyes fully, she saw Kate standing at her dresser. She was dressed, much to Callie's dismay.

"What time is it?"

"Seven thirty." Kate turned and smiled, but Callie recognized that smile. It wasn't one she liked. "I have a meeting at eight."

"Oh." Callie sat up and clutched the sheet to her bare chest. "I'm sorry. You could have woken me." She calculated times in her head. "I should get going, anyway."

Kate walked past the bed without a look at Callie, and on her way into the hallway, she said, "I know you don't have to be on campus until nine."

Ten, actually, due to a change in exam scheduling, but obviously Kate didn't know that. Chilled by the growing distance and its implications, Callie got out of bed and dressed. She was adjusting her ponytail when Kate came back into the bedroom.

"You didn't have to get up."

"No, it's okay. I have some things to do this morning."

"Some things," Kate repeated. "Okay."

Callie craved the morning-after from two weeks ago, when Kate had been comfortable and warm, even inviting. She took a breath and walked toward Kate, wrapping her arms around her before she could talk herself out of it. To Callie's surprise, Kate softened, her arms tight around Callie's waist.

Touch, Callie thought. *She just needs touch to remember.*

"I do have to go." Kate's voice was muffled, her face burrowed in Callie's shoulder.

Callie released her. Kate looked at her, emotion sliding off her face and into its hiding places. Callie supposed she'd have to get used to this mask. The touches didn't lie, even if Kate's face could.

Kate leaned in and kissed Callie, their lips meeting gently, allowing words to remain unspoken.

CHAPTER TWENTY-TWO

Callie didn't have "some things" to do. She had nothing to do before she was due at campus, but after leaving Kate's she went home and threw herself into cleaning her room. It was Friday, the semester was officially over in less than eight hours, and winter break stretched ahead, an endless (not really, but... semantics) space of time away from work. It was the perfect time for Callie to spend time with Kate, to nurture and explore the passion between them. She thought about inviting Kate over, maybe making her dinner, then—

"What? Asking her if she wants to come hang out in your room?" Callie dropped onto her bed. Having roommates had never bothered her before. It was temporary, a situation that benefitted Nikki and Callie especially and Maya as well, even though she was just along for the ride. But now? In the light of sleeping with a woman who was so established, so accomplished, Callie felt ridiculous to be thirty-four and living with a couple instead of on her own.

For a split second, she thought about asking Sadie to switch apartments with her. A studio would definitely look better than... this. Callie looked around her room. It wasn't a bad room. It was inviting and nicely decorated. It had the look of an adult room, complete with an expensive and supremely comfortable queen-sized bed. The decor was chill and, according to Sadie, "very Callie." This bedroom was a perfectly good place to bring Kate.

With an assured nod, Callie stood and went to shower. She'd spent too long cleaning her room and now she had to hustle if she was going to get to campus on time. After throwing on jeans and a Pennbrook quarter-zip fleece, she grabbed her things and headed to campus.

It would be interesting, she thought, to see what Kate would be like today. Callie was determined to find equal footing for them. There had to be a way she could help ease Kate into their blossoming relationship. She smirked. She wasn't entirely certain that's what this was becoming, but she knew without a doubt that her feelings for Kate were only increasing, and if she had to judge Kate's feelings based solely on their intimate encounters...then there was no question how Kate felt.

Everything else she did, though, was far too open for interpretation.

As Callie rounded the corner and Berringer came into view, she felt her phone buzz with an incoming text. Kate's name blinked on the screen; Callie smiled against her nerves. Kate wasn't the texting type, but this was not an unwelcome surprise.

I didn't want you to leave this morning.

Callie chewed her bottom lip, reading between the lines for meaning. She was working on her fourth interpretation when she stepped through the doors of Berringer. Finally, as she hit the steps that would take her to the English office, she tapped out a reply.

I didn't want *you* to leave this morning.

Confident that she'd be met with a more receptive, less closed-off version of Kate at work, she straightened her posture and walked into the English office, ready for whatever the day brought.

It brought a mess. Kate hadn't been kidding about the end of the semester being far more challenging and demanding than a newbie might expect. After discovering that Courtney had given her the wrong answer key for one portion of the final, Callie had to regrade a class's worth of tests. While she was proctoring the final for Intro to Lit Theory, she caught not one, but four students cheating. They argued with her, citing that her position as a TA meant that she had no idea what she'd seen and therefore they weren't cheating and she was dumb to assume they were. After corralling the suspects in the corner of the classroom while the rest of the class finished their exam, Callie dragged them to Renee's office. An hour later, her ears were bleeding from listening to Renee alternately lecture and yell. Callie was relieved to see the students get zeroes on their exams, but drained and irritated from the entire experience.

Just when she thought she'd have some time to herself, Courtney yanked her into her office to go over some discrepancies on the final they'd given in her Experiences in American Lit course. That took only a half hour, but battling and tempering Courtney's obsessive grading practices took Callie down a few more notches.

Before creeping out of Courtney's office, Callie poked her head into the hall and scanned the area for potential problems. Miraculously, it was empty and silent. She jogged to her own office and shut the door firmly behind her.

"Rough day?"

Callie nearly jumped out of her skin. She hadn't noticed Drew and Megan hunched at their desks in her rush to get into the safety of the office.

"Chaos," was all she could reply.

The shell-shocked looks on their faces echoed her sentiments, and the three lapsed into silence as they tackled tasks and put out fires. Every so often, one of the TAs would put on a tough face and leave the office, only to come back further scarred.

Callie was finishing up the Lit Theory exams when Megan slipped back into the room, her face snow-white and eyes tearing up.

"You okay?" Callie asked.

Megan nodded, then shook her head. She dropped into her chair, tears falling down her cheeks. "She's never been like that with me," she whispered, disbelief ringing through her voice.

"Who?" Drew asked, rolling across the room in his chair to comfort his girlfriend.

"Dr. Jory." The words stumbled out around a sob.

Callie felt her chest tighten. She waited for Megan to continue, not wanting to pry.

Megan shook her head again before rubbing her cheeks dry. "I need to get a grip. I just—she's always kind of distant, you know? And I've heard students talk about how harsh she can be, how she flips from being so cool to being, like, dismissive. I thought they were exaggerating. But that was—wow. Mean." Megan laughed through her tears. "I never thought I'd call her mean, but there's no other way to say it."

"She's probably stressed, like us," Drew said. "I'm sure she didn't mean to be rude, Megs."

Callie half-listened to their continuing conversation. She gripped the edge of her desk, her concern for Megan warring with her desire to check in with Kate. Something must have happened if she was going after Megan, since Callie knew that Kate quite liked her TA and respected her.

She glanced over at Drew and Megan. They seemed to be wrapped up in each other and Megan's tears had stopped. Callie, not bothering to make an excuse, stood and left the office, heading directly for Kate's.

Her door was ajar but no sound other than typing came from the office. With a steadying breath, Callie nudged the door open as she knocked.

Kate's head jerked up. The impassive mask was set in place. She didn't say anything, just looked at Callie, almost as though she was looking through her.

A voice in Callie's head yelled, "Retreat!" but she shrugged off the advice and stepped into the office, making sure the door was completely closed behind her.

As Callie walked toward Kate's desk, she saw a ribbon of emotion move over Kate's features. She didn't stop until she was standing next to Kate, and then she perched on the edge of her desk, angling her body toward Kate, who remained frozen in her chair.

"What are you doing?" she asked, her gaze fixed on her laptop.

"Checking on you," Callie said. "I heard some rumblings that you might be in a bad mood."

Kate didn't move, and she didn't reply. Callie took the lack of movement as a good thing, since Kate wasn't making a point to put physical distance between them.

"Anything I can help with?"

"No."

With dismay, Callie watched as Kate rolled her chair back, putting a solid foot of space between them. She double-checked to make sure the door was still closed tight.

"It's closed," Kate said. "But you shouldn't be this close to me. Not like this." She gestured to Callie's position on her desk.

The air between them prickled with tension. Callie felt the shift, not liking the way her body steeled itself. After a hesitation, she stood and moved even closer to Kate, then squatted down so their eyes were level.

"Callie." Warning threaded through each letter of her spoken name.

She reached over and took Kate's hand. "You said yourself that touch is what counts," she said, keeping her voice low but warm. "Talk to me. What's going on?"

A handful of seconds passed before Kate pulled her hand away, reestablishing the distance between them. "I told you, Callie. I told you we can't do this."

The words, familiar and still awful, knocked Callie back. She threw an arm behind her to brace herself, then quickly stood up. "You're doing this now?"

"I already did it," Kate said plainly. "And then I went back on my own words. I shouldn't have done that."

Arguments and challenges raced through Callie's mind, but for once, she stayed silent. Even she knew this was not the place to have this conversation.

Kate, however, had other ideas. She settled her eyes on Callie. "I don't think it's wise for people who work together to become involved, especially when our roles are as such. It's too complicated, and at some point, people would find out, which would make everything more complicated." She took a staggered breath. "You and I are on different paths. Sixteen years is a lot of life experience to overcome. This is simply not a good idea, and I'm sorry for not sticking to my word."

Callie waited for a slip of the mask, but none came. Kate's face remained stony, her posture rigid and unfeeling.

"Okay," Callie said as she walked toward the door, doing everything in her power not to look back at Kate. "I hear you."

With her hand on the doorknob, she couldn't resist. A look over her shoulder confirmed that Kate hadn't moved a centimeter.

"Nice speech, by the way. I can tell you've been rehearsing." With a final stomp, though it likely hurt her own heart more than it hurt Kate's, Callie pulled the door open and left, not bothering to shut it behind her.

All she wanted was to make it back to the safety of her own office without being seen or needed, but alas, that was impossible. Renee, coming out of Courtney's office, lasered her stare on Callie.

"My office. Now."

She dutifully followed Renee and tried to focus on the information she rattled off. Words like "schedule" and "class" repeated. Names were thrown into the mix, none grabbing her attention until "Kate" was said several times in a row.

"I know it's last minute, and this is entirely my fault for not telling you earlier." Renee shot an apologetic look Callie's way. "However, I have full confidence that you're already prepared for this class, and it's clear that you and Kate work well together, so I know it will work out."

Callie's brain rushed to keep up. "What course is this again?"

"It's a fiction workshop. Creative Writing."

"Right. Okay." Callie nodded. "And I'm, uh, Kate's TA?"

Renee cocked her head at Callie. "How much of what I said did you actually hear?"

"I'm really sorry. It's been a chaotic day and my brain isn't at its best."

"Well, this is also my fault for throwing it at you so late in the game. I thought Kate would have told you, but clearly I was wrong on that front." Renee shook her head. "Anyway. You'll be her TA, yes. Unofficially since you have the three courses, so we'll treat it as we did my evening course. Got it?"

"Understood." Callie left, having been dismissed with a firm nod from Renee.

Conversations and implications spun through her mind as she made her way back to her office, which was now, thankfully, empty. She fell into her chair and stared out the window. Things were certainly starting to become clear.

"Fuck," she said quietly as unwelcome truths lodged themselves in her brain. She was going to be TA'ing for Kate next semester. Not only would they continue to work on their project together, but they'd also be in a classroom...together. So much for having space to—

Callie groaned inwardly as yet again Courtney's warnings rang in her ears: *When she's your supervisor, totally off-limits.*

"Perfect," she muttered, throwing her laptop and papers into her bag, moving quickly to get far away from the English Department offices as fast as possible.

CHAPTER TWENTY-THREE

The whirring sound of an espresso machine filtered through the gentle hum of chatter filling the cozy space. Callie glanced around the coffee bar, anxiously waiting for Sadie to return with their drinks. She'd decided to cut back on her caffeine consumption over winter break. Her admirable endeavor was proving somewhat successful. It had been eight days since break began and she was just now giving in to her craving.

This break had been welcomed by Callie for numerous reasons. Since her parents had decided to go on a cruise over the holiday, she was staying in town and spending her time with Sadie, Nikki, and Maya. They were planning a haphazard Christmas dinner where it was likely more wine than food would be consumed.

Sadie pushed an iced drink toward Callie as she sat down.

"I may be hallucinating, but I'm pretty sure this isn't the hot Earl Grey tea I ordered."

"I've decided you need to leave your boring-ass tea comfort zone," Sadie announced. "Try it. You'll like it."

Callie gave her a wary look before taking a tentative sip of what appeared to be iced coffee. Her taste buds approved, realizing it was not coffee, but somehow tea? Iced and creamy? A mystery, but a tasty one. "Not bad."

"Wow, you're almost smiling. That's the happiest you've looked since break started."

"I'm fine," Callie said. "It's just been a stressful couple of weeks." She sat back in her chair and crossed her arms. She wasn't in the mood for this. Truthfully, she hadn't been in the mood for anything other than lying in bed, rethinking how she could have handled everything with Kate.

"Right, so, about that?" Sadie cleared her throat. "I was hoping maybe you'd want to talk? Because you've been so uncharacteristically quiet?"

With each question, Callie's defenses strengthened their reserves. Before she could respond with some biting remark about being silent for once, they were interrupted.

In a bluster of a thick winter coat and the unmistakable aroma of clove cigarettes, Nikki dropped into the chair next to Sadie. "Sorry I'm late, Sades. Did I miss anything?"

Callie looked back and forth between her friends as confusion trickled through her. "What are you doing here?"

"This is an intervention, my dear friend. We're intervening."

Sadie had the grace to look guilty, but Nikki appeared nothing but joyful. She leaned across the table and booped Callie's nose. "It's for the best, Cal."

Callie swatted her hand away. "And why the fuck exactly do you two think I need intervening?"

Nikki released a low whistle. "You didn't tell her?" she stage-whispered to Sadie.

"I didn't have the chance!" Sadie blessed Callie with an overly sweet smile. "You've been super unpleasant for days, Callie. And I'm worried about you but totally out of my league with this, so I, um, asked Nikki for help."

"You think I need a *therapist*?" Callie hissed.

"Wow, first of all, I'm not a therapist yet," Nikki said. "And secondly, since when are you anti-therapy?"

Callie took a calming breath. Her lashing out had a place, and it wasn't at these two well-meaning friends. "I'm not. Sorry. But I don't want to talk about anything."

Sadie and Nikki exchanged a look. "Nik," Sadie said, "why don't you start by telling Callie what you've observed at home?"

"Yes, of course. Well, Callie, you've been very quiet since break began. And that's weird, even for you. You've been spending a lot of time in your room and you're getting along really well with Maya, which tells me something is very wrong."

"And," Sadie interjected, "while you've been an amazing help at the store, you always want to stay in the stockroom. You seem paranoid when you're on the floor, like a bird that's constantly looking out for a predator."

"Hey, nice analogy," Nikki said.

"Thanks! I've been working on them. I feel like I could have used a stronger image than a bird, but it felt right to describe—"

"Stop," Callie said, her voice low, carrying a subtle threat. Nikki and Sadie snapped to attention, waiting for more, but Callie reverted to silence as she casually sipped her drink.

"It's Kate, isn't it?"

The conversational bomb dropped from Sadie's mouth and landed directly in a part of Callie's heart she swore she'd barricaded a week ago.

"Wait. Who's Kate?"

"Oh God," Sadie murmured. "You don't know?" She looked questioningly at Callie. "You didn't tell Nikki?"

"There. Is. Nothing. To. Tell." Callie looked back and forth between her friends. "I'm not doing this." She yanked on her jacket and grabbed her drink before hustling out of the coffee bar, leaving Sadie to explain.

Hours later, Callie was in a new bar nursing a new drink, one that had the potential to erase her mind far better than whatever iced tea concoction Sadie had given her earlier. She wasn't mad. Far from it, really. She'd been doing her best to tamp down her feelings and keep a brave, normal face painted on, but Sadie and Nikki knew her too well. It didn't mean she wanted to talk to them about it, though. There was only one person she was willing to bare her sad little soul to.

For the second time that day, Callie was greeted by a rush of cold air and wool coat as someone sat down next to her.

"You do realize I'm only here because you told me they have Hip Hop Horae on tap, correct?"

"And what riveting activity would you be engaged in if you weren't here with me?"

Courtney wiggled her eyebrows. "You really want me to answer that?"

"We've made it this far in our friendship without talking about sex, so no. Please keep it to yourself."

"Actually, I was going to tell you about the intensely difficult jigsaw puzzle Nick and I have been working on, but I'll let you keep whatever image is now haunting your brain." Courtney ordered her beer, then rubbed her hands together. "So. You slept with her, huh?"

Callie struggled between choking and spitting out her mouthful of beer. She settled for the former, gracelessly coughing until she could breathe normally. Courtney watched, sympathy on her features.

"I told you to be careful, Callie."

Having regained her composure, Callie cleared her throat repeatedly until she was confident she could speak without another choke-fest flaring up. "I was. I swear, I was careful. She—she did this."

"Don't pull that shit with me. You know better."

Okay, yeah. Callie did know better. But her current primary emotion was flat-out embarrassment, and her bad habit of pushing the blame on others had flared up in its wake.

"Leave out the details and tell me what happened." Courtney held up a hand. "And I mean it about the details."

With a sigh, Callie retold the events that led her to Kate's house, then to Kate's bed, on two occasions. Revisiting their last conversation was the most painful bit, and she knew her embarrassment-sadness combo was written all over her face.

When Callie stopped talking, Courtney sat for a while, drinking her beer and nodding every so often. As she waited for a response, Callie ordered another beer. Erasing her mind was starting to sound better and better.

"You're not telling me something," Courtney finally said.

"Other than the details?"

"You really expect me to believe that there's been zero attempt at communication from either of you since you spoke in her office?"

Callie's shoulders sagged. "That may not be completely true."

"Out with it."

This was, perhaps, the most embarrassing part, but Callie had to own it. "I texted her the day after we talked. I asked if we could meet up and talk, just to have a real conversation outside of work, since she's so much more open with me when we're not there. And she responded a day later, telling me she was looking forward to having me as her TA, since she's heard such great things about me and my work ethic."

"Oh, Christ," Courtney said. A pained look spread across her face. "That was cold."

"Icy. It's like nothing ever happened between us." Callie winced, feeling tears scraping her eyelids. "Courtney, I'm telling you, whatever happened was *not* one-sided."

"I saw the way she looked at you at Renee's party. I can assure you, from an observer's perspective, that you're not mistaken. She definitely feels something for you."

What should have been relief came on more strongly as loss. Callie hunched over the bar. She was so tired of feeling.

"But," Courtney continued, "she told you up-front, before anything happened, that it wasn't going to happen."

"And then it *did* happen. And *she* started it." Callie huffed, hating how pathetic she sounded. "I would have been fine knowing that there were feelings but nothing could come of them. But once she kissed me, I couldn't just walk away."

"And she wanted to see it through," Courtney said. "That much is clear. But maybe that's all it was, Cal. Kind of like scratching an itch."

"That," Callie said, looking at her friend, "may be the single worst thing you have ever said to me."

"Think about it. She told you she has feelings for you. She kissed you. It went further. It happened a second time, again with her initiating." Courtney shrugged. "Maybe she had to know what it was like, being with you."

Callie groaned. "And what? Now that she's ticked me off her to-do list, that's it?"

"Only she knows that. I told you before, and I'll tell you again: You need to be patient with her."

"Now is really not the time for you to defend the woman who recently ripped my heart out with her teeth."

Courtney whistled. "I'm going to let you be dramatic while I once again remind you of something very important. You're working as her TA next semester. Technically, anyway." She rolled her eyes. "The shit Renee comes up with. Anyway, you're the TA. She's the professor on record. That little mathematical equation adds up to the following phrase: 'No romantic relationships allowed.'"

"I don't think that's how math works."

"Close enough." Courtney shrugged. "But you're also still working on that course with her. You're going to have to deal with this and show her you can continue peacefully working with her."

Callie pressed the cool half-empty glass of beer against her burning cheek. "Do you think she feels I'm not good enough for her? Because I'm thirty-four and have roommates and I'm just now working on my PhD and I'm not established like she is?"

"Whoa, whoa, whoa. Don't do that to yourself." Courtney narrowed her eyes. "I thought you were over Kelly."

She was. Very much so. But the overlay of the shit her ex had laid at her feet as she dumped Callie had lingered despite her attempts to discard it.

"For the record, no," Courtney went on. "I know you're dying to know this, so I'll tell you." She turned to face Callie. "Yes, Kate and I talk about you. Yes, she has occasionally asked questions about you that led me to believe that she was interested in you. And because I respect her privacy, I'm not saying anything more than this. I can assure you, one hundred and one percent, that in no way does Kate view you as less-than. In fact, she's very impressed with you."

"Right," Callie muttered. "That's obvious."

"It is, dipshit. Have you forgotten about how she requested you to work on the course with her and then persuaded Renee to use it in place of your seminars?"

Callie looked up in surprise. "I thought that was Renee's idea."

"Hardly. Kate went to bat for you. She respects you, Callie."

As she rolled this information through her brain, she looked down the bar and felt a cold sweat come over her. Her stomach bottomed out as she looked more closely at the woman sitting at the other end of the bar. Nerves pounding, Callie scanned the woman until she was certain it wasn't Kate.

When she looked over at Courtney, she was met once more with a sympathetic look.

"It's not her."

"I realize that. Now."

"You've got it bad." Courtney rubbed Callie's shoulder. "I've got to imagine Kate's in a similar position, with what you've told me."

"I know you're trying to reassure me, but that doesn't help. She said it herself: She can't have me. But the reality is, she *won't* have me."

"I'm starting to get the feeling that you don't listen to anything I say." Courtney sighed heavily. "The best thing you can do is to let it be. Don't poke the bear."

With a roll of her eyes, Callie nodded. "I know."

"And look at it this way: You have almost a month to get over her." Courtney jostled Callie. "Plenty of time, right?"

"Right," Callie said, her body tensing. "No problem."

CHAPTER TWENTY-FOUR

As the spring semester began, so did the countdown to the end of the academic year. Callie, in her many years of schooling, had always viewed the winter holidays as a halfway point. When she was younger, she let herself progressively slack off as the calendar flipped closer to June. But here and now, in this multifaceted position as both doctoral student and sort-of-professor, she knew there would be no dropping of the proverbial ball. She had a job to do—several jobs, really—and there was no area in which she could ease up.

In fact, it seemed like everyone around her was working harder than they had during the fall semester. Returning to campus after winter break, Callie noticed a new layer of stress whooshing through the hallways, blowing lightly into classrooms and gusting through offices. The air itself was frantic, she thought as she sidestepped a group of chattering students. Classes had resumed a few days earlier, and with the weekend in sight plus an impending snowstorm, the energy in the building was rapidly rising.

Even the English offices were vibrating with a different, heightened feeling. As Callie entered, Audrey whirled around in her chair, the picture of panic as she gesticulated wildly. It took Callie a moment to realize she was on the phone and therefore oblivious to Callie's entrance. After grabbing a few envelopes from her mailbox, Callie slunk to her office, carefully dodging the line of open doors.

Drew raised a hand in greeting before leaning back and crossing his ankle over his knee, regarding Callie with interest. "What are you doing here on a Thursday?"

Callie kept her head down, already distracted by the mail she'd collected. "I have a meeting with Lawler and Jory in a half hour. Plus, I'm—they gave me an additional course to survey. That's at two."

"Heavy schedule," he remarked.

Callie glanced over at Drew, but he'd turned back to his work. She didn't feel great about appearing to be the favorite. Neither Drew nor Megan had been granted the same kinds of "extras" that Callie had, and they were all aware of it. Drew especially, since Callie was MIA from their doctoral seminars for the semester. Callie knew they all had enough on their teaching and studying plates, so it wasn't that kind of jealousy, but her connection to the professors wasn't going unnoticed.

She sat down at her desk and toggled over to her email. Before she realized what she was doing, she'd chewed so hard on the inside of her cheek that she tasted blood. All the pretending in the world couldn't hide the fact that she was nervous about seeing Kate. They'd gone the entire break, save for that initial awkward exchange, without any communication. Callie hadn't seen her in town. She hadn't even heard anything about her from Courtney. And despite being back in the same building, they'd somehow managed to avoid each other the entire week aside from two curt emails back and forth. Such a grand disappearing act should have been a salve for Callie's wounded heart and ego, but she found herself back to unsteady footing at the thought of sitting in a meeting with Kate.

Fitful thoughts about Kate, combined with plowing through far too many emails, made the time pass quickly. When Callie finally looked at the time, she grabbed her things and sprinted across the hall, seconds from being late.

She peeked into Renee's office to find that she was alone, typing madly on her laptop. She waved Callie in.

"Kate will be here momentarily," Renee said, barely glancing at Callie before resuming her keyboard abuse.

Callie's stomach flipped. Part of her had expected Kate to dip out of this meeting like she had the previous one. Another part of her had wanted her to. But some damn, obnoxious tiny part of her couldn't wait to see her. She silently cursed that part until it shut up.

She felt Kate's presence before she saw her, catching a whiff of her unmistakable scent before she walked into the office. Callie steadied her hands on her thighs, refusing to turn around. Kate slipped into the chair next to her. Out of the corner of her eye, she caught the movement of Kate's head as she looked at Callie for several maddening seconds, then turned away to face Renee.

"One second," Renee said.

Callie relaxed her posture, crossing her legs and pulling her laptop out of her bag. A particularly loud bang from Renee's desk caused her to jerk her head up.

To her left, a quiet laugh emerged, followed by the whispered words, "She might be rougher on her laptop than you are."

"It's a close call," Callie whispered back. The normalcy caught her off guard, but in a pleasant way. She still didn't feel brave enough to look at Kate, though, so she fixed her stare on Renee's poor laptop instead.

"I can hear you, you know." With a final powerful jab, Renee finished her task and focused her attention on Kate and Callie. "How's the course coming along?"

If Kate was thrown off, like Callie was, by the lack of formalities, she didn't show it. "Very well. Callie's pulled some great resources, and we have a working list of book requirements. The outline of how to move through the course is still in progress, but we should have that part wrapped up within the next month."

This was news to Callie. She stuffed her surprise in her back pocket and nodded. Renee cocked her eyebrow, clearly wanting to hear from Callie.

"Like Kate said, everything is coming along," Callie started. "The one area we need to spend more time on is the assessment portion. We've thrown around some ideas but haven't finalized anything."

Kate picked up where Callie left off, providing specific examples. Callie jumped in where she could, never once looking over at Kate. When they finished talking, Renee looked at them, curiosity flickering in her gaze.

"And you're still working well together?" she asked.

Before the question mark hit the air, Callie was nodding. Her peripheral vision showed Kate doing the same.

"No," Renee said, looking back and forth between them. "There's a problem here. What is it?"

Callie lost all the heat in her body. She could only flip her nodding to shaking.

Thankfully, Kate was ready. "There's no problem. We didn't get as much done over break as we thought we would, but everything is good, Renee."

"Great," Callie added. She felt the heat of Kate's gaze fall on her.

Meanwhile, Renee's eyes were glued to Callie. Unlike Kate's, Renee's face showed a wide array of emotions. Callie knew she wasn't buying whatever the two of them were half-heartedly trying to sell.

"I don't believe you," she began, flicking her gaze to Kate, "so I'm going to kindly ask you two to get over yourselves. I know you're capable of doing amazing work, and I also know how well you've been working together because *you*"—she nodded at Kate—"won't shut up about it. But something's wrong here." She paused, nodding to herself. "I want you to test-drive some of the new course material in your fiction workshop. Maybe that will help get you both back on track." Another nod. "Fix it."

"Consider it fixed," Kate said cheerfully before standing to leave. Callie followed suit, tossing a wide smile at Renee.

In the hallway, Callie stopped abruptly before she blindly followed Kate into her office. Just as she turned to head toward her own space, she heard Kate say her name.

It was impossible not to take her in, not to admire her quiet beauty. Callie held herself back from looking her up and down, but it didn't matter. Her heart was thrilled to see its object of affection again.

"We're good for this afternoon, right?"

Of course: work talk. Callie nodded. They would be meeting their fiction workshop class in about an hour; they hadn't met on Tuesday due to a midday sleet storm that had shut down campus early. Callie had no idea how this was going to be, the two of them in the same classroom, interacting as professor and TA. Kate had explained via her terse email earlier that week that she wanted them to function as equals in the classroom, wanted Callie to get a high-quality experience while she learned. Plus, Callie knew that Kate didn't know that she knew Kate was the creative writing pro between them. Turns out they both had plenty to learn.

Now, Kate seemed to be waiting for an actual response from Callie, because despite her nod of agreement, she hadn't moved or taken her eyes off Callie.

"Yes," Callie said. "I'll see you in 215 at ten to two."

Callie smacked down the urge to stand there for the next fifty minutes, basking in Kate's guarded stare. But the truth was, it hurt too much, so with a small smile, she turned and walked away.

Time was *not* on Callie's side. She'd mismanaged the entire fifty minutes between the meeting and class: Looping thoughts of how to approach this TA-professor relationship with Kate had kept her distracted from any real work. As she hustled down the hallway toward Room 215, she reminded herself to keep all the bullshit neatly packed away in its mental suitcase. She had a job to do, but more importantly, she wanted to prove to Kate how well she could do that job, even with her in the same room.

Callie's hustling came to a halt when she turned the corner and saw what awaited her outside 215. It wasn't right, she knew that. She'd checked the class list at least twelve times.

But there Maddie stood, hands clasped in front of her, eyes glued on Callie.

It was 1:51. Callie was a minute late and she despised being late. Being late for Kate was a terrible rhyme and a terrible feeling. But in order to get into 215, Callie had to first get past Maddie.

"Maddie," she said as she approached. "Nice to see you."

It was a weak attempt at avoidance, Callie knew, but she really thought she'd nailed it when Maddie didn't respond. Just as her toe hit the threshold of the classroom, however, a cold hand grabbed her forearm.

"Can we talk?" Maddie's voice was breathless, unnecessarily since she was standing still.

"I have class," Callie said.

"Not until two." A smile wound its way over Maddie's features. "Just a couple minutes, Callie. That's all I need."

Every inch of Callie's body sensed the underlying implications. After shutting her eyes briefly, she looked into the room. It was empty. She led Maddie down the hall a bit, keeping her eyes on the classroom door.

"You have two minutes, so make it quick."

"Wow, you're so forward. I like that." Her smile became noticeably less innocent. "I made sure I didn't take any classes that you'd be the TA in."

Callie took a small step backward. "I appreciate that."

"Right? I thought it was a really smart idea." Maddie took a large step forward. "This will make it easier for us to be together."

"You—what? No," Callie snapped. "Maddie. This isn't happening."

"But it's okay now! I know you feel it too. You always call on me in class and like my answers." She reached out and tried to grab Callie's hand. "I'm so excited to finally—"

"Maddie. Stop." Callie pulled her body away from Maddie's reach. "I have never given you any sign that I'm interested in you. Because I'm not. Please respect that. And please leave. I have a class to teach."

Resignation flashed over Maddie's face, quickly replaced by anger. "But you—"

"Nothing. I did nothing. You need to go."

Maddie's mouth opened and closed like a sad fish struggling to find food. Callie didn't wait to make sure she left. Instead, she kept her distance as she stepped past Maddie and went into 215.

Anger and frustration coursed through Callie as she stood in the room, taking deep breaths to get her bearings. *The audacity of that girl.* Callie shook her head.

"You handled that well."

Callie closed her eyes as a rueful smile made its way onto her lips. "You saw that?"

Kate moved next to Callie, close enough to touch but definitely not touching. "I did. I came around from the opposite direction." Kate's eyes searched Callie's. "Is that the student you told me about?"

"The one and only." Callie tried to keep eye contact but felt a bubble of sadness rising in her chest so she looked away. "Hopefully that's done with now."

"You were firm," Kate said. "Direct. It was polite stomping."

Before Callie could respond, she heard footsteps. She turned to see a handful of eager students entering the room. When she looked back at Kate, she found a genuine smile on her face.

"Showtime," she said quietly.

Callie learned quickly that working as Kate's TA landed somewhere between how Courtney and Renee worked her. Likely because they'd already established a working relationship, the two of them fell seamlessly into their roles. Kate dominated the class, giving Callie too much time to observe her. A new fire burned within her as she watched Kate come alive in front of the class. She had a cool presence, one that demanded respect but encouraged a collaborative environment. She was passionate, subtly animated when she hit something that she was invested in. Her words were thoughtful, smart as hell, and engaging. Callie watched several students fall under Kate's spell, smiling in sympathy for them.

During one of Callie's prolonged observations (Okay, fine, *stares*), Kate looked over at her, catching her red-handed. Callie flushed but didn't look away. She watched as several masks slipped over Kate's features before she landed on that good old impassive look. Callie sighed internally.

After a short break, Kate had the students working in pairs. She moved around the room, checking in with them. Callie tracked her movements for a while, then resumed jotting down some notes. She was thoroughly enjoying the comfortable chairs in this classroom: They were wheeled, thickly cushioned, and they swiveled. As Callie wrote, she shifted her hips back and forth, spinning slowly.

Suddenly, her spin was interrupted. She sat up straight. Her nose pricked to attention as the scent that brought her to her knees invaded her senses.

"Stop spinning," Kate whispered. She was behind Callie's chair, her leg pressed against it to stop the movement, and she'd leaned down to whisper directly into Callie's ear.

She was gone before Callie could react. A small miracle, indeed, since Callie's only response would have been to grab Kate and throw her (gently) onto the desk.

The rest of the class passed uneventfully, another small miracle for Callie's ego and libido. The students trickled out slowly, seeming not to want to leave Kate's powerful presence. Again, Callie smiled sympathetically. She was all too familiar with that desire.

"I think they'll be a good group," Kate said as she slid her laptop into her bag. "It's usually a good sign when they're so engaged on the first day."

"Are all of your students immediately enamored with you?" Callie kept her tone light and teasing. "Because I've never seen so much swooning in a first class."

Kate laughed and leaned against the table. "Very funny, Callie."

"I'm serious. I think I saw one of them writing 'I heart Dr. Jory' with like five exclamation points in her notebook."

"That would be a first." Kate idly played with the button on her blazer, one of Callie's favorites. "I do think this is a great group to test out some of our material."

"Speaking of…" Callie tilted her head and looked at Kate. "We should find time to meet, since Lawler's on to us." She cleared her throat. "Um, I mean, it seemed like she could tell we haven't worked on the project lately."

A barely perceptible nod later, Kate said, "Email me your schedule and we'll figure it out."

Something about Kate's body language had Callie on edge— not a bad edge, more like a captivated, anticipatory edge. She wasn't closed off. There was something undeniably open about the way she was facing Callie, about the look on her face.

When their eyes met, Callie nearly grabbed her and kissed her. The mask was gone, and in its place was pure yearning.

"Kate," she said, just above a whisper.

"We can't," Kate said with a tiny shake in her voice. "Callie, I told you. I can't have you."

"But you want me."

"That," Kate said softly, "was never in question."

"But—"

"I'm not going to do what I saw you do earlier, because, well, you understand the differences between the situations." Kate pushed her shoulders back. "I trust you, Callie. I know that this class will go well, as will the rest of the course planning. We have a great working relationship. I love—really like working with you." A faint blush splashed over Kate's cheeks. "And that's what we need to focus on."

"That," Callie echoed.

"Yes." Her tone was firm but kind. "And nothing else."

The words punctured Callie like a dull knife digging, searching for blood. She knew the unspoken implications, and yet—

"You want me to get over you."

A tiny gasp popped from Kate's mouth. It was so uncharacteristic that Callie found herself leaning forward, reaching to close the distance between them. When Kate sealed up her features and fixed Callie with yet another emotionless stare, Callie dropped her hand.

"Yes, Callie. That's what I want."

Never before had such empty words fallen so hard, so loudly, echoing endlessly in the silent room.

Not trusting her voice, Callie nodded. She wasted no time in grabbing her things and bolting, leaving Kate alone to absorb the painful reverberations of her own words.

CHAPTER TWENTY-FIVE

A new routine fell into place. It wasn't natural, but it worked. Callie and Kate found their footing, and to Callie's surprise, it wasn't entirely awful. Their easy banter returned, and while Callie couldn't say for certain, it seemed like Kate had accepted the fact that she was essentially unable to snap her fingers and get over her, but was doing her best to avoid her own feelings.

It seemed odd to Callie, the fact that she was magnificently heartbroken over someone that she didn't love. And yet she was. Her appetite vanished along with any impulses to engage in things that were good for her body. Her bed became her best friend, and when she couldn't bury her head under her pillow, she threw all her energy into working and studying. All in all, it was a manageable heartbreak, one that was proving productive in some areas, but it also hurt like hell in a way that she had never experienced before.

Callie normally scorned Valentine's Day, citing it to be "an utter load of shit," but she felt a different kind of angst when she saw how overboard Nikki went with spoiling Maya. Their entire apartment, it seemed, was filled with flowers and balloons. A colossal box of chocolates took up residence on the kitchen table. As the day went on, the gleeful squeals continued each time Nikki pulled out another surprise gift.

"Did you cheat on her?" Callie asked when Nikki made an appearance in the living room.

"You wish," Nikki retorted as she flopped onto the sofa. "You think I went overboard?"

"Uh, yeah. Just a little bit." She motioned around the room, which looked like a Hallmark store had thrown up repeatedly in it. "Are you seeing what I see?"

"Maya loves this shit," she said. "And if it's what I have to do to make her happy one stupid holiday a year, then so be it."

Callie grunted. She flipped the pages of the book on her lap, tired of trying to retain information that wanted no entrance into her brain.

"You got a date tonight?"

"That's a definite no." Callie shot Nikki a warning glare. She didn't know what Sadie had told her about Kate after their little attempted intervention, but Sadie was now required to stick to strict no-Kate-talk rules. She hadn't even told Callie about Kate coming into the bookstore and Callie was impressed with her restraint. Nikki hadn't so much as mentioned Kate's name to Callie, so she assumed she'd received the memo via Sadie.

"Great!" Nikki exclaimed, jumping back up. "We're having a party!"

"And I'll be going to Sadie's."

"You can't! I promised Hannah you would be here."

Callie groaned and threw her arms over her eyes. "Are we seriously back at this dead end? I thought I'd finally gotten you to understand I'm not interested in Hannah."

"You did. I mean, it took a while, but I get it now, *plus* Hannah's bringing a date, so you're really off the hook."

Callie peeked through her arms. "Seriously?"

"Promise," Nikki said. "And before you ask, no, we did not convince anyone else to come and try to sweep you off your feet."

Callie cracked a smile. "If you're lying to me, I'm moving out."

"I'm not, so since you still live here, how about you go buy some beer?"

Hours later, Callie idly wondered if Nikki had purposely double-dipped: Her obnoxious gifts to Maya had been promoted to party decorations. The balloons bobbed happily around the small group of people gathered in the living room, Sadie among them. She caught Callie's eye and maneuvered her way to the kitchen doorway where Callie stood guard.

"Great idea: You stop looking like it's paining you to be here and come join us. We're about to play that word game you like."

Callie cast a bored look at Sadie. "No thanks. I'm fine here."

"Yes, you're clearly having the time of your life." Sadie sighed and nudged Callie. "I know you're upset, but you could at least try to have fun."

"I did try," Callie said plainly. "I showered, I got dressed, I had two drinks. I even had a five minute conversation with that woman over there." They both looked over to the woman talking to Nikki. "She's in Nikki's doctoral program. Very nice. Dry sense of humor. Has a pet hedgehog. See? I tried." Callie put her arm around Sadie's shoulders and squeezed. "I'm not feeling social. Let me hang out with my busted heart, okay?"

Without waiting for a response, Callie ducked into the kitchen for another beer, then slipped back to her bedroom, shutting the door firmly behind her. She dropped onto her bed, propped her pillows, and stretched out. This getting-over-Kate business felt interminable, probably because she had to continue to see her almost daily and interact with her. She'd hoped the fluttering sensation in her stomach that rose every time Kate walked into a room would ease and disappear, but so far, it had only intensified with an underlying ache.

Callie poked at her phone, hoping against hope that Kate had reached out. She hadn't, of course. And Callie knew she wouldn't. She had made herself very clear, and there was no recourse, just the tired path of wearing down these feelings until they faded into the noisy background.

Having knocked back most of her beer rather quickly, Callie was contemplating venturing out for another when her door creaked open. She narrowed her eyes, expecting Sadie or Nikki and their pleas for her to join them in the festivities.

Instead, it was Hannah's head that poked into the room.

"Oh," Callie said, sitting up. "Hey."

"Hey yourself." Hannah stepped into the room, shutting the door behind her. "I heard you were hiding back here, so I thought I'd come say hi."

"Did you just get here? I didn't see you earlier."

"Yeah, about ten minutes ago." She perched on the edge of Callie's bed and regarded her with interest. "Why are you hiding?"

Callie rolled her eyes and tucked her legs under her. "I'm not hiding. I'm just not in a party mood."

"Wanna talk about it?"

"Nope." Callie forced a smile. "So tell me about your date."

"Oh God," Hannah muttered. "Did Nikki say I was bringing a date?"

"Yep."

Hannah shook her head. "I brought a friend. Not a date." She turned her gaze to Callie. "You know you're the one I want, Callie."

Callie fought back the laugh that bubbled up in her chest. First Maddie, now Hannah. The irony of being able to pick from two eager women while she was pining away over someone completely unavailable was not lost on her.

Unfortunately, Hannah mistook Callie's laugh-fighting smile for something else and moved closer to her. They locked eyes. Callie flipped through thought after thought, wondering why she couldn't feel something for this perfectly fine woman in front of her. While she was plunged in thought, Hannah made her move. Their lips connected before Callie noticed how close Hannah had gotten. It wasn't a new feeling, this kiss. Kissing Hannah was always enjoyable: She was skilled, seductive, and sexy.

Callie gave Tiny Brain Kate a mighty shove to the darker recesses of her brain. She grabbed Hannah and pulled her closer, digging her fingers into her back. She could do this. She could absolutely make out with someone who wasn't the woman who had consumed her.

And it was fine, perfectly fine, until Hannah's hands moved to more sensitive parts of Callie's body. The intimate touching was enough to ring warning bells in Callie's mind, and she pulled away abruptly.

"What's wrong?" Hannah breathed. "You were so into that."

"No," Callie said. She stood up and paced across her bedroom. "That's not happening."

"Sure seemed like you wanted it to."

Callie stood at her window and pressed her hands against the chilled sill. "That's just it, Hannah. I *don't* want it to happen." She turned and faced her. "I'm sorry. I thought we were on the same page."

"You're *sorry*," Hannah spat, standing. "I'm so sick of this back-and-forth bullshit with you."

"No," Callie said again. "I've always been up-front with you, from the start."

"And then you kept coming back for more."

A shiver ran through Callie's body. "We agreed to be friends," she said weakly. "We definitely had that conversation."

"So then why did you kiss me back?" Hannah asked, her voice raising.

Callie laughed, the sound sad and tired. "Because it felt good." She shook her head. "I shouldn't have kissed you back. It won't happen again."

At Hannah's silence, Callie peered at her. Her eyes were steel.

"It's Kate. Isn't it?"

The punch of her name set Callie a step backward. "I don't know what you're talking about."

"Yes, you do. I saw it that day at lunch. I should have known." Hannah cursed under her breath. "Theo told me Kate's totally hooked on someone. Never thought it would be you."

Callie fumbled to make sense of Hannah's words.

"You should have told me you have feelings for someone else."

"Okay, stop. That's irrelevant, Hannah. I stopped things between us before I developed feelings for her. And I stopped things between us because I realized we're not compatible. So please don't turn this into something it's not."

Hannah glared at her. But there was a softness beneath the glare, a flicker of understanding that Callie hoped would grow with time. She left without another word, and Callie locked her door before throwing herself back onto her bed.

It was Kate's words ringing loudly in her head, not Hannah's. *I can't have you. It's not a matter of want—because I do want. I can't have you.* They repeated endlessly, a forlorn soundtrack, as she burrowed under her covers and fought to sleep.

* * *

Callie stuffed half an English muffin in her mouth as she opened the newspaper to the crossword puzzle. Nikki had left her a note, claiming she needed Callie's "massive brain" to complete the puzzle. It was rare that one of them admitted to needing help, seeing as they were each annoyingly competitive with word-related games. Callie figured Nikki was still, a couple weeks later, making nice for having invited Hannah to that ill-fated Valentine's party.

As Callie filled in the Z and D for "Jazz Age literary wife," her phone buzzed with an incoming email. She glanced over and saw Jana had sent her a file. Callie ignored the email, scribbling in the G, I, and A for "Good Witch of the South." She steamrolled ahead, knocking out several more clues, before her phone buzzed again.

Need this one done ASAP, sorry for the short notice!

Callie stared daggers at Jana's follow-up email before reminding herself that this was a paying job and completing the crossword puzzle was not.

Back in the quiet of her bedroom, Callie opened her laptop and clicked on the waiting submission.

The rain came on an otherwise clear day. The clouds didn't bother with much warning or prelude; they simply burst and shattered. What started as a quiet drizzle soon became a full-blown rainstorm, the kind that simultaneously makes you want to seek shelter and stand in its soaking glory.

This wasn't the storm I'd been expecting. It wasn't one I was seeking. Thick, bulbous clouds paraded across the sky, hiding light and harboring truths. Cupped, my hands gathered droplets, rivulets streaming down my wrists as I tried, over and over again, to hold this impossible ocean as it fell. I fought against nature and its primal need to escape, to be made of chance and encounter. I sought permanence and ran from it, too, when the water became too deep.

Drenched and awakened, my senses were alive when shelter found me. The rain continued, beating endlessly, and in it, a soothing rhythm began. The storm rose and fell, reaching unparalleled heights and dropping to cavernous depths. Clouds parted just enough for moonbeams to filter through, illuminating the quietest, gentlest corners of thoughts unspoken.

With her, it is rain and words, paragraphs and storm. She is shelter and lightning. In her, there is warmth and light, distant trails of thunder. Her touch is a flash flood of sensation, a mirror to my own desires.

She is danger and exhilaration, promise and impossibility. She is the very hurricane I've dreamed of, the one full of tempestuous destruction and irresistible pull.

I never loved the rain until I learned the beauty of the storm.

She didn't need to search for the author's name. Every syllable, every twist of vowels, every painstaking weight of consonant revealed it: It was Kate.

To Callie's surprise, tears pooled in the corners of her eyes. It was the mark of good writing, she knew that, but more so it was everything Kate wouldn't say to her, spelled out right in front of her. It was the darkness that she kept hidden from Callie. It was her *why*, naked and unveiled.

Callie swallowed hard. Yes, there it was. There also sat the fact that Kate had absolutely no idea that Callie was editing the very things she couldn't or wouldn't say to her.

CHAPTER TWENTY-SIX

"Don't bring it up."

Callie kicked the toe of her shoe against Courtney's desk. "I was hoping you wouldn't say that."

"Well, you came to the wrong place, then." Courtney raised her arms up, locking her fingers behind her head. "You truly cannot bring it up."

"Okay, but here's the thing. I don't think she knows that I'm an editor for *Sapphisms*. Don't I owe her that honesty?"

Courtney kicked her feet up on her desk, completing her picture of relaxation. "Kate's not stupid. She can read a list of editors. What makes you think she hasn't?"

Callie felt the color drain from her face. "She's never mentioned it."

"Why are you whispering? No one can hear us."

"Because," Callie hissed, "I feel like I've invaded her privacy. That last piece was like reading her journal."

"She's a writer, Cal. She knows what she's doing by publishing pieces like that."

Callie groaned and slumped in the chair. She hadn't been able to get that piece of writing out of her mind since she'd read it four days ago. Fortunately, she hadn't been acting like too much of a spaz around Kate, but she had a nagging feeling that she needed to confess to the entire situation.

"You're not doing anything wrong," Courtney said, her voice gentler than before. "Do your job, and let the pieces fall."

"What if she knows I'm an editor, and she purposely wrote that so I would read it and now she's waiting for me to come to her and tell her, 'Hey, I read your—'"

"Take a breath. You're going off the deep end."

A staggered breath, better than none at all, shook through her lungs. It wasn't a big deal, Callie reminded herself. Kate was writing. She was a writer. That's all!

"I told you, you need to be—"

"Careful. I know." Callie kicked the desk again, a bit harder than necessary, and received a contemptuous look from Courtney. "Thanks for your shitty advice," she said as she stood and stretched.

"Shitty, and yet you keep coming back for it!" Courtney called to Callie's retreating form.

"No idea why," she muttered as she walked toward the main area of the offices. She could hear several voices chattering. When Callie approached the mailboxes across from Audrey's desk, Megan waved as she excused herself from the conversation and disappeared down the hall. Low murmurs of conversation continued behind Callie. She scanned a flyer in her mailbox while half-listening to Renee explain something to Audrey, who clearly wasn't getting it.

Callie took a step back as the door flung open and hit the right side of her body, landing hard against her hip. She gasped and dropped her mail, cupping her hands around her throbbing hip.

"Oh my God," Kate said, concern weaving through her words, "I'm so sorry, Callie."

"You've really mastered the art of opening these stubborn doors," she said as she massaged what was sure to be a spectacular bruise.

"This one doesn't normally open so…powerfully." Kate scanned Callie. The compassion in her eyes was almost too much for Callie to see. "Are you okay?"

"I'll be fine." She crouched down to pick up her dropped mail. "Maybe use a little less force next time?"

Kate laughed. "I'll go slow."

Callie's breath caught in her throat. The simple phrase carried sensual weight, and she turned quickly to hide her blush from Kate. It was then that she remembered Audrey and Renee were in the room, and both were watching the show unfold before them, attention rapt.

"Oh," Kate said softly, apparently also realizing they were being watched.

Renee's expression was priceless, and Callie hoped Kate wasn't reading it the way she was. Audrey was fighting a large smile.

"Show's over," Callie said, and the two women let their smiles relax into something more normal.

"Dr. Jory," Audrey said, "don't forget about the Peabody Foundation reception this weekend."

"Yes, Kate," Renee said as she began walking away, "they're expecting you."

"Shit," Kate mumbled. Callie glanced at her and saw the chagrined look on her face. "I completely forgot."

"That's why I reminded you! It's a very important event." A devious glint appeared in Audrey's eyes. "Who are you taking with you?"

"No one," Kate said quickly.

"That's preposterous," Audrey announced. "You should definitely take someone with you! Those events can be so awkward when you go alone."

"Preposterous," Callie agreed.

Kate put her hands on her hips and looked between Callie and Audrey. "I never thought I'd see the day when you two ganged up on me."

Callie held her hands up innocently. "There's no ganging happening. I'm nothing but a fan of Audrey's vocabulary."

"Why don't you take Callie?"

Silence splintered the room in half, sealing Audrey safely with her goofy smile on one side, leaving Kate and Callie caught motionless, shocked, on the other side.

Audrey quickly took advantage of the stunned lack of responses. "I think it's a great idea! She's good arm candy, but she can also hold a conversation. She's very smart. Not the best people skills, but you shine in that area, Dr. Jory, so it's a perfect combination!"

A surprised laugh fell from Callie's mouth. Kate whipped her head around and stared at her. She shrugged and mouthed, "Arm candy." The corners of Kate's mouth tugged upward.

"But, Audrey," Callie began. She couldn't resist, even at the risk of angering Kate. "I thought you were against inter-office romances?"

Sure enough, Callie felt the wave of irritation flow from Kate. Audrey's expression made it worth it, though.

"I didn't say anything about *romance*," Audrey said defensively. "I merely suggested Dr. Jory have you accompany her to an event that she doesn't want to go to."

The irritation changed to resignation. "It's not that I don't want to go," Kate said. She toyed with the thin gold bracelet on her left wrist, sliding it back and forth. "It'll be a very nice evening, I'm sure."

"It would be even better with Callie by your side."

Callie shot Audrey a warning look, but Kate was already on the move, heading toward her office.

"What's wrong with you?" Callie whispered loudly.

"Nothing! She doesn't want to go alone," Audrey whispered back. "You should ask her."

"It's her event!"

Audrey rolled her eyes so hard Callie was surprised they didn't end up on the floor. "Go back there and talk to her."

Callie pressed her hands on the edge of Audrey's desk and leaned in close enough to see the faint line of freckles trailing across her cheekbone. "What are you doing?"

"Nothing," she squeaked. "Nothing!"

With a parting sneer, Callie stalked down the hallway. Both she and Audrey knew she was, in fact, going to Kate's office—but not because of that conversation.

After grabbing her laptop from her desk, she backtracked to Kate's office. Without a word, she nestled into her favorite chair and opened their working document for the course. Kate passed her a thick file of articles, and as Callie sorted through them, they fell into a peaceful working silence.

"Let's go over the two essay topics you added," Kate said after some time. "I like the ideas, but I have some suggestions."

"Lay it on me," Callie said.

Kate slid her glasses on, a weak attempt at hiding her reaction to Callie's words. They worked through the suggestions, finalizing requirements and timelines. Callie suggested they talk about one of the articles they'd both read recently.

"Before we do that," Kate said, a nervous note in her voice. "Do you want to?"

"Talk about the article? Uh, yeah, seeing as I suggested it…"

"Not that." She couldn't quite meet Callie's eyes. "The reception. This weekend."

Callie waited, but nothing else came. "What about it?"

"Come on, Callie," she said. "You know what I'm asking."

"Maybe," she said kindly. "But I'm not reading between the lines with you anymore."

Kate's expression mirrored that of someone who had been doused with ice-cold water. She couldn't hide it, which gave Callie a strange sense of relief and pain.

After a moment, Kate nodded once, then cleared her throat. She met Callie's eyes, her expression back to something unreadable, and said, "Would you like to go with me on Saturday?"

"Sure," Callie said immediately. She sat back, surprised by her answer. Kate, too, looked incredulous.

"It's not a…you know," Kate attempted. "It's work-related."

Callie held their eye contact. "I'm well aware of what it is and is not."

"Okay then. Good." Kate looked away. "Pick me up at seven."

* * *

"This is a terrible idea," Sadie moaned. "And just when you were turning a corner!"

"It doesn't sound awful to me," Nikki said. "It might be the kind of closure you need."

Callie wrinkled her nose. That didn't sound accurate. She sipped her beer, the newly tapped Prometheus' Pear Porter, and relished the flavors swirling in her mouth. She wasn't a huge porter fan, but this smoky-sweet winter beer was delectable.

"Whatever it is, and whatever it will be, I agreed to go, so I'm going." Callie patted Sadie on the back. "The worst of it is over, Sades. I can handle one evening with her."

"You say that now."

"What's the worst that could happen?" Nikki asked. "She can't break up with you again, right?"

"For what? The third, fourth time?" Callie shook her head. "Besides, it's technically a work-related event. We still work together and will for several more years. The more opportunities we have to adapt to that the better."

Sadie leaned forward on her stool. "But can we be honest about how much you still like her?"

"Why?"

"I think you need to admit it," Sadie said firmly, nodding. "Yes. Say it out loud. Get it off your chest! Sing it out to the universe!"

"You're weird," Nikki said. "Like way weirder than I ever realized."

"Fuck off, Nikki. Go ahead, Callie. Let your feelings out!"

Callie rubbed the back of her neck. "I'll pass, but thanks for the idea."

"See? Weird." Nikki reached around Callie and flicked Sadie. "Do you, though, Cal? Still like her, I mean?"

Probably. Maybe. Clearly. *Obviously.* Callie swirled more beer in her mouth before answering.

"Yes. But I'm learning how to be normal with her while keeping my feelings tucked away. It's for the best."

"For you? Or for her?"

Fucking Nikki, always with the obvious but avoided truths. Callie shook her head.

"For both of us."

CHAPTER TWENTY-SEVEN

As Callie stood, hands on her hips, debating her choice of outfit, Nikki knocked, then entered her bedroom, two glasses of wine in her hands.

"Thought you might need this," she said, handing Callie a glass. "A little something to take the edge off."

Callie smirked before taking a sip of the cold white wine. "I'm the one on the edge."

"So...it would be a bad idea to take the edge off?"

"I think that means I'd fall. Hard." Callie cocked a half-hearted smile at Nikki. "But I also think it's too late for that. The edge has crumbled, leaving me scrambling for footing on extremely unsteady ground."

Nikki shook her head and leaned against the wall. "You and Sadie take this whole English nerd thing too far sometimes." She watched Callie for a moment, then said, "You love her."

The words pierced every pin-sized hole in Callie's porous heart. She wanted to deny it, plainly and coolly, but it was no use anymore. She'd stopped being able to lie to herself. No sense in trying to keep up a lie for her friends.

"Yes," she said, shrugging. "Apparently I do."

"And you've told her?"

"No." Panic traipsed through Callie's nerve endings. "No way. That's—no."

"I really thought you had that heart of yours sealed up. I gotta say, I'm surprised."

Callie snorted. "You and me both." All the time she'd spent chastising herself for being heartbroken over someone she didn't love had turned into a hot mess of denial. The instant she saw that flicker of yearning in Kate's eyes as they stood in Room 215, Callie knew she had to own up to her feelings. At the very least, she could be honest with herself—despite Kate's continued refusal of her, and her own panic and fear over the very existence of her attachment.

As it turned out, admitting to herself that she loved someone who maybe, possibly, loved her too but would rather choke down those feelings than air them out was...not a pleasant experience.

Attending an event with that person was also not Callie's smartest move. But it was too late to back out, and she wouldn't put Kate in that position anyway because, right, she loved her.

Callie pointed at the three outfits laid out on her bed. "Please pick one while I shower."

Nikki clapped her hands in delight as Callie left the room. By the time she returned, Nikki was gone, and she'd made an entirely new outfit from the pieces of the options Callie had left her with. As usual, she'd nailed it.

Callie stood in front of her mirror, admiring herself. The skinny blank pants worked perfectly with the pale pink button-up. Seeing that Nikki had put out a belt, Callie tucked the shirt in before winding the belt around her hips. She pulled on her best pair of motorcycle boots, the low-cut pair that managed to look fancy and cool at the same time. Her hair, dark blond now from losing all its summer highlights, went into a smooth low bun, a few wisps escaping around her face. Callie stared herself down in the mirror, silently reminding herself to keep all her raging feelings tied down neatly and out of sight. With a firm nod at her reflection, she grabbed her black wool peacoat and left, hoping for an easy night.

The moment Kate stepped onto the front porch, Callie knew she was destined to ogle her all night long. She, too, was wearing black pants, but hers accentuated every tantalizing curve of her legs and hips. A silky white camisole was topped by a black blazer with velvet-lined lapels. Heels, higher and far sexier than any shoes Callie had ever seen Kate wear, completed the look. The extra height brought Kate nearly to eye-level with Callie, giving her an obstructed view of delicate, pale skin and shining hazel eyes. She didn't dare drop her gaze to look at Kate's lips. Okay, yeah, she couldn't resist, and yes, they were stained just enough with a darker shade than her natural color, full and highly kissable.

Callie nearly dissolved into a puddle on the spot.

"Thanks for picking me up," Kate said, turning to lock the door. "Parking can be difficult."

Suddenly unsure of how to stand and have arms at the same time, Callie punched her fists against her hips, the movement causing her coat to rustle and flare awkwardly.

Kate eyed her. "Are you okay?"

"Are you going to be warm enough?" Callie blurted. Not her smoothest moment, but thank God she'd swallowed the litany of compliments that threatened to spill from her lips.

"I think so." Kate started walking toward Callie's car, leaving her to follow mutely. "We won't be outside for long."

Callie turned the heat up, just in case, once they were in the car. Kate hummed appreciatively. Basic small talk consumed the first ten minutes or so of the drive before a quiet eased over them. It wasn't uncomfortable, but it possessed threads of unspoken sentences that bent and waved in the puffs of heat pushing through the vents.

The silence allowed Callie to relax, perhaps too much. As she drove, she didn't forget that Kate was next to her, because that was impossible, but she managed to sideline the tension and uncertainty, the heartache and sadness. She was simply happy to have Kate with her, even if it meant she could never confess the intense feelings she harbored for her.

Lines from that latest damn Katherine Pearl essay blew into Callie's mind. She chanced a look over at Kate and found her staring peacefully out the window at passing traffic. There was some sad comfort in knowing that, if Kate's essay rang true, they were both harboring feelings that would never see the light of day.

"Callie." The word was hushed and for a moment, Callie thought she'd imagined it.

"Kate," she said back, just as quietly.

Kate shifted in the seat so she was looking at Callie, who kept her eyes focused on the road. "I need you to understand that my feelings for you are real."

One more conversation like this and Callie's heart was going to fully capsize. "You don't need to explain anything to me." She did her best to keep any sign of bitterness out of her voice, but seriously, she couldn't do this again.

"I do," Kate said. "I really think I do."

"No. You don't."

The bitterness must have leaked out because Kate stared her down for a solid minute before finally saying, "Maybe I don't, but I want to."

"Kate." Callie's voice was low, weighed down with buried feelings and unspoken words. "I've heard you every time you've explained something to me. I get it. What's done is done."

Still staring at the road, Callie heard the movements indicating Kate had turned in her seat and was no longer looking at her. The loss was acute and her fingers gripped the steering wheel tightly.

"Okay," Kate eventually said, right as Callie turned into the parking lot of their destination. "You're right."

Callie hadn't known what to expect, but she was impressed with the Peabody Foundation's dedication to creating a night to remember. They'd gone with a winter wonderland theme, and everything was in harmony with it, including the drinks. Callie immediately snagged one from a passing waiter, admiring the aesthetics of the frosted glass and sugared cranberries pierced through a toothpick hanging over the vodka drink.

Kate passed on the drink but gave Callie a pointed look. "Do I need to remind you that you're driving?"

"No," she said after a luxurious sip. "We just got here. If you haven't noticed, there's a ton of people here, and you're the one with people skills, not me. This will help take the edge off." Callie bristled, hearing Nikki's words from earlier emerging from her own mouth. The edge seemed long forgotten, having been replaced by a never-ending tumble down a rocky cliffside.

"Give yourself more credit, Callie. You're very good with people." Kate's eyes settled on a group standing nearby. "And here's your chance to prove it." She cupped her hand around Callie's elbow, the innocent and friendly touch sending sparks raging through Callie. "I want you to meet some friends of mine."

And so the night went, with Kate guiding the way. Callie found she enjoyed being the arm candy, but also begrudgingly realized she had decent people skills after all. Kate made it easy for her: She was seamless with introductions, engaging and confident. Plus, it turned out she knew a lot of people at the event, which surprised Callie, given how new she was to the area. As the hours ticked by, it became less of a surprise. Kate was a networking genius. Seeing evidence of that unfold before her was a massive turn-on, and she had to practice keeping a neutral look on her face.

But Kate was...beyond beautiful. She was fucking flammable. She eased her way in and out of conversations with the skill of a seasoned talk show host. Her smile dazzled. Her posture commanded respect and admiration. Her words cascaded over everyone who dared cross her path, leaving them spellbound and aching for more.

Or perhaps that was just Callie.

Needing a break from the intoxicating draw of Kate, Callie excused herself to the bathroom. On her way back into the crowded room, she searched for Kate. She was exactly where Callie had left her, thoroughly engaged in a conversation with two professors from a nearby college. Watching her from a distance did little to temper the powerful feelings that had taken up permanent residence in Callie's heart.

"She's stunning, isn't she?"

Callie whipped her head around, thrown off by the familiar voice. "Who?"

Renee laughed lightly. "You know exactly who."

"I wasn't expecting to see you here," Callie said, trying to buy time.

"Oh, yes, of course I'm here. I do the background work and send Kate out there to do the networking."

"She's got a knack for it."

"She does." Renee's smile was cocky, and Callie knew what was coming. "Yet again, I have to congratulate myself for finding her and dragging her halfway across the country."

"Congratulations," Callie said drily, dodging the nudge that was thrust her way.

"You should be thanking me." Renee's smile turned into something more teasing. "Don't you think?"

Callie laughed nervously. "I guess so. I'm learning a lot from her. And without her, I wouldn't be getting the experience of—"

"Oh, Callie, cut the shit. Neither one of you is good at hiding things, though I admit Kate's far better at it than I would have expected." She fixed her stare on Callie, seeming to wait for her full attention before continuing—or perhaps she just wanted to make Callie sweat, which was proving a successful endeavor. "I trust that you'll do the right thing."

Callie glanced over at Kate, whose stare was now fixed on them. Her eyes didn't waver even as she continued talking to the people around her.

Renee leaned in close and whispered, "You two will make a gorgeous couple someday." With a wink, she walked off, leaving Callie in a daze.

After holding Kate's stare for a few seconds, Callie forced a smile before breaking eye contact. She backtracked to the bar for a glass of water and wasn't surprised when Kate appeared next to her a few minutes later.

"What did Renee say to you?"

A short laugh burst from Callie. "Nothing. Nothing important, anyway."

"You looked like you'd seen a ghost. I don't think it was nothing."

"She surprised me. That's all." Callie looked at Kate and was instantly warmed by the emotions visible in her eyes. "It's not a big deal, Kate. Really."

"I don't believe you, but I do believe you'll tell me when you're ready." Kate leaned against the bar. "My feet are killing me. Come with me for one last conversation and then we'll go. Sound good?"

Callie could only nod and follow her across the room. She couldn't avoid spending most of the walk admiring Kate's round, sexy ass, though.

"Wow," Kate breathed, wrapping her arms tightly around herself as they walked to Callie's car. "It got a lot colder, didn't it?"

Without hesitation, Callie shrugged out of her jacket and set it around Kate's shoulders. She avoided catching the look Kate sent her way.

In the car, Callie busied herself with adjusting the temperature. She sighed dramatically when the forced heat created a thick fog on the windows.

"Careful, people will think something wild's going on in here," Kate said, her voice low and teasing.

Callie cut a look at her. "The horror," she stage-whispered.

"Far from horror," came the reply.

"Kate," Callie said, warning in her voice. "You can't say things like that if you expect me to get over you."

"Right," she said. After a pause, "I'll do better."

When the windows were clear, Callie began the half-hour drive back to Kate's house. Kate filled most of the drive with chatter about the evening, the people they'd met, the impressions Callie had made. Listening to her, Callie began to see herself the way she saw her. It was a glimpse at something she couldn't fully envision, but Kate's words had a way of burrowing under Callie's skin and bringing her new levels of awareness.

Callie pulled up to Kate's house and put the car in park. Kate fell silent for the first time since they'd left the event. She rested her hand on the door and watched Callie run her fingers through the keys dangling from the ignition.

"Thank you for tonight," Kate said. "I'm happy you came with me."

"Thanks for inviting me."

"I can't wait to get these shoes off," she mumbled.

"Then you better get inside."

Kate laughed, but there was an undertone of emptiness in it. "You're right. Thanks again, Callie. Good night."

Her departure from the car deflated a balloon of happiness in Callie's lungs. Again, she found herself gripping the steering wheel as a shiver ripped through her.

Right, she thought. Her coat.

She made her way up to Kate's front porch. Just as her foot hit the top step, the front door flew open. Kate stepped outside, Callie's coat hanging from her fingertips.

"I almost forgot," she said with a sheepish smile. "Though I wouldn't have been upset if you'd had to come back for it tomorrow."

Taking her coat and pulling it on, Callie stayed silent.

"I know," Kate said quickly. "I did it again, didn't I?"

"Remember how I told you how confusing you are? The hot and cold? The talking around things instead of saying them clearly?"

Kate nodded, her eyes shining in the moonlight.

"You're not making this easy for me," Callie said, doing her best to keep her voice level and free of the pained emotions that were striking hard inside of her. "I am doing my absolute best to—to hold back, to get over. But every time you say something that leaves room for wonder, I trip over myself and fall back several places. And I know… Kate, I know that's not what you want."

Kate reached up and stroked Callie's cheek, a touch filled with longing and regret. "I'm sorry, Callie. I am so sorry."

Her touch lingered, and Callie shut her eyes briefly before she brought her hand up to cover Kate's.

"Renee said we would make a gorgeous couple." Callie kept her eyes shut, unwilling to see Kate's reaction. "I wish you could accept how true that is."

Callie lowered her hand, taking Kate's with her, before opening her eyes. Kate pulled her hand back, a stricken look on her face. Unwilling to hear the surely painful response to her proclamation, Callie spun and took the steps two at a time, hurrying to the security of her car and its isolation, its barrier from the tangible cause of her heartache.

CHAPTER TWENTY-EIGHT

Callie reached across the table and snapped a piece of the puzzle into place. She patted herself on the back as she scanned the pile of dark blue pieces waiting to be added to the night sky.

"How is it that you've been sitting here for five minutes and you've already put six pieces in?"

"She's the fresh set of eyes we needed, honey." Nick looked at his wife adoringly. "Plus, she's younger and your eyesight is deteriorating more rapidly than hers. Have you called the optometrist? I left you a note on the fridge with the number of a great doctor."

"He's right, Courtney." Callie batted her eyelashes at her friend. "You really should get those old lady eyes looked at before it's too late."

While glowering at Callie, Courtney said, "Hey, Nick. Ask Callie how her date was last night."

"That's low," Callie said at the same time Nick cheered. "Sorry, Nick. Your wife is a liar. No date was had."

"That was very much a date," Courtney remarked, sorting

through the snow-colored puzzle pieces. "And a good one, from what I was told."

Callie felt the color wash from her face. "What are you talking about?"

Her shrug was innocent, but the look on her face was devious. "I may or may not have spoken to Kate today."

Nick gasped. "Your date was with *Dr. Kate*? Details, now."

"It was not a date!" Callie kicked Courtney under the table. "Kate and I aren't—we're not—fucking shit," she said, exasperated. "It's not happening. Okay? And if she said it was a date—which I highly doubt, by the way—then I want no part of that."

"If you say so," Courtney said, exchanging a look with her husband.

They worked in silence for some time, the only sounds coming from pieces snapping into place and logs crackling in the fire behind them.

Eventually, it was too much for Callie, and her restraint broke.

"Did she actually say it was a date?" she mumbled.

"Sorry? Did you say something?" Courtney leaned closer, cupping her hand around her ear. "It sounded like you asked me something about a date?"

Callie rolled her eyes. "Looks like your hearing is deteriorating along with your eyesight. Tell me everything she said."

"Well, that I cannot do. But regarding your inquisition about labeling your outing as a date, I can tell you her exact words were, 'It felt like a date, and a good one.'"

"She told you that?" Callie pushed the words around in her head, struggling to make sense of them, especially considering how the night had ended.

"She did." Courtney held up a hand. "And no, I'm not going to lecture you right now. So you guys are cool then, right?"

She shrugged. All things considered, nothing had changed: Feelings remained smashed up against stubborn impossibility. And they both knew it. So… "Yeah. I mean, I think so."

As if on cue, the doorbell rang. Nick bounced out of his chair and made for the door. Callie looked questioningly at Courtney, who hadn't wiped the devious look from her face.

"What did you do?" Callie asked through clenched teeth.

"Me? Oh, nothing. Nick thought it would be a great idea to have a wintry afternoon with friends, drinks, a fire, and a puzzle. Oh, and snacks. He's making a charcuterie board. He's very excited."

An all-too familiar laugh trickled from the foyer, followed by a louder guffaw from Nick. Callie's stomach did a backflip. She leaned back in her chair and could just see Kate taking off her heavy winter coat, brushing snow from her dark hair. Her cheeks were pink from the cold, and she was the picture of happiness.

How she could look so carefree and peaceful after the way they had left things last night made zero sense to Callie, who was doing her best to keep a smile on her face as Kate and Nick came into the dining room.

"Let me get you a drink," Nick said, continuing into the kitchen. "Courtney, come show me which bottle to open next."

Left alone at the table, Callie tapped a puzzle piece against her hand, debating on how best to say hello to Kate. Courtney's little announcement about the date-thing had knocked her off balance yet again.

"Hey you," Kate said.

Taken aback by both her tender tone and the words themselves, Callie jerked her head up. She was met with a sweet smile.

"Hi." Not her best opening, but it would have to do. "You still have some snow in your hair."

Kate ran her fingers through her cropped hair. "I think this storm is going to be bigger than they predicted."

"Relatable," Callie said, the word slipping out without warning. Her eyes were on Kate, but her head was back in that poetic essay. She shook herself out of her brain fog. "That's New England for you. We never seem to know exactly what a storm is going to do."

"Storms can be unpredictable. That's part of the romance of them, don't you think?"

She heard Nick and Courtney coming back into the room, but Callie couldn't take her eyes off Kate, who was staring at her with raw intensity. They held still in their reverie, each waiting for the next move to be made. Kate broke the moment first, accepting a drink from Nick and pointing out a particularly challenging area of the puzzle.

With a short, forced exhale, Callie refocused her attention on the dark skyline of the puzzle. The four worked together steadily, though they were distracted often by winding conversation and bursts of laughter. To Callie's confused delight, Kate remained close to her, sharing some affectionate touches. It wasn't anything monumental, and after each brief brush of Kate's fingers against her arm, Callie reminded herself it was simply the mark of close friendship. Nothing felt awry; the energy coming from Kate was calm and happy. Despite a lingering sense of confusion, it was the most at ease Callie had felt in a long time.

Later, when Nick took a break to go create his charcuterie masterpiece, Callie excused herself, citing the need for some fresh air and to check the snow accumulation. Both Courtney and Kate gave her curious looks. They fell into their own conversation as Callie zipped up her jacket, pulled on her boots, and stepped out onto the back deck.

Yep, the predictions were wrong: There were at least six inches out there already. Callie kicked at the snow, testing its weight. She wasn't in the mood for back-breaking snow shoveling and was happy to see that it wasn't heavy.

She tilted her head to the sky. There was nothing like the illuminated gray sky of a snowfall. Callie knew nothing about the science behind it, but she loved the way the world glowed while the flakes spun down.

The door closed behind her and she knew Kate would soon be by her side. She was caught off guard by the closeness of her when she left a mere inch separating them, but she told herself to enjoy it because friends can do that.

"Definitely bigger than predicted," Kate said.

"And no signs of stopping." Callie continued staring up at the endless sky. "Do you really think unpredictability is romantic?"

Kate laughed and bumped her shoulder against Callie's arm. "Have you forgotten how I wouldn't know romance if it smacked me over the head?"

"I don't think that was exactly it. Didn't I call you a jaded realist?"

"Yes, but that was after you accused me of being a cynical isolationist."

Caught off guard by the power of her laugh, Callie bent over with her hands on her knees. "Shit. I had you pegged early on, huh?"

"You certainly did." Her tone melted into something lacking humor. Callie heard it and righted herself, looking at Kate, who was gazing out at the snow-covered line of trees at the edge of the property.

"But about storms," Callie said, throwing caution to the wind. "You prefer rain over snow."

"Oh, it depends on my mood. They both have their allure, and they both have their downfalls."

"Or their own promise and impossibility." Callie steeled herself, hoping that was enough and she wouldn't have to recite the entire damn essay back to its author.

Kate didn't respond. When Callie gathered the courage to turn and look at her, she was met with a slightly bemused expression.

"Danger and exhilaration, too," she added.

"How?" Kate shook her head in disbelief. "Seriously, how?"

Callie pulled her phone out of her pocket and tapped until she found the *Sapphisms* website. It wasn't flashy, but it had the information she needed. She tilted the screen toward Kate, who nodded and watched as Callie pressed on the "Team" link, scrolled down and stopped when she hit her name, sitting third under "Editors."

The seconds ticked by as the snow fell, blurring the words on Callie's phone. When her screen went dark, Kate remained standing, stock-still, until a loud peal of laughter burst from somewhere deep inside her. Callie couldn't help but laugh as well despite the tiny bit of panic she was feeling.

"All this time," Kate said once she regained her composure. Her eyes were sparkling, her eyelashes shimmering with snowflakes. "Why didn't you say anything?"

"You use a pen name. But then Audrey put some of your mail in my mailbox and I saw your middle initial. And when that last piece came through…" Callie shrugged. "I was never certain. But I had a pretty good feeling that I was your storm."

Kate gripped Callie's forearms, sliding down to clasp their hands together. "Callie. You read it. Don't you see? You're my storm, but you're also my shelter."

"So I…destroy you and keep you safe?" Callie raised her eyebrows. "Seems a little contradictory, Dr. Jory. It's not your best analogy."

"You don't destroy me." The unspoken hung between them, swinging patiently back and forth.

Callie nodded, the pieces clicking together. "I scare you."

A breath rushed from Kate's lungs. "Deeply."

"But even though I scare you…"

"You're where I feel safest and happiest." Kate's eyes shone with emotion. "I am utterly consumed by you, Callie. And I can't push that away anymore. I can't push *you* away anymore. I was trying to tell you that, even show you that, last night, but you kept stomping on me. Not that I can blame you." She laughed as tears gathered in the corners of her eyes. "I don't want to push you away. I'm quite afraid I want you, and need you, as close to me as possible."

Callie leaned over and pressed her lips against Kate's, not needing to hear another word. The sweet gasp that came from her only made Callie kiss her harder, her arms wrapping tightly around her waist and holding her firmly.

"That," Kate said, breaking the kiss, "is just one phase of the storm, but it is by far one of my favorites."

A commotion from inside was loud enough to grab Callie's attention, and she turned to look through the kitchen window.

There stood Nick and Courtney, huddled closely, clapping and cheering.

"You better be sure about this," Callie said, looking back at Kate, "because we're never going to hear the end of it from them."

"Oh, let them enjoy it. They've been waiting for us to get our acts together."

Callie tugged on Kate's hand. "Wait a minute. Just how much have you shared with Courtney?"

Kate grinned and shrugged, her mock innocence matching Courtney's from earlier. "That's for me and Courtney to know."

Stroking Kate's cheek with the same gentle caress she'd given Callie the night before, Callie looked deeply into the eyes of the woman she loved, rather hopelessly. It wasn't the right time—or was it? What did time even mean in the grand scheme of falling and declaring?

"I know," Kate said in a voice filled with tenderness. "Callie, I know. I feel it too. And I am so sorry for, well, being an asshole with your heart."

"You haven't been an asshole. You've been...challenging. Moderately infuriating. Borderline impossible at times."

Kate winced. "Wow, don't hold back on my account."

Gripping Kate's shoulders, Callie pulled her closer so their noses were touching. "I forgive you."

"That's very kind of you." Kate rested her forehead against Callie's and closed her eyes. "I'm ready for this, Callie. I'm ready for us."

The words, though she felt them and knew they were coming, still knocked her back a bit. "You're sure?"

"More than sure." Kate cradled their hands together and held them against her chest, peering at Callie with naked adoration. "You can say it, you know. I'm ready to hear it."

Callie grinned. "Nah, I think I'll wait. I can't be sure you're not going to give me another speech about how you want me but you can't have me, and—"

"Never again," Kate interrupted. "I'm all yours."

"Well, in that case," Callie said, pressing her lips against Kate's cheekbone. She pulled back to meet her eyes. "I love you, Kate. Kind of a lot."

"Yeah," Kate said, her eyes shimmering once again. "I kind of got that impression. And I love you, Callie. More than a lot."

Callie nodded. "For two people who are so good with words, we're really not doing them justice right now."

"We've got time," Kate said as she brushed Callie's hair away from her face. "And I know we'll use it well."

EPILOGUE

A precariously piled stack of papers teetered at the edge of Callie's desk. Why some professors—i.e., Courtney—refused to give in to the neatness and efficiency of handing in essays electronically was beyond Callie, and she was glad the days were ticking down to the end of the semester so she could stop lugging around file folders filled with essays about American Modernism.

Well, at least for a couple of months, anyway. The curse of being in academia, Callie was learning, was that even as one semester closed, another loomed in the distance, impossible to ignore. She planned, however, on ignoring the shit out of the next academic year to the best of her ability over the summer…

…except for that damn doctoral seminar she'd enrolled in.

"The hits just keep coming," she said to the empty office.

As if summoned by her words, Drew threw open the office door, generating enough wind to dangerously flutter the edges of Callie's pile. She slammed her hand down on the top of it before disaster struck.

He smiled sheepishly as he made his way to his desk, which was also cluttered with piles of papers. "You think she'll ever make the switch?"

"Not until she's forced to, much like your counterpart."

"I could see Lawler enforcing it, the whole electronic system. Then they'd have to get on board."

Callie laughed. "Courtney won't go down without a fight. She'd write an entire dissertation on the merits and joys of swiping her pens over pristine typed pages."

"Speaking of dissertations…"

"Let's not!" Callie exclaimed as she stood. "I truly hate to avoid this hot topic of conversation, but I have somewhere to be."

"Callie," he said, sounding decades older than his twenty-some years. "You have to make a decision before August."

"Yes, *Dad*, I know. That's what the summer seminar is for, okay?" Callie stopped at the door and looked back at Drew. "We can resume this parental argument then."

She shut the door on his response, shaking her head with a smile. She was well aware of the decision she needed to make regarding her dissertation, but she had a few things to work out before she declared her topic.

Callie poked her head into Kate's office, taking a moment to admire her before disrupting her concentration. Kate's skin was just slightly sun-kissed, the result of having attended a conference in Florida the week prior. She was tapping a pen against her lips while she focused on her laptop screen. Callie grinned, remembering fondly her desire to be anything that touched Kate's lips, including that very pen in Kate's hand.

"Are you going to stop staring at me like a creep and say hello?"

"No," Callie said as she stepped into the room and leaned against the shut door. "I happen to enjoy creepily staring at you."

"You always have," Kate said, a smile teasing the corners of her mouth. "Lucky for you, I like catching you in the act."

Callie tapped her watch. "As much as I'd love to continue this flirtatious banter, we have an appointment, Dr. Jory."

"You're correct, Professor Lewes." After sliding her laptop into her bag, Kate met Callie at the door.

"You know damn well I'm not a professor. You can't call me that."

"I think," Kate said, her mouth enticingly close to Callie's ear, "that I can call you whatever I want."

A shiver cascaded through Callie's body. One thing certainly hadn't changed, or diminished, in the last several months: Kate still had an unearthly effect on Callie, and she relished every blissful second of it.

Callie mustered the most serious face she could manage. "That's enough of that. Go." She gestured toward the door. "Lead the way."

"I know exactly why you want me to lead," Kate whispered as she opened the door and brushed past Callie. She did, in fact, lead the way, much to Callie's delight.

The two arrived at the conference room to find Renee. Resplendent in a canary yellow suit only she could pull off, she was already seated, legs crossed, fingers rapping on the table. She looked pointedly at the clock when they entered.

"We're right on time," Kate said while Callie got her laptop connected to the projector. "I know what a tight schedule you have, Renee."

The tapping stopped. "Watch it, Jory. I'll send you right back to Tennessee."

Kate smiled broadly. "You wouldn't dream of it."

"You're right. Okay! Let's get this show started. You've kept me waiting long enough."

Kate gave Callie a short nod accompanied by a genuine smile. She'd put up with Callie's need to practice this presentation upwards of five times, and Callie was pretty sure she'd driven Kate crazy in the process. She was also sure the practice was going to pay off, especially since she felt not an iota of nervousness as she launched into the introduction.

Twenty minutes later, Kate wrapped up the final details of the course she and Callie had created. The time and enthusiasm they'd put into it had certainly paid off: The material was engaging, contemporary, diverse, and high-interest. Renee had nodded so much during the presentation that Callie was certain she'd pulled something in her neck.

"Very impressive. Not that I had any doubts about what the two of you could put together, but I have to say, you've wowed me."

"Thank you," Kate said. "We worked very hard on this."

"I can tell. So, we'll run a section in the fall and one in the spring. You'll each take one."

Callie darted her eyes at Kate, who was nodding at Renee. "Wait. You mean Kate will teach them both, and I'll be her TA. Right?" Discomfort rumbled in her gut. They'd come so far even while putting so much on hold until the end of the semester—she couldn't go backward again.

"Is that what I said?"

Callie perched on the edge of a table. "No, but what you said doesn't make any sense."

"Actually, it does," Renee said as she slammed the innocent keys of her keyboard. "There's a part-time position being posted tomorrow. You'll apply right away. Are we clear?"

Callie leaned back as she absorbed the meaning of Renee's demand. She glanced at Kate, who was unable to hide the huge smile on her face. "You knew?"

She shrugged. "I heard a rumor."

"We all know you're above the position of a TA, Callie. This is the perfect opportunity for you to gain some real ground in the classroom while completing your PhD." Renee shut her laptop. "Everyone wins. Now that we're clear on all accounts here, I have another meeting to get to."

Kate shot a slightly nervous look at Callie. "Renee, there's one more thing we should discuss."

Renee stopped at the door and focused on Kate. "Well? Go ahead."

A rare sight graced the room: Kate, at a loss for words, looked panicked. Callie's heart thumped harder at the image, wanting to scoop Kate up and comfort her, but she sat back and enjoyed the uncommon vision, knowing it wouldn't last.

"Callie and I…" Kate stood up straighter, strengthening her composure. "In the interest of full disclosure, I think you should know that Callie and I are involved. Romantically."

"I see," Renee said after a prolonged silence. She remained standing at the door, expression unchanged.

Callie bit the inside of her cheek. Kate had slipped on her blank mask and wouldn't make eye contact with Callie.

"That's…well. That's unexpected." Renee nodded slowly. "I'll have to reconsider Callie taking that open position."

"No," Kate said hurriedly. "That's not necessary. We—we can be professional. The truth is, we have been. Involved, that is. For months."

Renee settled her placid gaze on Kate. "Months? This has been going on for *months*?"

Callie crossed her arms and pinched the most sensitive skin she could find.

"Yes," Kate said, drawing the word out. "Please know that we have always upheld professional boundaries. And since you clearly didn't know, then you understand there's no reason to—"

"Kate," Renee interrupted, her resolve breaking as she let loose a laugh. "Relax. I've known the whole time. Quite frankly, I knew before you did." She tapped the toe of her turquoise high heel on the floor. "Why do you think I didn't ask you to evaluate her?"

Callie exhaled and let the smile she'd been fighting back emerge. She loved Kate, very much, but it was fun to watch her squirm—especially when Callie knew what was going on.

"I thought the evaluation—you—oh my God, Renee, seriously." Kate threw her hands against her hips. "You let me go through all of that, and you *knew*?"

Renee laughed again before she squeezed Kate's shoulder. "I've been waiting for you to catch up. It certainly took you long enough." With a parting wave, Renee left.

Kate turned to face Callie. "Don't even tell me you knew that she knew."

"I won't." But her smile gave her away.

"Unbelievable," Kate muttered.

Callie crossed the room and tilted Kate's chin up. "I told you she said we would make a gorgeous couple."

"Yes, but I thought she was just saying that, not that she actually *knew*." A surprised laugh accompanied a quick shake of her head. "All that stressing for nothing."

Callie rubbed her thumb over Kate's bottom lip. "You're exceptionally cute when you're freaking out, you know."

"That's a strange compliment." Kate pressed her lips together to kiss the pad of Callie's thumb. "But I'll take it."

"So," Callie said, dropping her head closer to Kate's. "Now that Renee knows…"

"We're not getting into the habit of kissing at work," Kate said. Her eyes glittered with emotion. "But just this once."

"Just this once," Callie repeated before lowering her mouth to meet Kate's.

Bella Books, Inc.

Women. Books. Even Better Together.

P.O. Box 10543
Tallahassee, FL 32302

Phone: 800-729-4992
www.bellabooks.com